Night Children

Wings Press, Inc.

Charles McRaven

Night Children

They were near the path again when a sudden voice rang out ahead, stopping them dead.

"Don'tcha move!" A match flared from behind a big tree. A lantern was lighted. A man stepped out, shotgun aimed right at Susan in the lead.

She knew the man. He'd been with that Holtz at their farm years before: a slave catcher. Was he just out hunting? Doubtful. Either way, there was absolutely no time left. And yes, he was looking hard at her face, remembering.

He was about to exclaim, when Susan's hand whipped around and she shot him through the heart. His cocked shotgun blasted down into the ground as he fell. The lantern tumbled into the dry leaves as the woods echoed the gunfire. She snatched it up, stamped out flames.

"Git his gun," she snapped. "An' enny money, shot an' powder he's got."

She reloaded her pistol, scanning the forest, tumult raging inside, but outwardly cool.

The runaways were shaking, eyes wide, but they moved. Susan doused the light then, and led them quickly away, heedless of the leaves crackling underfoot. *Not as noisy as th' gunshots...*

Night Children

Charles McRaven

**A Wings ePress, Inc.
Historical Fiction Novel**

Wings ePress, Inc.

Edited by: Jeanne Smith
Copy Edited by: Brian Hatfield
Executive Editor: Jeanne Smith
Cover Artist: Trisha FitzGerald-Jung
Images:

Wings ePress Books
www.wingsepress.com

Copyright © 2025 by: Charles McRaven
ISBN 979-8-89197-974-1

Published In the United States Of America

Wings ePress, Inc.
3000 N. Rock Road
Newton, KS 67114

Dedication

To my Southern ancestors who freed their slaves.

One

The path was a gray-brown twisting of August dust, hot between Susan's bare toes, drifting a little still from the passing feet of the other children out of sight ahead. She was used to being alone with her thoughts, and there was no hint of evil in the still air. The dust-filmed leaves of bushes reached out, no longer the yellow-green of spring, but deep, leathery in the waning summer.

Pickin' time soon, she reflected, which would take them out of the hot, gray-boarded subscription schoolhouse with its smells of sweat and dust and ink and chalk. She rubbed her thumb; it was all grown back to normal now, nearly a year after the endless picking of the fluffy cotton off the rough stalks, that after the soreness left your thumb slick and callused hard. She remembered the backaches, the stooping, dragging the tarred pick-sack down the rows.

The slaves sang at picking, she remembered, spread out over the fields like a formation of dark, melodious birds, on the bigger places, the plantations. Seemed to enjoy it, someway. No, more likely just making the hot, aching, endless time pass. *Thank the Lord we ain't got a big place. No need fer slaves on 160 acres, an' some of that woods.* She avoided a scraggly branch where tiny, biting seed ticks could swarm on you the second you brushed it.

Why God ever made ticks—and mosquitoes and flies—she'd never know. About plagued a girl t'death, those did. Snakes, too. Now what good in this world was snakes? Not s'posed to know about such, the teacher, Miz Albert, told them. Said if you're smart 'nuff to know that, you'd be smart as God who made 'em, and wouldn't be th' need to be in school.

Maybe so. Preacher said about th' same, over at th' meetin' house on Sundays. Pa made them go t'church, same's Ma had, and said they'd need all th' school learnin' they could get t'make it in this world. Unless they married rich, and he let it show he didn't much count on that.

Susan barely remembered her mother, and the image of her worn hands and thin face sort of merged with that of the schoolteacher when she tried to bring it up. Consumption had got her, like it had a lot of their neighbors six years back, when they had that epidemic. Doctors couldn't do much, and folks died coughing, wasting.

Zachary Blaine had about gone crazy at the loss of his wife. Left him with the three girls, and Susan only four, the boys gone as babies. He took to the whiskey in his sorrowing, and would've let things slide on the farm if it hadn't been for Kate.

She was seventeen and a woman grown at the time, tall as he. Kate had faced her father down on a night heavy with oppressive heat and the new loneliness they all felt that ate at you, gnawed you till your bones ached. She'd shamed him and put a set in his spine with her blazing eyes and her bony grip like a man's on his shoulder, talking to him like no daughter ever talked to her pa.

Zack had stumbled from the little farmhouse then, in the shadowy smoky oil lamplight, leaving the door open, heading for the barn. Jenny had started after him, but Kate held her twelve-year-old sister in a vise-grip.

"He'll leave us!" Jenny wailed, a cry that cut the night like that of a lost soul.

"Mebbe so. Mebbe not. Got to sober up first, though, an' then we'll see." Kate shut her face, her mouth a grim line.

"But if he don't come back...?" Eyes wide, hand to mouth.

"Then he won't. Reckon we c'n manage." Then the features softened. "But he will. We're all grievin', Jen, but grievin' time's over. Been over."

"He won't forgit Ma!"

"No, and neither'll we. But we'll go on livin'."

Susan hadn't known why her father had gone, and remembered little now but her sister's words, and her tall, harsh stance against the light. But Zack Blaine had come in next morning, sober, and hugged them all.

And then they'd gone out again to the unforgiving fields.

~ * ~

Remembering, she'd let the other children go on further ahead, stopping, watching a black crow on a black gum branch. A few of its leaves were beginning to turn that deep red that warns of the coming of fall, even in this sun-slanting, stifling heat. Now she rounded a turn in the path, where it skirted the Talbot plantation, fenced off at this back corner. *Not too far now, only about a mile.*

Susan's feet stopped. She wasn't sure at first whether she heard, or just sensed the sounds, faint but jarring and out of place in the soft afternoon. But yes, they were real, and they sent a chill up the back of her ten-year-old neck. There is no other sound like the smashing of fists into flesh, and every animal instinct in her sharpened.

Then a cry, scuffling feet. A whimper, a grunt. She wanted to run, but her feet rooted her to the ground like cypress knees immobile in the deep mud of the swamps. Then she could see movement through brush at the edge of the Talbot field, and she shrank back, holding her spelling book close. It smelled of sweat and chalk.

From behind a pin oak tree, Susan could just see the man—Talbot's overseer it was—Saul Avery. He was dragging something that whimpered and cried toward the field-side bushes. It was a Black woman, she could see now, who fought against the big man, clawing, writhing. Susan saw red, raked blood on his bare arms.

Who was it? She didn't know all the Talbot slaves, but ...yes, it was Juno, the pretty one, grown up, but still small. A torn piece of her pokeberry-juice-dyed shirt fell to the dirt as the man hauled her up. Susan caught a glimpse of her face, twisted, bloody, before the man struck her again. She cried out and slumped.

"Black devil," he snarled. "Fight me, will yuh? Teach yuh, I will. Actin' like you's too good fer some white. I know whut's been goin' on with them bucks. Think you's somethin' special, do yuh? Teach yuh, I will..."

Susan could smell the whiskey even from her hiding place, on the faint stir of breeze. She smelled something else: raw fear, brute power, evil like the blackness that clamped down on you when you blew out the last candle, and the room peopled itself with ghouls.

The man Avery looked back across the field, then dragged the stunned form a few feet further to one side out of sight behind brush. Then he flung off his hat, loosed his galluses, began tearing at the woman's clothes.

My Lord, what's he doin' t'her? Susan was at once drawn to and repelled by the thrashing beyond the brush. Then she knew— she'd heard the older girls talk; she knew what a farm girl knew about breeding animals, but this was ... Her legs grew weak; she staggered, settled on her knees, biting her knuckles. The woman cried out in pain.

"Quiet, you Black bitch!" And the sound of blows again. More crying. "I'll choke yuh quiet, then." An ominous stillness, with only the heavy breathing and faint struggling.

Susan lurched to her feet and ran, but not on toward home where the man could see her. Back down the path toward the safety of the big trees. She did not feel the exposed roots under her bare feet, the reaching briars catching her dress. Her heart pounded inside her ribs as she slid behind a great oak.

That was what brought babies, she knew. But the beating, the blood, the raw violence of it—people didn't do that, and neither did animals. The man Avery was crazy, then. Crazy and drunk, yes.

I got to get home. Late. But I cain't go past...them. Go 'round, th'u th' woods, but I might step on a moccasin snake. Hafta wait. They'll go on soon, sure.

She could tell the sun had moved when she crept back up the path to the fence corner turn. How long had it been? How long did such as that take? She peered through the leaves.

The slave woman Juno lay where she'd been attacked, eyes staring, tongue swollen, distended, her legs bare, scratched. Green flies were beginning to buzz around her body. The man Avery was nowhere in sight.

Susan gagged, ran past, then turned off the path and vomited, going to her knees. She couldn't get her breath for long moments, the horror paralyzing her. Finally she got air, in great heaves, almost choking her. She stumbled to her feet, the spelling book still clutched tight, and ran.

~ * ~

"Where you been, girl?" Jenny was peevish, driving the cows back through the break in the cypress-rail fence. "These cows has got into th' garden while you was dawdlin' 'long." Then, seeing Susan's trembling, her red, streaming face, wide eyes, "What's wrong, Susie? What is it?"

"Th' man..." her breath couldn't come fast enough; her legs ached. She'd stubbed a toe, fallen twice. The taste and grit of the Delta dust was still in her mouth.

"Man? What man? Susie, what's happened t'you?" The older girl knelt before her, took her trembling shoulders. "Baby, tell me. Did a man hurt you?"

"No, not me ...Juno. Mr. Avery, he ...Oh, Jenny, they was blood all over..."

Zachary Blaine and Kate drove up in the wagon at that moment, the mules eyeing the late sun, knowing their day was almost over. The jingling of harness penetrated Susan's rigid mind, and she turned toward her father.

"Whoa, thar. Whut's th' trouble here, girls? Susie, you all right?" Then he was off the wagon seat, his long arms about her, worry in his faded blue eyes.

"Oh, Pa..." She clung to him, her dress wet and sticking and the smell of him was all tobacco and sweat too, and gentle strength.

"Tell me, girl. Y'didn't git a whippin'?"

"No, Pa..."

"A man, Pa," Jenny said. "Somethin' 'bout a man."

The eyes hardened. He picked his daughter up, strode to the sagging porch, set her down.

"Bring a dipper water, Jenny. Katy, take thet wagon to th' barn, unhitch." But Kate looped the reins over the wagon brake and came to them, taking the gourd dipper of well water from her sister. She held it for Susan.

"Now, little un, tell us whut happened. Y'said y'saw a man. Who?"

"Mr. Avery, over at Talbot's. An' he was beatin' on Juno..." Her voice choked as the image came again. The blood, those eyes...

"Juno. That one of their wimmen?" Zachary asked gently.

"Is, Pa," Jenny answered. "Growed up, but little, pretty. Got Indian blood, they say. What'd he do t'her, Susie?"

"He ...he was tearin' her clothes offa her ... He..."

"All right now," Her father realized what she'd seen. "Did he hurt *you*, Susie?"

"Never saw me, no. I was hid. But Pa ...Pa, he *killed* her." The child's voice broke into sobs at the remembered eyes, sightless, bulging. She was shaking. Her father held her close. Kate and Jenny looked at each other. Jenny's hand went to her mouth, and Kate's clenched, hard.

"An' you *seen* this, baby." Zachary's voice was sad, angry at the same time. His shoulders slumped, as the weight of this realization settled on him, a numbing load added to that of the endless day.

"Yes, Pa. I was comin' 'long at th' corner there, an' I heard 'em. Others gone on ahead, an'...I was 'fraid they'd see me, so I hid out."

"All right, now. Jist you set here a spell, girl. You're hot, must'a run all th' way in this heat. Jenny, git a wet rag, cool her down some. Let's us git th' taters off, Katy, then we'll think on what's t'be done. Let her he'p you in th' kitchen, Jenny."

At eighteen, Jenny Blaine knew about men—normal men— about their stud-dog appetites. But this was different, strange, frightening. *And he killed her...*

She'd set her cap for Darrel Hedges, who worked at the livery stable in Hernando, but he was slow coming around. Jenny would have liked to go off to Memphis or Jackson to see the world, but she knew she'd best take any man she could find. Kate had never seemed attracted to the boys, but Jenny longed for arms around her, a place away from here, with all this hard work.

But this thing with Susie, now. Wasn't right for her to've seen that...

Just a slave woman, and such as that happened sometimes with the Black girls, though the Talbots were known for treating their hands well. Old Avery drunk, for sure. But that Juno, couldn't been but ...no, she was full-grown. Then she remembered the man's leering at her and her sisters too, times they'd see him in town. *Lay a hand on one of us, Pa'd shoot you, sure. Or Katy'd break your neck.* She shivered.

Susan had quieted, going about the familiar tasks of peeling potatoes, shucking the late sweet corn. Jenny hadn't tried to talk to her much, let this wear off some.

Suppertime and the milking over, Kate helped Susan with her spelling words, then sent her to bed. Then she pulled a kitchen chair up to her father's rocker and sat. *Here it comes,* Jenny thought, watching. *Saul Avery's gonna catch hell.*

"Well, Pa?" The blue eyes sharp, the yellow hair pulled back and tied severely. The planes of her cheeks, already sharp at twenty-three, showing an iron will.

"Well what, girl?"

"You gonna wait till that crazy drunk Avery gits ahold of Jenny, or even Susie?"

"Woman was jist a slave, Katy." The eyes evaded hers.

"We never held much with ownin' slaves, Pa."

"No. An' no, it ain't right: I know that. But well, I been studyin' on how t'handle it. I tell Everett Talbot Susie saw it happen, Avery's liable t'come back on her some way. He is a drunk, and he's 'parently funny-turned, but Everett says he gits th' work outta the hands. Doubt if he'll do a thing to 'im."

"Sarah Talbot won't stand fer it."

"No, reckon not. Takes good care their people." He rose wearily, stooped as if the low ceiling with its circle of light from the oil lamp had already pressed down on him. "Well, guess I'll go on over in th' mornin', talk with Everett some."

"You don't, I will, Pa." It was matter-of-fact, but he knew his daughter meant it.

"What I'se afraid of. Saul Avery's lucky he ain't tried to tangle with you."

"I'd kill him."

He knew she meant that, too.

Zachary Blaine wasn't afraid of this daughter, but he respected her mightily. Outwork any man, shoot straighter than most, run this place by herself if need be. *Well, that might jist happen, way these pains been comin' on. Girls all a comfort, since Aggie went, but life's still empty 'thout her. When I go, I'll know they c'n manage.*

~ * ~

"Meanin' to send word, Zack," Everett Talbot told him. "One of my women ran off, an' need to tell folks to keep an eye out. Strange that, the way Sarah fusses over 'em. Wanted to take Juno—that's th' one—into the house, train her up. Won't get far, though, slave catchers get after her. What brings you, now? Seen her?"

"No, but she ain't run off, Mr. Talbot. One of m'girls saw yore man Avery beat her t'death, down by yore back corner. Reckon she fought him." Zack had his worn shotgun with him, and his flat statement matched the dull but no-nonsense metal of it.

"Don't say?" The planter's face tightened, whether from surprise or insult, Zack couldn't tell. "That's a mite strong, now. I know Saul's had an eye for the wenches, an' yes, there've been other rumors, but Juno was so little ... An' well, that's accusin' my man of murder, even if 'twas a nigger girl. Reckon we oughta go talk to him, hear his side of it."

"No disr'spect, Mr. Talbot, but let's you'n me ride on back there first. Man's already spread it she's run off, an' that ain't it atall."

"Well, Zack, you're sure not one to go makin' empty talk around. Yes, let's go see what we can find, then."

They took a shovel and rode for the distant back corner. Talbot had 400 acres of good land, mostly clear and in cotton. Not a large plantation, but a prosperous one.

"Sure hope you're wrong about my man, Zack. Gets more work out of my hands than anybody I've had."

"Got th' cotton lookin' good, all right. But my girl was some scared, comin' on that from school. Still cryin'; cain't git it outta her mind."

"Oh, bad. Your least one? Susie?"

"Yes. Girl her age oughtn't had t'see such as that."

"No. And Juno was one of my likeliest ones. Saul prob'ly on the bottle again." The planter sighed. "Guess I'll have to let him go then, if what you say's true."

"Girl wouldn't hardly have made th' story up, thang like that."

Zachary Blaine was a small farmer, but he was not in awe of the planters hereabouts. He owed not a cent in this world, and was beholden to no man. Talbot was, despite his limited acres, an upstanding citizen in DeSoto County, and on the social scale well apart from this neighbor. But Zachary didn't really care about that. His vote was as good as anyone's, and he'd speak up and act as quick as any when need be. Everett Talbot knew this, and couldn't discount the man's accusation. *Damn bother, though...*

"Path from th' school cuts close y'know, up ahead. Susie said she heard 'em, then saw him draggin' th' woman, hittin' her. Should be about there..."

The ground was scuffed near the rail fence corner, and brush had been strewn over a mound of fresh dirt back in the bushes. Without a word, Zack dismounted, pulled limbs away, began to dig. Talbot's eyes hardened when a dyed piece of head rag came up. He got down from his horse.

"Let me spell you, Zack. *Damn* the man..." And he took the shovel, moved dirt.

It was a sickening sight, and both men turned away.

"Her sister'll be torn up," Talbot reflected, after getting himself under control. "So will Sarah."

"Oughta hang th' bastard," Zack opined.

"Never get a conviction, slave and all. But Sarah won't let me just run him off, either. Her people didn't have slaves, and she'd set 'em all free if I didn't stop her."

They rode back toward the house, the planter muttering to himself. He was angry, but unsure of just what action to take. He took his pistol out, checked the prime. Zachary Blaine said nothing. The Black woman had been just a little older than his Jenny, Kate had said. They came in sight of the field hands then, scything the late hay, the women in colorful headcloths, bending, swaying with the men in an uneven line. The scythe blades caught rays of the morning sun, and the long grass lay flat behind them. The overseer Avery rode among them, urging them on. There was a bottle in his hand. Talbot headed toward the man, who, seeing them, hid the bottle quickly, turned his horse and rode to meet them.

"Yessir, Mr. Talbot? Howdy, Zack." The man's eyes were shifting.

"Got something you need to see, Saul. Back by the corner." The planter's eyes were hard.

"Corner?" Avery licked his lips. "Which corner, sir?" Zack could smell the whiskey on the overseer, and it was still early in the day.

"Just come along, and we'll see what's to be done."

"Yessir. Ain't been back there fer awhile. Fence down? Somebody's stock git in? I'll git th' hands, git after it, if y'll jist tell me..." Chattering, eyes moving. Zack let his horse fall a little behind, cradling the long muzzleloading shotgun. Talbot led the way, knowing now what he should do about this, but reluctant to act. *After all, just a slave woman, not married yet...*

As they neared the corner, Avery began casting around as if for a place to run. He seemed to have forgotten Zack. Then he slipped a pistol from its holster.

"Wait!" he commanded suddenly, and Talbot turned to see the gun coming up. The planter's eyes widened in disbelief. His hands went out, as if to push the sight away. His overseer's eyes were slits, his mouth grim. Whatever misgivings he might have had before, now he was going to kill the planter.

And Zachary Blaine shot Saul Avery off his horse. The blast, at close range, tore a hole in him you could put both hands in. He tumbled to the ground, the eyes wide in astonishment. Talbot was shaking.

"He'd have shot me, Zack! Fool to let him behind me like that. Man, I owe you my life! He'd really have *shot* me..."

"Reckon so." Zachary reloaded the shotgun almost casually, pouring in the powder, shot, ramming the wadding, priming the pan. He wasn't as calm inside as he looked, but his hands were steady. He glanced at the fallen man.

No need now to worry about the overseer ever finding it was Susie had seen him, and told.

Two

Susan was fourteen when her father died. The chest pains had come, then gone, for months. Then come again, until he'd collapsed coming in from spring plowing. She would always associate the smell of newly-turned earth with the memory of him after that. Catching at his chest, pitching forward, face-down in the black soil, as if trying to get into the ground he'd worked all his hard life.

That was the last time for many years Susan Blaine cried, at the funeral. Kate sat dry-eyed, stern, while others also wept. And some of her older sister's strength flooded into the youngest, some of the need to go on, to dig in and survive, to bury the past with her father.

As time passed, Susan would actually take the lead in the family, young as she was. Life needed a hard eye if you was to get ahead, she knew, hard hands and no weakness. She reckoned she had 'em. Jenny, though strong, had never filled out, but Susan was now blocky, muscled, and an easy match for wiry Kate at farm work.

At a conference around the supper table it was decided that each would take turns at all the chores, from cooking to haying, instead of filling separate roles.

"Keep it f'm gittin' too old on us," Kate explained. "Don't reckon any of us be marryin' off soon."

Jenny had bitten her lip at that, since Darrell Hedges still hadn't made a move toward the altar. She wanted desperately to be away from this farm, to have a real life, with a real man. But all right, she guessed she could do this for a while longer till then. Least till Susie got her growth. Be harder though, with Pa gone.

Susan had already experienced the advances of boys, clear back in school, which she left shortly after the Talbot incident. Older Bobby Tellis, who caught cats and turpentined their rear ends, had whispered in her ear on a dare, and she'd knocked him on his backside.

Bobby hadn't liked being shown up before his friends that way, so he brought two of them along to surround Susan in the brush near the schoolhouse. She took the biggest one out with a savage kick to the groin, and chased Bobby and the other one under the schoolhouse.

After that, the boys left her alone. And memory of the little slave woman kept her from seeing any good from any relationship: boys—men—just had too much of that stud-dog in them, and it looked like it made some of them crazy.

So it was Susan who began making decisions. She suggested they cut down on the cotton crop, raise more corn, beans, squash, to live on, maybe sell a little in town.

"Ma's old spinnin' wheel's still good, an' we c'n patch th' loom up. I don't see killin' ourselves on a crop that'll jist buy us a few purties we don't have th' time nor place t'wear."

"Oh, but I do so like cotton print, Susie. How's a girl ever gonna look nice in homespun?" Jenny objected.

"Save yer butter 'n egg money, then. We've watched th' price of cotton go up an' down like a seesaw: more we raise, th' less it brings. Put up plenty t'eat, we'll be all right."

"But we won't have any money!" A wail.

"Hire out, then. Easier'n choppin' cotton. I aim fer us t'git t'where we don't depend on ennybody or ennything t'git by. 'Sides that, if a man don't look at you in homespun, he ain't much of a man."

Kate had smiled a rare smile at this no-nonsense sister. *She'll change, if th' right feller comes along; most of us do. But fer now, she's right: tell 'em all t'go to hell.*

No one knew, or would ever know, the currents beneath Kate Blaine's hard exterior. Had she ever loved anyone? A man, even secretly? Had her heart broken? Doubtful, her sisters reckoned: Kate was Kate, an' never 'nother'n like her.

If there were rocks in DeSoto County, Mississippi, they were deep down, but their view of their big sister was that: a rock. To steady yourself to, to lean on, maybe even to hide behind, if need be. And it really didn't matter what was inside her. They both loved her as she was, as another mother.

Despite the grinding, unremitting toil, Susan's sensitivities weren't crushed out in the daily round of work. She took time to move a turtle out of the road, to pick yellow flowers for the table, enjoy the red flare of sunset over the Delta. Jenny might be the romantic one, but all the women loved the land, and the patterns in its changing face.

They learned to trade a lot. Neighbor Isaac Ingrum was a born trader, and could somehow manage cloth for quilts, or even dresses, along with pots and skillets from his forays into Hernando and around. If the Blaine sisters had cut and split a good locust fencepost tree, they could swap Ingrum for things they craved. Or if the cows produced an extra calf, it could be traded.

"We'll make it fine," Kate assessed, after a year by themselves. "Annie Ingrum's a help an' got a good heart, an' she likes us: no little uns left. Got t'watch Isaac in a trade, though ...skin you quick."

Susan doubted if any man alive could skin her sister in any trade. *Me either.* She learned early never to want something more than the other fellow wanted what you had. Walk away, that was how you kept from gettin' skinned. And like as not, the fellow'd come back after you and wanta deal when he saw you meant it.

~ * ~

She was sixteen when they found the runaway slave in the barn hay. The girl was maybe Susan's age—hard to tell, she was so skinny, so weak. March, and the Delta winds were still sharp over last year's cotton stalks, and she hadn't a coat at all. Just a twisty dress and a ragged shawl, bare feet cut up bad from running through fields of stubble.

All she had was a name, memorized from the slave grapevine. That and a fierce determination to be free. She'd tried to run when the sisters found her, but had stumbled weakly and fallen. *White women: they'll send me back...* But she could only glower, clutching the shawl tightly.

Kate looked at Susan, Jenny, her mouth that straight line. The wind whistled around the corners of the barn. The girl shivered, coughed.

"She'll starve, reckon, if we don't feed her." A statement, devoid of emotion. Susan looked at Jenny, who was shaking her head.

"Y'd take in a sick bird, Jenny, er a hurtin' dog. How's this enny diff'rent?"

"B'longs t'somebody."

"Not no more. Now, I'm fer feedin' her up a bit, find out what she c'n tell us, see where t'go after that. Enny argument?"

Jenny lowered her eyes.

"Reckon not, then." And Kate had moved ahead of her sister, lifted the starved girl like a gunnysack, carried her into the house.

They spooned broth into her, talked soothingly. The big, dark eyes darted to corners, expecting pursuit, danger. These women were feeding her, true, but so had her masters back home, if never enough. She must regain strength, then run, before they could tell. But her limbs were not responding. Her legs, arms, felt a massive weight on them, and the warmth of the kitchen stove made her drowsy. The broth ... so good...

"Now, girl," Susan told the girl two days later, "you run, an' th' slave catchers'll have you in a minnit, an' we cain't do a thing for you." The eyes were still hunted, furtive. "What's yer name?"

"Celie. You know I run off. Couldn't take it no mo', not feedin' us regular, ever'body gittin' beat on." Susan had never seen any human so skinny, and the anger had risen in her like a towering, black cloud. *Saul Avery, beatin' little Juno...* This girl was pretty, too. That'd mean she'd soon be singled out, by the master maybe, or his sons, or the overseer if they'd had one. She hoped that hadn't already happened.

"Know where you're headed?"

"Nawth. Memp'is."

"Ever been there?"

"Naw. But I knows a name. Figger to git there, then ask 'roun'."

Susan marveled. Memphis was, in 1843, a huge river town, a center of cotton commerce, teeming. This girl probably thought it was a village, like the cotton gin towns from wherever she'd come. Just where was that?

"I come Wes', 'cause I knowed they'd look nawth first. On pas' Tupelo. I los' th'dogs in a creek, an' I strike out wes'. But I knows th' big river not far now, so I go nawth by th' Drinkin' Gourd stars t' Memp'is."

"Do you even know where you're at, Celie?"

"Figger I'se close to Hernando, whar th' roads go nawth. Only I don' go on th' roads."

"No." Susan got a picture of this desperate girl, running, hiding, searching out the way by the North Star at night, the Dipper, the Drinking Gourd, holing up in daylight, growing hungrier, weaker. Alone in a hostile world, with every hand raised against her. But determined, steeled against every barrier, not realizing how hopeless her flight was, how doomed to failure, recapture, to being stolen, almost surely to a worse fate than the one she'd fled...

"Leave your baby?"

"Baby died, las' fall. Then they sold my man, 'cause he say somethin' 'bout freedom, an' somebody told. Wanted 'em to sell me 'long with him, but they wouldn't. Figgered they'd wanta pair me up agin, git more field hands."

They held a meeting that night, around the supper table. The girl Celie sat with them, her fear mostly gone. These women could've turned her in, but they hadn't. Could she trust them? Could she trust *anybody*?

Something told her she could.

"Won't be long, somebody'll find out yer here, Celie. Neighbor's wife pokes her head in all hours," Kate began. "Now, I don't reckon there's enny way you c'n get t'Memphis 'thout gittin' stole. You'd hafta have a white man er woman with you, then find where this man you're lookin' fer is. What's his name?"

"Brannon. Tom Brannon. All I knows is, he teach at some school 'r other. Heered he was with folks he'ps niggers hide, git away nawth."

"All right," Susan spoke up. "Who d'we know would know 'bout schools in Memphis? Ain't that far."

"Sarah Talbot, fer sure," Jenny stated. "Sent her young uns up there, 'member? But there's lotsa schools, town that big. How'll we find th' right one?"

"We?" her older sister queried. *"We* gonna do this?" She looked from one to the other. Susan was watching the girl Celie.

"Reckon we are," she said.

~ * ~

Sarah Talbot had raised her family well. The daughters had attended normal school in Memphis and had married businessmen and Delta planters. The sons had gone on to college at Clinton or in Memphis, then into business there or in Jackson. None wanted to stay and till the soil he'd been raised on, which annoyed stern Everett Talbot considerably.

"Too much education," he grumbled. "Make sissies out of our boys, up in those towns."

Sarah had let him grumble. She was glad their offspring had gone on to better things. There was opera in Memphis, concerts, lectures, and she often visited her children and grandchildren there. Sometimes Everett would go along, still grumbling, anxious to get back home.

Until the first grandchild climbed onto his knee.

Sarah Talbot always got what she wanted, eventually. And since the children had grown, she'd focused on caring for their slaves. It was generally known that she wanted Everett to free them, and she was sure he would, in his own time. Even in the face of severe opposition, even ostracism, from their neighbors. *Well, to hell with the neighbors*, she thought, in her genteel way. But so far, the best she'd gotten was a promise from her husband to free them upon his death.

But that was a start. More would come later. And with an empty house, she and Everett could manage with just a few hands they could pay. Or share the crop with. She'd heard of a family, the McRavens, fifteen miles to the east, who were doing just that. She'd see that Everett met them.

Yes, she would.

The fact that the woman had been beaten, raped and killed on her plantation still sickened Sarah. She missed the bright Juno, quick, smart. She'd wanted to train her for house duty, but her husband had been planning to match her with one of the men, get more field hands.

And if Zach Blaine hadn't shot the overseer Avery, she, Sarah, would have found a way to do it herself.

So when young Susan Blaine confided in her, she listened eagerly. She liked these rough girls, who asked nothing of anyone, farmed their own place, owed no one.

"She's there, now?"

"Yes'm. Couldn't hardly turn her out, starved down thataway. They prob'ly beat her a lot."

"Ohh. I've never let ours be beaten. Except..." and she covered her mouth, remembering Juno.

"No'm, I know. But she sez there's folks in Memphis she's heard tell of, helps runaways. Man name of Tom Brannon, teaches at some school there. All she knows. Figgered you might know more."

"I've never heard that name, no. But I suppose one could ask around. I'm told there's even been an effort to start a charity school for young Blacks somewhere there, but I don't know if it's been built, yet."

"Now, that'd be th' likely place, if 'tis there. How'd we go 'bout findin' out, reckon?"

"I could go for a visit, I suppose, then ask around. Yes, that's what I'll do. Susan, this is noble of you and your sisters. But you—we—absolutely mustn't get caught. When we find the place—the people—I know I can brazen my way to them with the girl as my maid. But do you really think there's an ...organization there? I've never heard of one."

"Couldn't be none, if folks knew it, ma'am." The simple logic of this took a moment to soak in.

"You're right. Oh, Susan, if we can do this, it'll mean so much!"

"Mean prison if we don't do it right. Or hangin'."

"We'll do it right."

Three

The Talbot carriage rumbled up the road from the Blaine farm. Jenny Blaine, in her best dress and hat, sat beside Sarah Talbot. The sisters had talked it out, and Kate had insisted Jenny go. It had been only four months since Darrell Hedges had been kicked in the head by a horse at the stables, and died. Jenny's world had come apart.

Prob'ly what's softened her up so she changed her mind an' wants t'help this runaway, Kate theorized. *Wants to do somethin' with her life, an' mebbe this'll do her good. Might do us all good.*

Celie had worked alongside the sisters in the fields the past days, with the story that she was on loan from an obscure family beyond Hernando. Even the ever-curious Annie Ingrum believed it. *Not right anyways, those girls havin' to work that place by their selves. Need at least one of 'em t'git herself a man. An' that Jenny, she ain't so bad-lookin', put some weight on her. Or young Susie'd make some man a wife. No hope fer that strict Katy, though: men 'bout scairt of that'n.*

Memphis was a long half-day journey, and for Jenny the trip itself was a sort of revelation. The only other times she'd been to the town were with her father and sisters, in a wagon filled with produce for sale. They had normally sold their garden vegetables in Hernando, but Zack had wanted to show his daughters the city, and they'd looked forward to the trips. This time, however, Jenny was riding in a carriage with fine horses and the liveried driver Jesse, with a plantation mistress. All the difference in the world from peddling garden sass from a wagon.

The miles rolled away, and the green up countryside, newly-plowed ground, prosperous farms, built an anticipation in Jenny. Maybe this trip would hold the magic of opening a door to her way off the farm. Maybe there'd be some sort of ...miracle. You had to believe in miracles, or what was there to look forward to? She'd read enough about miracles in the books she'd traded for, stories of maidens and heroes and a fairy-tale existence.

By the time they reached Sarah's son Brady's house, it was afternoon. Early flowers bloomed in well-tended beds, perfuming the air. Huge trees bordered the streets, their new leaves just unfurling. This part of Memphis was already old, with elegant houses hiding down long walks and an air of prosperity. Planters lived there, with their cotton land out from the town, down in the deep Delta soil along the river.

Sarah's daughter-in-law Stella greeted them, noting Jenny's plain clothing and country talk. Stella was tall, with prominent front teeth. *Like a beaver*, Jenny thought. She was also a bit of a snob, Sarah had told her guest, but was really ...tolerant. *Don't matter*, Jenny had reasoned, *I ain't tryin' t'push myself onto s'ciety here*. She was excited though, to be in the big town with a pleasant place to stay and sights to see. Maybe hiring out in a place like this to keep house wasn't such a bad idea...

But where to begin their search? Jenny wondered. They couldn't very well visit each of the many Memphis schools for a list of its teachers. Or maybe that's just what Sarah had in mind.

But Jenny really began to feel, now that they were actually here, as if this would be as far as they'd get.

Sarah Talbot seemed undismayed. Her attitude was that they'd find the man, and it would simply take as long as it took. And yes, they might have to go through a list, travel all over this big town. But they'd reasoned that the supposed new school for Blacks would be the best place to start. Maybe get a clue there, anyway. Surely these school people knew other teachers, headmasters from other schools, talked to them, maybe even met with them on occasion.

Inquiry revealed that yes, some sort of school for Black children was newly open, in the southern part of town. No, no one Stella knew had heard the name Tom Brannon. And why on earth would Sarah Talbot care? Stella's smile was indulgent, but she was curious.

"I've this one girl, Stella, who's very bright. Just a thought, but I've learned that some Blacks can be taught, and well..."

Taught? Surely get you into trouble. More like, now Brady and the others are gone, you need something to occupy your mind, her daughter-in-law reasoned. *And you'll probably free the wench afterwards, and bring more scandal onto the family. And whatever possessed you to bring plain Jenny Blaine to town? Well, no harm, just being nice to the poor folks, I guess.*

~ * ~

Professor Archibald Bancroft, short, round, energetic, greeted his visitors with his English accent and a discerning eye. The Shelby Institute was dependent on contributions, and yes, the one lady looked prosperous. The other ...perhaps a companion, housekeeper. His smile was genuine however, and he bowed over both ladies' hands, which flustered Jenny.

"As you can see, we're building on here, ladies. Our enrollment is small yet, but we have the core of an excellent faculty, and we shall expand."

"I have heard of a man whose reputation as a teacher is excellent, sir. Tom Brannon? Is he by chance one of your instructors?"

Oh, ain't gonna be that easy, Jenny thought; *ain't nothin' comes easy. First place we go an' all, but here we are...*

"Oh, yes, ma'am. Mr. Brannon is our mathematics specialist. Late of Chicago. Very accomplished young man, and dedicated to the advancement of the colored race. Now if you'd care to, we can make a brief tour of the premises. I regret that my time is short today—must meet with a group of benefactors. I'm happy to say that support has been good for our institution, despite the prevailing and shortsighted belief that Blacks cannot be taught."

The tour was indeed brief, because the place was small, and was busy, actually still under construction, with lumber stacked around and additions being put against the main brick building. But the ladies were able to meet some of the few faculty, including a spare, intense Tom Brannon.

Jenny was immediately drawn to this young man, as she was indeed drawn to most single men. But, she told herself, it was just because he was involved in such a worthwhile cause. Teaching repressed children *and* helping runaway slaves escape, if Celie's word could be believed. His accent was strange to her, and his manner brusque, which put her at a loss as to how he was to be approached with their delicate mission. *But leave that to Miz Talbot...*

Fortunately, Mr. Bancroft had to excuse himself soon for his meeting, and Sarah led Jenny back to the teachers' shared office space. Brannon was there.

"Mr. Brannon," she began, "could we have a moment more of your time, please? Miss Blaine and I have further questions." She inclined her head toward the door in an unmistakable meaning.

"Of course, madam. Let's step outside for a moment, shall we? This room grows stuffy." He rose and led them to an outside door.

"Now, Mr. Brannon," Sarah began, "if we are mistaken, please understand that we shall deny that this conversation ever took place." Sarah looked about quickly, as Jenny noted a sudden wariness in Brannon's face. Then, lowering her voice, "We know of a runaway slave girl who knows only your name, sir. We are unsure how to proceed, but you may trust us completely in this matter. I can bring her to Memphis as my maid, but no farther." She looked sharply at him. "Are we mistaken in telling you this?"

Oh, now: th' fat's sure in th' fire now, Jenny thought. *If he ain't th' man, we jist stuck our necks out a mile on this'n, an' no tellin' what'll come of it* ... She twisted her hands in the fabric of her skirt.

It was Brannon's turn to glance about them. Evidently none of the others here were part of whatever movement existed.

"You are not mistaken, madam, but if *I* am misled, *I* shall deny this conversation. We must be very, very careful in our work—God's work, if you will."

"I understand. Give us a time and a place, and we'll trust you with the rest." Sarah knew to keep this contact short.

"You're near Hernando ... Could you arrange another visit in exactly two weeks? After dark? I can meet you, and we'll go together to the safe house. It would be unwise, begging your pardon, to disclose its location so ...soon, you understand."

"Completely. Yes, in two weeks. Should you prepare a bill of sale perhaps, in case we are apprehended? Conveying ownership of the girl to you, or to another? Is that how it's done?"

"Yes, that'll work. But you can surely bring her to town without suspicion as your maid, as you said. Can your husband know of this?"

"I'm afraid not, no. And we must not use the mails, I realize. But tell me, Mr. Brannon, how could this girl, from east of Tupelo, have heard of you? Do you have a large organization?"

"We are developing branches, yes. But understand, Mrs. Talbot, we cannot disclose the details of our ...procedures. I can tell you this: if others of this oppressed race can contact you, we will arrange to move them to freedom in the North safely. That is our mission."

Time and place were agreed upon, and the two women took their leave.

"Now we shall spend some time with my daughter Audrey, Jenny, and perhaps see more of Memphis, to justify our trip. I'll see the others next time. What did you think of our Mr. Brannon?"

What Jenny actually thought, she was sure Sarah didn't want to hear. She had fantasized him as a sort of knight, albeit not upon a white horse, who could sweep her up in his arms ... The young man was the polar opposite of the farmers' sons she knew, and with his education and his passion for social justice, she'd found him extremely attractive.

"I never heard a Yankee talk b'fore, Miz Talbot, but past that, he seemed real set on helpin', so reckon we got t'trust him."

"Yes, without him we've no way to ensure that Celie has papers, or that they wouldn't be stolen if she did. You know, I've often tried to imagine myself as a slave, with no choices, no options at all, no future. It's terrible, oppressive, inhumane."

Jenny hadn't thought much about that. Susie had, she knew, remembering that about little Juno: she'd get riled about that all over again, time to time. *But that's just how things are: some folks er slaves; some er owners. An' some er crazy, like that Avery. Then there's them like me and m'sisters, and Isaac Ingrum, an'—well, most of th' small farmers around—don't think much about it, one way or 'nuther.*

But yes, maybe it's time t'take a stand on it. Legal an' all, ownin' other human bein's, but not right, fer sure, way some of 'em gits treated.

No, not right...

"I've never been able to make Everett see it clearly," Sarah went on. "He's so set on the system, so sure we couldn't survive without it, like most masters, I'm afraid. Yet there are those prospering with hired labor, or sharing the crops. What do you think of the slave system overall, Jenny?" She knew many small farmers would like to expand, own servants, but she also knew the Blaines weren't of that stripe. Not at all, she now knew.

"Wal, we been pushed about that, since Celie's come. Best way t'say it'd be it just ain't *right.*"

"No, not right at all. And this undertaking will be dangerous, you realize of course, but it is also *very* right."

Up front, driving the carriage, the slave Jesse had heard snatches of their conversation. Now he smiled, broadly.

~ * ~

Back on the farm, Jenny regaled her amused sisters with tales of the city, and her infatuation with the personable Tom Brannon was plain.

"Abolitionist, that's what he is," Kate stated.

"But he's not makin' speeches an' wringin' his hands like I hear they do up North. He's *doin'* somethin'", her sister defended.

"Well, I'll jist be glad t'finally git Celie safe somewheres, so's we can git back t'normal 'round here. Longer we keep her, more chancy it gits fer us."

Kate's plain talk disguised the fact that she felt real sympathy for the Black girl. That she'd been severely mistreated, surely along with all the slaves there, was obvious, and the older sister could easily imagine the life she'd led: always harder if a girl were pretty. They hadn't asked specifically what she'd suffered, and they wouldn't, despite their suspicions.

The days passed, the girl gained a little weight, lost her suspicions entirely. Jenny realized Celie was actually a beautiful young lady. Something like the ebony maidens in the books she read: a Nubian princess maybe, forced into slavery ... No, that was the stuff of writers' imaginations, she suspected. Celie was a field hand with absolutely nothing but her beauty. But that might be a help now, and she supposed in the end it might open some doors for the girl up North. Down here it'd just mean some white man would buy her for his personal bedroom toy. She hoped Celie wouldn't get into that kind of trap wherever she'd end up.

And then Sarah Talbot's carriage came to take the runaway on the next leg of her journey. The sisters hugged her, sent food with her. They understood she'd come close to asking to stay with them, so much better was her lot here. Kate had forestalled this.

"'Twouldn't be th' same as freedom, girl," she had told her. "No way fer us t'set you free, here. We ain't all that far f'm Tupelo, y'know."

"Won't never fergit y'all," was all Celie could reply, through tears.

Sarah returned in a few days, and stopped by the farm to tell the Blaines all had gone smoothly. Jesse, her carriage driver, knew, of course, what this had all been about, and he regarded the sisters with a new appreciation.

"What's gone with yer nigger gal?" Annie Ingrum queried on her next visit. "She run off?"

"Owners had t'sell her t'some Memphis folks," Susan told her. "She was good help, but Lordy, we couldn't afford nobody, an' they couldn't even keep her fed."

"Wal, y'done right by her here. 'Bout starved, she wuz, all right. Wisht Isaac an' me c'd git us one, but that's fer folks with money. Wouldn't want one that good lookin' ennyway; give m'man idees." She winked slyly and cackled.

Afterwards, in the now-strange emptiness of her absence, the sisters often speculated on Celie's probable fate.

"Afraid they ain't much better off up North," Kate remarked. "Hear them factories works 'em cheap, an' th' stores charges 'em high for ever'thing."

"Maybe she's got work in a good home." Jenny was hopeful.

"Freedom's s'posed t'mean y'got choices," Susan mused. "But if y'got nothin' t'start with, ain't much t'choose from. Still, we done right, no doubt. An' that Sarah Talbot, she's got gumption. Worried 'bout trustin' her at first, but 'twas th' best way, turned out."

~ * ~

Jenny Blaine's trip to Memphis did perk her up, but only for a while, her sisters observed. Getting over Darrell's death took some time, even though she'd apparently understood beforehand that the relationship was never to flourish. Now however, at twenty-four, she was clearly facing spinsterhood, and was acutely unhappy. Susan or Kate would find her crying silently while milking one of the cows, her head against the warm flank of the animal, tears coursing down her cheeks. Or they'd come upon her stopped in mid-task, her eyes beyond the tree-line that bounded the Blaine acres, her hands holding whatever she'd been about, now forgotten. Repeatedly she speculated aloud about going back to Memphis as a housemaid.

"Seems like there's just so much goin' on there, y'know?"

"Mebbe so," Kate would remark, "If y'wanta spend yer life scrubbin' other folks' floors." And she'd dismiss her sister's fantasizing.

"Way I see it, Jenny," sixteen-year-old Susan observed, "is, we got this place free an' clear, t'do with jist what we want. We c'n work our ground hard, an' have a little spendin' money, or we c'n lay back an' jist git by, pay th' taxes. Or anywhere in b'tween. Thing is, we got th' choice, th' whole choice. An' no way d'you git a choice if yer slavin' for somebody else, gittin' paid pennies.

"So, you got t'make up yer own mind, Jenny, but I see th' three of us havin' it better here, t'gether, than scattered out, each one grubbin' fer other folks. We care 'bout you, girl, an' don't th' rest of th' world, much." She stopped, spread her strong hands. "An' that's jist how I see it, I reckon."

Kate loved both her sisters, but this declaration warmed her anew toward Susan. Both of them looked at Jenny, and felt some of the distress in her. Everyone was silent for a time, during which the middle sister's plain features showed her emotions. Then a new light kindled in the pale blue eyes, and grew.

"Reckon maybe you're th' best I c'n hope fer, then," she sighed. "An' besides, now we're abolitionists together, ain't we?" The three of them hugged each other.

And it was only three weeks later that Sarah Talbot called on them again, with another plan to transport another runaway slave North. This time it was a nervous middle-age field hand named Cabe, who fidgeted constantly, eyes moving from one suspected danger point to another. He looked about to bolt from the Talbot carriage.

"I can't hide him at our place," she lamented. "Could you maybe keep him a day or two until I can take him to Memphis?"

The sisters looked at each other. The barn or sheds would be the first place slave catchers would look. Could they pretend he was on loan, as they had with Celie? Risky, with Annie Ingrum sure to show up unannounced. There *was* that dense briar patch away from the house. Maybe, for just a couple of days...

Or they might cram him up in the attic, keep him hid up there, just long enough. Sarah was waiting for an answer, not sure if this would work.

"Reckon we c'n think of somethin'," Susan assured her. "Where's he from?"

"On east, close to Pontotoc, so the catchers shouldn't come here. Minister brought him, and nobody questioned him. I'll try to get away tomorrow, though mustn't let Everett suspect. I'd be so grateful, girls. I'll tell anyone on the road I'm taking him to the market in Memphis to sell, then get him to Tom Brannon."

"Folks'll wonder, jist you with him," Jenny warned. "Figger he might git away."

"Have him chained, just for show. He knows that'll be necessary." The runaway nodded. *These folks he'pin' me, spite of mebbe gittin' caught theyselves. Th' Lord, He's lookin' after this boy, He sho' is.*

Cabe helped Katy hoe the crops that day, while Susan and Jenny kept watch at the road toward Hernando and toward Ingrum's place. He slept in the attic, grateful for a roof over him. When he'd run the two days to the minister's house he'd heard of, he'd hidden in a swamp, leaving no trace for dogs. And it'd rained steadily that night.

Sarah took him to Memphis the next day, meeting Tom Brannon just after the Institute closed. He unlocked the chains to lead Cabe to the safe house, but told her that this could not continue. There was soon to be another way, he told her, one carefully planned that could move more runaways at a time.

"I can't tell you much just yet, but you can be assured that our work will be more efficient, and completely safe. You won't be exposed at all, the way we'll set it up; other volunteers will aid us."

"Mr. Brannon, sir, this work you and the others are doing is vital, and I'm so very glad you're willing to do it. But you must take every precaution, not risk getting caught. Without people like you, we'll never free these oppressed people. I cannot let even my husband know of this." She patted his hand, watched him conduct his 'slave' down the street. Then directed the driver Jesse toward another of her children's houses.

Four

Tom Brannon was only one member of a tightly-run abolitionist cell newly-operating out of Memphis. Farther east, other groups were active, notably the Underground Railroad itself, with members such as the celebrated Harriett Tubman.

Picklock historians disagree on whether there actually was such an organization in Memphis, which most doubt, although at least one safe house was later discovered, and a second rumored. Another root cellar, rare in Mississippi, was also used, according to descendants of its owners, who insisted on this in 1960. These historians' negative certainty is based on the fact that no further shred of other evidence has surfaced, a fact the group members' ghosts no doubt revel in.

The Memphis apparatus was never disclosed, because these conspirators were sworn upon their lives to secrecy. And mishaps were so effectively sealed off, there was never any link to a central operations center; slave escapes were considered individual efforts. And even after the conflict, the defeated Southerners for the most part resented anyone who'd aided in such a venture. The term 'abolitionist' was perhaps the greatest insult one could apply in the region, for many years thereafter.

The cell called itself the Cotton Route, but seldom used the actual name. Its organizer was one Hiram Hyde, late of Massachusetts, who ran a mercantile business dealing in wholesale goods with country stores in northern Mississippi and the area of Tennessee south and east of Memphis.

He had logically sought out the staff of the new Shelby Institute for recruitment, and had found the willing Tom Brannon. So far, he was the only member of the Route at that school. After the most discreet overtures, it was learned that headmaster Archibald Bancroft would not risk his fledgling establishment with illegal activities, no matter how idealistic.

"Spineless," had been Mr. Hyde's evaluation of the Englishman. "How can he profess to help this disenfranchised race if he will not aid in freeing them?" His thin lips had curled in contempt. One was either for freeing the Blacks by any means, or against. No gray areas existed for Mr. Hyde.

The Route eventually developed a *modus operandi* that consisted of escorts for legs of the journey north, with the Tennessee city the first-stage hub of operations. But such well-intentioned citizens as Mrs. Talbot could not continue indefinitely transporting individuals openly for two reasons, Mr. Hyde pointed out to his new staff.

"First, the obvious repetition will attract notice. Each run becomes more dangerous, subject to detection. Second, one runaway every few weeks or months is not satisfactory. As we establish contacts on farms and in villages in the South to aid in the slaves' escape, we must be able to move them in groups quickly, and of course, secretly.

"To that end we are establishing way stations on two routes to begin with, down into Mississippi, our primary working area." He produced a map. "One from here down to the Hernando area, which will be actually the last leg of that route. An escort can shepherd a group from there to a safe house here in the south part of town in one night, arriving well before daybreak. The courier from Senatobia will have brought the group to that 'station', and so on, from Batesville, Grenada, etc.

"So also, the route southeast from Olive Branch, Byhalia, Holly Springs, toward and from the Tupelo and Oxford areas. Each stage must be accomplished in a single night, and a safe haven available until the next night." He paused. "Any questions?"

"Who establishes the havens ...stations?" Tom Brannon asked. "And who collects the runaways at the various starting locations?"

"It is of no concern to this group who handles those branches of the operations, sir. The less any one member knows, the better, if apprehended. I am afraid we must operate in that manner, so that any ...mishap, can be contained, and not endanger the entire enterprise. Next?"

"Yes," queried a Baptist minister from a prominent church. "It seems the distance would be too great from say, Olive Branch to here. Any delay, for any number of reasons, would jeopardize nighttime arrival here."

"Very good, Reverend. The locations I gave are not specific. Actually, in the instance of Olive Branch, that village would be approximately mid-point in that leg of the journey. The escort would be based there, but would pick up the group beyond, and transfer it to another location and guide well this side for the last miles to the safe house here."

"What is the nature of the stations, sir?" asked a shipping clerk, a worried-looking older man.

"They vary. We are trying to find remote farmhouses, but that is extremely difficult, given the attitude toward our efforts in the region. I am afraid most of our hiding places are, at first, to be abandoned barns, derelict houses, sheds, even unfortunately, the deep woods in places. We hope to rectify this state of affairs soon, but count the slaves' freedom a higher priority than their temporary discomfort *en route*."

"Who stays with the group at each location?" from the same clerk.

"The escort to that location. He, or she, will know the area, and will monitor the site closely to avoid suspicion. The transfers will all occur quickly and quietly, with the object of leaving the stopover point as soon as possible. And though none of you has asked, we will not use *any* major roads, ever. Each guide will work out his or her most secluded path, varying that as necessary. I needn't remind you that hunters are out at night in season and other times, as are late visitors, travelers, and of course, the slave catchers."

Mention of the catchers, those bounty-hunting scourges, quieted the assembly. Entirely within the law, these men, sometimes known as patrollers, could, and had, shot to kill anyone aiding escaping slaves. The slaves were their source of payment, but to those assisting, they often showed no mercy.

"We all know the attitude of these men," Hiram Hyde continued. "They hate Blacks, and are eager to hunt them. With dogs, on horseback, in large search parties if necessary. And they hate us more. I would venture to state that the only ones they hate more are themselves."

"And perhaps God," the minister offered.

"And perhaps God."

~ * ~

As a result of their having harbored the girl Celie and the runaway Cabe, the Blaine sisters were among the first approached, by Mr. Hyde himself, to act as guides on the Hernando route. The aging Sarah Talbot, though sympathetic and of use in other contributory ways, was not escort material under the planned system.

He called on the women after the crops were laid by in early summer, 1844. Jenny welcomed this stranger, noting his accent and dark clothing.

"My sisters er close by, sir. C'n I tell 'em yer business?" The man made her nervous, seated rigidly in the proffered chair, stovepipe hat in hand, eyes sharp.

"Of course. And yes, I would like to address all of you together, if I may. It concerns my associate, Tom Brannon who, with me, is very grateful for your past help."

"Um. Well, I'll git 'em. Jist you make yerself to home, sir."

Now what'er we t'do, here? Could this man be th' law, someway? Had they caught that nice Tom, and were they t'be next? *Git Kate an' Susie first: they'll know what t'do, what t'say an' what t'keep quiet about.*

Hyde had evaluated the young woman as being perhaps too timid for the work at hand. *But perhaps the others...* He took in the plain but clean house, the garden and fields beyond out the window. Barn was not a proper one, by New England standards, but these in the South never were.

The women filed in, greeting him warily, and he rose, bowed slightly. They offered him well-water-cool tea, and arranged themselves afterwards about the tiny front room. Then they waited, each with her eyes fastened onto his. And what he saw in tall Kate's and stocky Susan's faces reassured him.

"Ladies," he began, "let me first assure you that I mean you no harm whatsoever. My name is Hiram Hyde, and I am the organizer of the group in Memphis that transported young Celie, whom you sheltered, and the other, Cabe, as well as runaways you do not know of, to safety in the North. They are now in Illinois, free, working in a mill owned by a kind and generous man who helps finance our operation. This gentleman has built housing for the people we send to him, and provides medical care, in addition to the wages he pays.

"It would be foolish of me to expect you to trust me, a stranger, in this ...business, since what we do is clearly against the law—man's law, not God's law—as the Apostle Paul separates the two in the Holy Book. But you will not be betrayed, by me or any of us in this work, as you will see with the passage of time.

"I am here to propose that we work together in this most vital cause: freeing God's children whom their misguided masters hold in bondage. There will be a small regular payment made to cover food and a few necessities, but the work itself must be voluntary.

"Now, if you are interested, I can give you further details. If not, I can understand fully, given the nature of the work and its risks. Of course, if you choose not to join us, I cannot give you information that could harm us. So we must trust one another." He stood.

"Now, why don't I wait outside while you discuss this among yourselves. May I admire your garden? It appears, this early, to be quite bountiful." He paused a moment, looking at Kate, obviously the leader among them. But it was Susan who spoke.

"Mr. Hyde, I didn't follow all y'said ...some of them words was big. But I got a question."

"Certainly, if it doesn't reveal too much for our safety."

"Shouldn't. Would we hafta go t' Memphis, er out through th' county gatherin' up runaways?"

"Oh, not at all, either one. Those would be the tasks of others. What we would need would be simply a guide for this part of the journey, around twelve miles, to a safe location where the next guide would take over."

"At night, fer sure."

"Yes, for obvious reasons. Shall I go now?"

"No need," Kate spoke up. "Like you said, we'd hafta trust you, an' you us, if we do this. If we don't, we still got to trust each other not t'tell. Reckon we c'n talk this out amongst us all, cain't we, girls?"

They agreed, and for the next hour the grim Mr. Hyde satisfied himself that these independent women would do nicely indeed. And they, ever mindful of the mistreated Celie and the brutalized Juno and the frightened Cabe, agreed to become a link in the chain of Black freedom in Mississippi. A huge and dangerous step, given the times and place, but one they felt was, as Jenny had told Sarah Talbot, *right.*

"I will leave you with this assurance, ladies: we never take a direct route north. The groups you will be guiding will be from either far east or far west, even Arkansas or Alabama. Slave catchers naturally expect runaways to head north, so often our people will actually start in another direction at first. We pray their hunters never learn better. So you should never be in real danger, unless you are careless.

"But if you *are* caught," and he raised a cautionary finger, "we cannot acknowledge you or aid you in any way. Understand that. Once exposed, our entire operation would be stopped, and we cannot allow that. You simply must *not* be caught."

The sisters looked at each other. Susan felt a hot surge of righteous challenge in the prospect. Jenny thought of meeting Tom Brannon at a remote station still to be located. Kate saw the justice in the proposal, which they'd already agreed to in principle, after all.

"Reckon we'll hear from you then, Mr. Hyde," she said, rising. "Now we'd best be stirrin' 'bout supper. Will you stay?"

"Thank you, madam, but I am overdue in Hernando to meet a contact. You will send word by Mrs. Talbot when you have located one or more safe stopovers, and she or another will bring you further instructions. Now, please take this money for food for the first groups in advance, which will be of five to eight. More will be sent as our work progresses. Good day." He bowed, departed.

As the hoofbeats of his horse faded, the three stood silently, emotions clear on both Susan's and Jenny's faces. Kate wore her habitual set expression, but her thoughts were far from serene.

What have we gone an' got ourselves into now? she wondered.

~ * ~

During the next few weeks the sisters, one at a time, scouted suitable routes north and south to the approximate areas Hyde had given them. The exact location of the south exchange station would be given to them later, but they must find the north ones. At first, Kate felt she should be the only one to guide the runaways, but Susan set her straight.

"We're all in this, Katy, an' we'll all do it, right f'm th' start. If yer worried 'bout me bein' too young, jist stop. I'm seventeen, an' I c'n whip most men, 'cause I won't fight fair. An' I wanta go see Isaac, t'git us a good pistol—you know, t'shoot snakes with. We'll all practice with it, an' all of us'll git as rough as we got to, t'git this job done.

"Way I see it, we got enough t'feed a few folks at first already, so we c'n use th' money Hyde give us t'wards th' gun an' powder. I'm thinkin' one of them with two barrels, if he c'n find one."

"Or maybe two of 'em," Jenny suggested. "Snakes bad, this year." She grinned at her sisters. Kate wondered if Jenny could ever shoot a slave catcher if cornered. *Prob'ly could, since it'd mean hangin' if she didn't.*

~ * ~

"Small gun'll do, Isaac," Kate told him. "I stepped right on a moccasin snake down by that marshy place, watchin' fer briars. Wonder he didn't bite me. Cain't lug a shotgun ever'where we go."

Isaac Ingrum was a stooped man of sixty, with a bulbous nose, red from too much whiskey. His dark eyes were sharp, though, always on the lookout for a trade, a sale, any way to make a dollar. Everything he owned was for sale, "'Cept th' ole woman an' th' cat," and he was the man to go to. He traded his wife's handmade quilts, her laying hens, his dogs, whatever he and she could do without, for what might be better.

"See what I c'n find, Katy. Cap an' ball cost ye, though. Them old flintlock uns cheap, but hard t'keep yer powder dry, carryin' it around. New uns bein' come up with all th' time, but couldn't none of us pay fer such as that." He knew the women couldn't afford much.

"No, but we got a little money, Isaac, f'm those heifers we sold. Jist don't want one of us bit, er run on a panther cat er somethin'."

"Reckon not. Wal, I'll see. Goin' t'town ennyway." Kate reflected that Isaac was always going to town. Trading constituted most of his income, and the rundown state of his farm showed it.

The sisters knew their neighbor wouldn't limit his trading forays just to Hernando; he'd find an excuse to go to Memphis if necessary, for this and other pursuits. And they also knew he'd be relatively fair with them: his wife Annie would see to that.

And the two-barrel pistol he eventually found was percussion cap-and-ball, so it would be more dependable than a flintlock. And two shots would be much better than one.

"Got th' bullet mold fer it, too," he showed them. "Y'got powder, lead?"

"Some. Pa always said that'uz one thing he'd never git low on, God rest him. Reckon we'll practice with it some then, so's we c'n hit close t'what we're aimin' at. Y'll prob'ly hear us at it." She counted out their hoarded money for the gun.

"Jist don't shoot yer foot off, Katy," Isaac grinned.

~ * ~

Surprisingly, Jenny became the best shot with the new pistol. Maybe it was from resentment at her station in life, but she strove for competence in everything she did, from cooking to weaving to this new adventure they'd taken on. And it was she who stitched a holster that could be hidden at one's back under a cloak or shawl, supported by a reinforced waistband. She showed her sisters how to distract a watcher's eye for an instant, during which the gun would appear as if by magic in her hand.

"Well!" Susan applauded, "you c'd be a good stagecoach robber, girl. Show me that agin, now." Kate smiled in approval. Jenny would do to tie to.

Practice sessions were ongoing, and soon each sister wanted to take the pistol on cow hunts, berry-picking and nut-gathering. They asked Isaac to watch for a second gun.

"No hurry," Jenny told him, "ain't got th' money yet ennyway, but Susie, she shot a swamp rattler t'other day, an' it's mate'uz right there. Got it too, but didn't have no more powder nor ball on her, an' was spooked comin' home."

"Y'all gonna be th' meanest wimmen in th' county, girl. I'll keep my eye out, then." He grinned after the departing Jenny. *Glad t'see that'n's perked up some, after that Hedges boy got hisself kilt. Mopey fer a while, she wuz.*

Susan located not one but three decaying sheds and barns on the way north, back from the Delta farms. The land had been taken by the first wave of settlers a score of years earlier, but the rising low hills didn't grow the long-staple cotton like the flat, black bottomland the big planters had claimed.

Small farmers had moved west, across the Mississippi into Arkansas in search of land, independence, or just out of love for the wilderness. The cabins and outbuildings they left began to rot and fall quickly, as the forest moved to reclaim the land. Back from the main route to Memphis the scrub brush grew, the domain now mostly of wildlife and hunters.

She was unworried, despite her motives for this search, knowing she could explain to any curious farmer she might meet that she was cow-hunting. And she enjoyed these outings in the newness of summer, with green leaves open, and forest flowers blooming. The music of the birds never ceased here, and she might surprise a turkey hen on its nest, or see a blue heron rising from a swampy place. There were snakes, and she reminded herself to have all of them get high boots for this work. *More money t'be spent, but better'n gittin' bit.*

Susan mapped the locations after they'd received word of the pickup points south, and the three agreed on the best routes to each. These stopovers of theirs were numbered, in their directions to the guides on the Memphis leg of the trip, with instructions to use them in sequence, minimizing trampled ground and tracks.

By early August, the tension grew among the Blaines as they waited for word. They'd received the location of the first south hiding place (there were more than one of these, too) and each had devised her route to it. The moon would be dark soon, so any day... They scythed late hay, dried vegetables, waited some more.

Then Jesse, the Talbot's carriage driver, slipped up to the back door of the farmhouse just before dusk on a Tuesday. His was a privileged position on the plantation, and he was trusted to leave on errands and given the run of the place.

"T'night, Missis say. She porely, so she send me t'tell y'all. Tha's all she say, jis' t'night. Figure y'all know whut t'do." And he was gone.

They knew. Without a word, Kate holstered the pistol, took powder and ball, the pack of bread, cheese and meat. She slid a long knife into her waistband, hugged her sisters, and paused at the door.

It had been agreed that she would take the first trip. The others had argued for strength in numbers, but Kate had pointed out that more people meant more trail left for enemies to follow. Plus, their absence might well be noted while hidden the next day, waiting for the next escort.

"Back t'morrow night. Tell ennybody wants t'know, I'm tendin' Miz Talbot." And she set out on her perilous journey.

She had traced the route south to the exchange barn both in daylight and at night, and the miles passed quickly under her long stride. The way was well east of Ingrum's place with its dogs, in the low hills, down past the Talbots', cutting across the path to the subscription school. From there, it was due south through woods by the compass two miles, then through a farm gate into a cornfield. That farmhouse was distant, but there were dogs there, too. This was a danger point, and would be worse when fall came, with its hunters, and the cover of the cornstalks gone.

Beyond this field, the trail crossed a narrow road into woods again, with a twisted oak as guidepost. The trees soon thinned past a stream, into a meadow. Skirting this, Kate kept to the edge of the forest, walking alongside a dusty cattle path that would show tracks. Manure patties were darker patches on the dim ground, and weeds scratched at her skirt. Her boots were good, among the few items she and her sisters had spent that money on. She hoped they'd protect her against unseen snakes.

The slaves would probably be barefoot, unless Hyde had provided for them. She doubted it: the humorless New Englander was a zealot, probably not overly concerned with what he'd termed the discomfort of his charges.

But I reckon their whole lives er a risk, she thought. *Ever' day not knowin' if they'll be sold away, whipped, sometimes even whether they'll git fed. Though any fool master'd oughta know he's got t'keep his workers fittin' to work. Course, some don't care.*

She was mindful of night noises: of cicadas responding to the cooling air, a distant owl's call. And sudden movements in the brush, which startled her, but which she recognized as rabbits, 'possums, other nocturnal creatures.

Despite her high nerves, Kate could appreciate this nighttime world, so different in its relative silence from the sounds people made just in their surviving in the daytime. Then, despite the comparative remoteness of the holdings, one could usually hear axes in the woods, plowmen calling faintly to their teams, roosters crowing. This path had to twist and wind itself among the darkest cover, and absolute quiet would be...

A horse's hooves sounded on this road ahead. She melted into trees, froze. *I'm downwind: good. Could have a dog with him...*

The horseman passed, and she waited a full two minutes before venturing out from hiding. Her heart was still churning, her breath shallow. *Mightn't been such a fine idee, this business. Git us all killed...*

But once past the road and along the edge of another field, her confidence returned. She walked faster, mindful of the passing time. *Have t'keep 'em movin' on th' way back. Lessee: if I git helt up, I wait 'nuther day. If we all git helt up, we got t'make do, some way. Deep woods, I reckon, er th' swamp on north, an' pray a lot. Well, I'm close now...*

The old barn was in a thicket of briars and brush, its roof sagging precariously. She slipped to a rear door that was a dim rectangle, knocked twice, waited, pistol out.

It opened, a hand reached gently, pulled her inside, closed the door. A sulfur match flared, lit a candle. A circle of frightened black faces watched her, eyes wide. She saw her counterpart.

She knew him.

"Shelby? Shelby Coulter? Why, I never s'spected you..."

"Me, neither, Katy. I'm 'bout as flustered as you." The farmer's eyes bulged. He was lean, in overalls and a patched shirt. He was a widower, around forty, and had actually danced with her twice the year before at Hernando. The sisters had teased her about becoming the new mother of the man's three children, but she'd scotched that speculation.

"Reckon not," she'd told him and her sisters, too. Now here he was, a slave-freedom runner. This was for sure a crazy world.

"All right. They've et t'day. Traveled good; won't be no trouble t'you. You git, now. Don't waste a minnit, case y'git helt up."

"Thanks, Shelby. Pray fer us."

"I will, that. God's work, fer shore. Now git, girl." He blew out the candle, opened the door, checked the surroundings. "Go fur 'fore yuh stop, case ennybody seen th' light." He squeezed her hard hand in his equally hard one.

There were two men about thirty, one teenage girl, one heavyset woman maybe forty, and a ten-year-old boy. All had shoes, she'd seen in the brief candlelight. *Thank God:* He and somebody else had provided.

They set out at a brisk pace, retracing Kate's footsteps. One of the men took the food pack without a word, for which she was as silently grateful. They had nothing with them, nothing but the ragged clothes they wore. But all of them had the same eagerness, the same look of resolve. *Freedom.* Freedom for now was this tall white woman and miles more of walking, hiding.

It was a scary thing, having to trust your life to these strangers who didn't let you talk much, didn't let you stop until you had to. But they were deep in it now, and trust them they would.

With no moon, the stars burned whiter than Kate had ever remembered them. She hadn't taken time to look at stars for many years. That was something you did when you were young, sitting out in the yard among the fireflies. Wondering at the spangled canopy above you, that made you feel so small, with so much up there, out there. And yes, there was the North Star ahead of them, pointed to by the Dipper, the Drinking Gourd, that was said to have guided those slaves who'd escaped.

They said God was up there somewhere, and maybe that was right. Didn't seem closer, the way Preacher was always claiming. Not there to help with endless chores, making do, doing without. Up there somewhere, watching maybe, as she and her sisters patched and plowed, scrubbed and dug and chopped and hoed.

Maybe God, up there in His stars, was glad at what He saw them doing tonight: leading His people to freedom. Like Moses, maybe. But something they had to do, either way. Not the way the law saw it, for sure. Owners robbed of their property. Slave catchers be out all over, hunting human prey, punishing folks like her, those who dared go against the system of master and slave.

They passed east of Isaac Ingrum's place, beyond where his dogs would scent them or hear the rustle of their feet in the grass, in the weeds, in the forest. They followed paths made by cattle or deer, or no paths at all, guided by dark tree-shapes against that glittering sky, by fences and gates and thickets. A few times Kate would crouch, risk a match flare to read her compass, the slaves a silent, shielding circle around her.

There were probably snakes, and she was glad of her boots, in the lead that way. Some snakes would slip away at the sound of heavy feet approaching, but some would not. For the simple reason that they knew they didn't have to: they were deadly, and to be feared and avoided. Kate tried not to think of them.

They heard scurryings in the brush, and sometimes the crashing flight of deer as they approached. At such times she'd freeze, sure they'd been discovered, expecting harsh, challenging voices, lanterns flaring, guns.

None of that occurred.

The night wore on, to the steady pacing of tireless feet. They waded streams, and stopped to scoop water and drink, then off again. The boy would lag behind, tiring, until one of the men would swing him up onto his shoulder for a spell, and he'd doze off. Kate marveled that the stout woman could keep up, but she never faltered, never complained. The girl, maybe fifteen, moved up alongside Kate and whispered questions: Where were they? How much farther tonight? Where would they stay this time?

"Best if we don't talk," she told her, stepping out and away. Voices, however muffled, might startle animals that in turn might alert some out-of-season hunter, some late-returning farmer, some traveler. Some robber on an errand as stealthy as theirs. Or some slave catcher, warned by a slip of a tongue or just a suspicion. The night was peopled with threats, if you thought on it too much.

At last they reached the first of the sheds, still before the stars told them dawn was near. Most of the roof was intact but sagging, along with two walls which formed a corner they settled into. This was closed in by a pole gate, and that had kept deer away from hay the sisters had spread there earlier. Soon the runaways slept, while Kate, her nerves still tight, kept the first watch.

The light came up stealthily, in that chill that signals the ending of summer, that will be gone in burning-off sun in an hour. Dew-smells lay on the weeds, the surrounding brush, the old boards of the shed. The coming hours would be the most dangerous, with people out for any of a hundred reasons, in daylight. Lost cows, tree-cutting, going from place to place. The old wagon ruts to this place were grown over in sprouts and briars, but this had been someone's cow shed once, and people would know of it. A chance, but all this was a chance.

She watched the sun: red, spiked and crisscrossed with limbs, screened in leaves, tethered in trees, break finally into copper sky. The heat rose in shimmers then, not intense yet, but moving, building. It would be a long time before dark again, before Tom Brannon or whoever, crept to this lost hideaway, and the beginning of his own perilous journey.

When Kate had judged three hours had passed, she turned to the others, and found them all awake, watching her. She managed a brief smile, and opened the food pack. A covered bucket of water with a dipper sat against a wall, hidden in the hay. Quietly they ate, drank, turning eyes often to the surrounding trees, overgrown field, thicket.

Kate and the other women went to relieve themselves, then returned. She felt it was safe to talk a little now, if they kept it low.

"Memphis tonight. There'll be a house there, where y'can clean up, sleep, git clothes. Don't know for sure how they git y'on past there, but they do. Prob'ly hafta pretend t'be bought, an' goin' to some plantation. Where y'all from?"

The men were brothers, from near Columbus. The woman had joined them from south of there, a place called Green Tree, which Kate had never heard of. The girl was her niece, from the same place. The boy was an orphan who'd slipped off from a storekeeper, told by a customer of a name and a place. Kate wondered how many more had tried and failed to reach whatever haven the Route people had provided.

They'd moved west quickly, in forced stages to cover as many miles as possible, across most of the state, till the turn north days before. Now, with Memphis near, the excitement was in their eyes once more, the growing assurance that they'd really escaped, were beyond capture. It was wishful hope still, but hope nonetheless. There were so many miles to go, so many dogs to elude, chances for discovery. But there'd be some daylight travel too, with papers in the hands of supposed owners, men who could appear legitimate, unsuspected.

Kate talked with the inquisitive girl some more, softly, reassuringly. Then she let one of the men keep watch, and settled for sleep. She drifted off to the hum of insects in late weeds, the twitter of curious birds. It was fitful sleep, with always some movement, some sound rousing her, but all remained secure.

Finally, with the sun slanting, she sat up, brushing hay from her hair and clothes. Some of the runaways slept, others sat passively waiting, thoughts to themselves. *Not long now, an' they'll be off agin. They must be tired still, sleepin' in snatches, feet burnin'. Rest in Memphis, though, for sure. Easy t'hide in a house basement er attic.* She pictured an old couple, with maybe just such a place, feeding these people, clothing them, hiding them, all at their own peril. *Has t'be th' one south side: too far t'that other'n, up on Second Street. Prob'ly 'nuther route to that one.*

She wondered what drove them, these faceless Samaritans, like in the Bible, to this work. This chain of joined hands leading to freedom somewhere far off. Well, what drove her and Jenny and Susie? Sure a lot of trouble to get into for just a handful of runaways, when there were thousands more who'd never have the chance to get away. She'd never see these again, up in Illinois or wherever, never know how this boy was to grow, or what kind of man this girl would marry, or whether the others would succeed or fail in whatever they would be able to do.

Don't matter, she told herself. *Jist do what y'can, if it's right. An' this's right. All there is to it.*

Darkness came, and deepened. Tension built. Brannon could travel in daylight, but he'd surely want to make certain the route was clear by dark.

Any time now.

Kate remembered the procedures: if a guide got held up on the way down, he'd wait as long as he could, still to be able to reach Memphis before daylight. If that proved impossible, he could only wait another day, with the runaways and their escort hidden where they were. Past that, it was up to that person to find a way to continue to hide them as long as necessary. And if there had to be a change beyond going to the next numbered shelter, he or she'd have to find a way to get word north.

The guide came, silently, with only a rustle of weeds that set them on high alert, and the swift knock. Kate lit a candle.

"You coulda come in day, couldn't you?"

"Yes, but we save those trips for when there's no other way. Can't do that often. I'm Tom Brannon."

"Figgered that. I'm Kate, Jenny's sister. How far y'got t'go?"

"Just under fifteen miles. House is on the south side. These travel all right?" His accent was strange, quick.

"Did. Good folks. Take care now, an' y'd best git goin'."

They faded into the night that closed in after the candle was snuffed. Kate took up the empty pack and bucket and set out for home.

One trip completed. Five former slaves headed for freedom, if the rest of the trip went as well as this. Her feet felt light and the stars smiled overhead.

Or could that be God?

Five

The next trip was Susan's, a few weeks later. Rain had come and gone, and now the nights were cool and the leaves crisping, if hardly turning yet. The temperature was welcome—no snakes out—but eager early hunters might be. Kate had primed her sisters with every detail of the route, and Susan had but to watch for dim landmarks, and consult the compass a few times.

Amazingly, an entire family of six had escaped in different directions from a plantation in western Alabama, joined again in the forest, and were moved, again laterally. There was a prized blacksmith of forty, his wife, cook in the Big House, and all four children, from eighteen down to twelve. One of the girls, at sixteen, had been a maid in the house, and with her mother, had learned the routines, the weaknesses of the planter's operation. The fourteen-year-old boy had been apprenticed to the aging carriage driver, and had traveled with him over much of the nearby territory, so they knew where to go, and how to reach the Cotton Route contacts.

Their plans had been well-laid, and when the guarded message had come from the contact, each family member faded away into the darkness. Each had a hand-drawn map, and each reached the rendezvous ahead of the alarm. The smith hoped to be able to practice his trade up North, and to be able to educate his family. Susan had hopes for them, because they seemed better equipped and more aware than most field hands.

The night passed with only a few tense moments: a distant dog barked, they lost the way twice, had to retrace steps. Susan remained optimistic. It was to her as if this perilous journey would simply succeed, no matter what. And she had her pistol and a long knife to help it along, if need be.

Spirits were high, in spite of the many miles these people had already traveled, the many more ahead of them. Theirs was an outlook she'd never seen: they were to be free, thanks to this sturdy young woman guiding them, and to all the others. No power on earth would hinder them with anything more than minor inconvenience. No imagined hardships in the North dismayed them. They would overcome, and an innate joy radiated from them. Susan caught their enthusiasm, and it buoyed her, carried her along.

She was aware of the dangers, yes: cracklings in the brush that raised the hair on her arms and neck, unexplained sounds that could be pursuers, the chance of sudden surprise. But this trip would succeed, as would those following, she was certain. The *rightness* of it all gave her added confidence, and she silently hummed an old hymn in time to her steps.

At their destination, a better but more secluded barn, she learned more about her charges. They kept voices low, but with one person always on guard, there seemed little chance for discovery.

"Wisht I could answer yer questions better, but truth is, I dunno what's ahead, beyond Memphis. I do know there's factories an' such in Illinois, but I hear they don't pay much er treat real good. Course y'got to take what you c'n git at first, till mebbe y'git some ahead an' c'n go out on yer own. Wouldn't doubt but there's need fer a smith most anywhere, though."

Susan was, overall, friendlier than Kate, but more reserved than Jenny. She was genuinely concerned for this family's welfare and future, and wished she could be sure they'd prosper. She knew enough of the world however, even at seventeen, to have her doubts. Southerners in general pictured Yankee factories as inhuman, drafty, crowded places where people were worked till they dropped, for little in wages. With a supply of even more dependent labor in these runaways, she feared their exploitation.

"So, I dunno what to expect for y'all. Might be worse'n bein' slaves, though I sure hope not."

"No," said the smith's wife, "nothin's worse'n bein' slaves."

The guide who came from Memphis was John Kellog, the Baptist minister, but he wore a gun and carried a big knife. *Looks like he ain't dependin' on jist th' Lord to pertect him,* Susan observed. *Well, neither'd I. Mebbe he c'n pray 'em into a good life North.*

~ * ~

Jenny Blaine's confidence rose as she practiced with the pistol. Not naturally as fearless as either of her sisters, she nevertheless took heart from their successful runs, and began to look forward to her turn with the runaways. This was a different kind of excitement from that she'd always craved, but it *was* exciting. And she was buoyed by the belief that what they were doing should have been done a long time ago, no matter the law.

The second pistol was her favorite, although only one-shot, but long enough for some accuracy at distance. She pondered long on the prospect of actually having to shoot a slave catcher if discovered. What would it be like to take a life, however depraved? Would that condemn her to Preacher's hell? It'd only happen if there were absolutely no other course: discovery would doom her and her charges, for sure. But the shock, the blood, the violence of it: could she? She prayed it would never come to that, but if it did...

Jenny imagined such disaster: there'd be more than one enemy, and they'd have light. Maybe they wouldn't shoot her on sight, being a woman, but maybe they would, too. She'd have to kill the leader first, then whoever was the next biggest threat. She'd have to be fast, and accurate. She was both. So, take the two-shot gun, then.

She had learned to reload in the dark. If a man grabbed her, she could get her knife into him, she was sure. The myth was that women were defenseless, but the Blaine sisters would destroy that myth. One thing was deadly certain: once discovered, none of them could leave an attacker alive.

Jenny Blaine would not be shamed by her tougher sisters, she vowed.

~ * ~

It was October, and much of the harvest was done when the next word came, Jesse slipping from the Talbots' place. Sarah was weakening, he reported, and Susan prepared to go back with him to tend her. Jenny hugged her sisters and set out on her own journey.

The air was heavy in clouds, and the night was as black as she ever remembered it. Would she get lost? Couldn't afford that. No, the way was clear in her mind, but would she be able to follow it? Trees were only slightly darker shapes against the sky, still with leaves clinging, as she set out on this familiar first part. Her feet must feel the way then, for all those miles. Thinking about it could almost make you give up and go back.

Almost.

~ * ~

Susan and the carriage driver reached the Talbot place easily, she having the candle lantern. The slave slipped away as she approached the tall house. She mounted the high porch to the opening of the front door by the aging butler.

The smell of boxwoods permeated the night air, and she'd seen a lot of late coreopsis and chrysanthemums still blooming. She was not intimidated by this grand house, but she appreciated it and all it stood for: the South, her South, with but the one canker of slavery. And that was being undermined, if only a little at a time. She knew Sarah Talbot would succeed in her quest to free the plantation's slaves, even if Everett hadn't realized the fact yet.

"Evenin', James. I hear Miss Sarah's porely."

"Shore is that, Miss Susan. She be right glad t'see you." There were some poor whites James had no respect for, but the Blaine sisters were not among them. While hardly quality, only the most pretentious plantation families—and their prideful servants— looked down upon these independent women. They were favorites of the ailing Sarah Talbot too, and that counted much in their favor.

Everett Talbot greeted the visitor with a tired smile.

"Thank you for coming, Susan. Sarah's been asking about you."

"How is she, Mr. Everett?"

"Not well, I'm afraid. She's insisted on going to Memphis often this year, and I fear it's weakened her."

"Had to see those young uns I know. She eatin' all right? I've brought some of Jenny's broth."

"Hardly anything, but I know she'll welcome you, and perhaps you can get her to eat."

Susan climbed the wide stairs carrying the reheated broth. James showed her in, where pale Sarah lay propped by pillows in her canopied bed.

"Susie, come here, girl. You're a sight for these tired eyes."

"Miss Sarah, what in th' world you doin', here? In bed? Why, I figgered you'd be out dancin' someplace, drag that old bear of yours out t'th' bright lights." She set the tray down, took the older woman's hand, kissed her.

"Oh, you. You're like fresh air, Susie. What's this you've brought me?"

"Jenny's special cure-all broth, that's what. Won't let me'n Katy in th' kitchen when she makes it, but it'll do you, for sure."

"Well, I'll have some, then. You girls are sweet to think of me."

During the visit, Susan was able to whisper that Jenny was out guiding runaways that very night. That news brightened Sarah more than any jollying the girl could offer.

"I'll be praying for her, Susie, and for all of you. You're doing God's work."

Everett was grateful for his wife's radiance following Susan's visit. Sweet girl, that one, and been really good to Sarah lately, spending time with her. Sure found a lot to talk about, those two. Almost like another daughter, uneducated though she was.

~ * ~

Jenny, lacking much of her sisters' boldness, took longer to follow the tortuous path to the barn pickup site. She was greeted by the farmer Shelby Coulter, with six runaways from across the Mississippi in the Arkansas Delta. They had crossed the big river in a perilously leaking boat, missed their next guide for hours, and found alternate hiding in swampland at the last minute before dawn. Finally they'd made contact west of Clarksdale, then farther east, to turn north.

Five of these were field hands, two women in their twenties and three men a little older. The sixth had been a butler in a house south of Helena, and at fifty, had been hard-pressed to keep up. His eyes shifted constantly, fearing discovery.

"How's Katy?" Coulter asked, as they were leaving.

"'Bout th' same, Shelby. Katy don't change her mind."

"Reckon not. Well, best hurry, now. Long way."

It was, and though she tried to hurry, Jenny often froze at sounds of wildlife, imagining hunters, slave catchers, even the rare panther. She found she must put such thoughts out of her mind and push ahead, even in the face of imagined danger.

Her evident fear and hesitancy communicated themselves to the runaways, who became even more fearful as the night wore on. Finally the butler moved up beside her. He spoke quietly.

"You doin' good, Miss Jenny. You knows th' way, an' you ready fo' trouble. Jis' don' you borrow no trouble. We doin' fine, an' we knows you take care of us. Sumpin' happen, we ain' gon' run. We jump in, don' matter how many come down on us. Jis' you keep on now, an' don't fret none."

Jenny thanked this man so out of his element, so scared himself. She stepped out then, showing a confidence she hardly felt. And even when she must kneel and risk a match to read her compass, she quickly stood again, set off purposefully, scanning the dark tree line for guiding shapes. She even tried to ignore the occasional deer crashing away in the brush, although it made the hair on her neck stand and her heart quicken.

Nerves were on high alert when they finally reached the third hiding place, a moldering log cabin, as the sky was graying. No rain had fallen, but the air smelled as if it would come any moment. This worried Jenny as they settled into the scant shelter, since early-season hunters would surely know of the place and seek it. She took the first watch, scouting the area as the light came up full.

The rain came then, softly at first, then harder, saturating the leaves that had crackled all night under their feet. She finished her circuit of the woods and thickets and headed back to the shelter. She moved silently from newly-acquired habit, imagining herself an Indian maiden from one of her books, slipping through the dense trees on some romantic errand.

So it was that the lone hunter did not hear her as he made his way toward the cabin, rifle partially under his coat to keep it dry. Jenny clutched her pistol, heart racing. She must not let him open the sagging door, and he was only yards away. She would have to kill him then: no help for it. But this was no slave catcher, alone this way, a game bag over his shoulder.

Could she do it? Shoot him in the back? She cast about for some other way. *Any* other way…

She could leave them all. Just turn and slip off through the rain back home, leave all this: the risk, the tension that made your nerves jagged knife-edges, your heart racing. She could…

She saw the section of fallen porch post. It was cedar, the heartwood knobby with knots with the sapwood rotted away. Something had broken it recently, showing the solid, red hardness of it. She holstered the gun, reached, lifted the piece, and moved swiftly up behind the hunter.

Strangely, time slowed to a molasses crawl for her: the hunter shifting his rifle, starting to reach for the door, her feet stepping as if with a mind of their own, in dead quiet on the wet leaves. Her arms raising the makeshift weapon as if hindered by a great weight, but higher, higher. The whole like a macabre dance of movements, blurred in the falling rain, otherworldly…

As he stamped clinging leaves from his feet, Jenny brought the club down on his head with all her strength. He collapsed with a grunt, and she grabbed his rifle, backing to see if he moved. He did not. Adrenaline sang in her body, propelling her, strengthening her, making her, it seemed in that moment, invincible.

She pushed the door open, motioned to the men. They came, eyes large at sight of the fallen white man. He was about thirty-five, bearded, medium height, not heavy. Jenny didn't know him.

Her mind worked as she searched the man. *Make it look like a robbery.* He hadn't seen her, or any of them. If they could get him away, or get away themselves... That might work, but this was morning: how could they stay hidden away from the cabin till dark? And how could Tom Brannon, or whoever the next guide was, ever find them? This man would bring others, try to find who'd attacked him, robbed him...

All right, first step: get him away, maybe tie him to a tree while we make a plan. She motioned the men to carry the hunter into the woods. There was no rope or wire in the cabin, though.

"Vines," whispered one of the field hands. They propped the inert body against a tree. Jenny gave one of them her knife and he slipped away. She held her pistol on the man, shielding it from the rain, knowing she'd have to kill him if he roused.

He did not. They bound him to the tree with vines, stuffed a rag into his mouth, tied it with a strip of cloth torn from her dress hem. She sent the men back to the cabin, checked the hunter's breathing. He would come around, but what then? The rain fell steadily, muffling sound. She feared another traveler, seeking shelter.

What to do? She was suddenly confused, as if this situation were not real: a dream, a bad dream. How had she come to be here, even? From day-to-day farm work, predictable, a numbing but comforting sameness, to this: a man unconscious, while runaway slaves crouched in leaky shelter. Outside the law, all of them, the law that could get her hanged...

"Cain't stay heah," the butler stated when she'd rejoined them. "What y'all do when sump'n go wrong?"

What do we do? Her mind was blank. Where was the action Jenny of a few minutes ago, driven, purposeful, able to do whatever was necessary? Gone. She was as if alone, adrift with no clear way to proceed. She tried to will herself back to the task before her. *What...*

But they *had* another plan, if... Then it came: the other shelters. Next in the sequence: the fallen shed. *Of course! Where's my head been? Git 'em outta here, now.*

But as they left the cabin, she thought of the tied man. He might die. Motioning the runaways to wait, she slipped back to the tree. He was still slumped, unseeing. Yes, it'd only been minutes. She crept up behind him, cut the vines, her other hand on her pistol. Then she backed away, turned and moved quickly to join the group. Let him explain it however he might, they were away, and she hoped, safe. She was ashamed of her weak resolve earlier, but refused to dwell on it.

The butler carried the hunter's rifle, one of the field hands the food and water bucket Jenny had brought, leaving no trace. They walked quickly the mile and a half to the shed, just visible in the rain, where she motioned them to stay hidden. She crept forward, gun in hand but still shielded. If someone was here, too...

No one was. They crowded into the one dry corner, ate and drank. Two of the men stood guard then, while the others slept. Jenny lay between the women, and their body warmth soon put her to sleep, despite her nerves.

It was late afternoon somehow when she awakened. The rain was still steady in that soaking, chill prelude to winter that sometimes sets in ahead of time. There would be dry, windy days to come, but this rain promised to go on at least through the night. She thought of these people and their next guide out in it, hidden by it, yes, but weathered-down, unsheltered.

Just now all of her world was this crowded shed, hemmed in sluicing water drumming on what was left of the roof, with these fugitives. The universe seemed focused in on this one sagging corner, this tiny spot of life, in a lowering crush of the elements determined to blot them out, make it as if they'd never existed. Never moved, talked, laughed, loved, regretted. But they were alive, a spark still, in the vastness, a shiver of hope...

The light was fading into early dark. She worried that Tom Brannon, if it were he, would walk into an ambush at the cabin. No, he'd as much right to be there alone as anyone. Could well have missed the way, stumbled on the place following the old, dim track. It was the northbound trip that was dangerous, with this human caravan.

Jenny reflected on the fact that Brannon could move so much more freely than she or her sisters. A woman just wasn't out at night, without a light, alone. For any reason. Oh, maybe an emergency of some sort, seeking help, desperate...

So Tom would know to come here, but that would put him that much later. Well, no help for it. At least he wouldn't be burdened with food and water, and could perhaps travel faster. And the safe house in Memphis would be dry and warm: there'd be clothes and good food. What lay beyond, she couldn't know.

She told the runaways this, and that there should be a day or more of rest for them there. But she worried too, about what lay past that for them. Would there be jobs, indeed? Decent treatment? What could the butler do, unused to hard work? And the others: uneducated, easy to manipulate.

Like her sisters, Jenny wondered how much better off they'd actually be. And that made her doubt the real worth of what they were doing, with it all. What good, if it put these people, so full of hope, into another life of exploitation at the hands of greedy men? Again, it was almost enough to make her give up... *No, best not to think that way.* They'd come this far, after all.

At last came the knock, and she lighted the candle, to see pale Tom Brannon, in an oilskin raincoat, his face anxious.

"There were men at the cabin, and a fire. I didn't know what I'd find here, or if I'd find anything. Thank God you're safe. We must leave now, Miss Blaine. And you must stay well away from there. Is it a hunting party?"

She told him of the lone man, who must have revived, then brought others in search of his attacker.

"Then we must not use the cabin again. And with hunting season upon us, I hope we can wait before the next trip. I'll talk with Mr. Hyde. You'll receive word. Now we all must go, quickly." He offered her his hand.

Impulsively, in a release of tension, in gratitude, and perhaps from some other emotion, Jenny hugged the surprised young man quickly. He was wet, but warm.

Then she stepped out into the rain.

Six

Winter wore away. The Blaine sisters carded and spun, wove and knitted and cut firewood. And on a cold February day, Sarah Talbot died quietly, grateful for the work she and they had done together. Her last request to her husband was that he fulfill his promise to set their slaves free. And he had done so, torn in his grief at losing her.

Little changed at the Talbot place, however, except that Everett let his overseer go. The man hadn't wanted to work hands who could walk off when they wanted to. Intolerance for free Blacks was so intense in the region that almost all the hands had stayed, to work for scant wages. This was preferable to facing the hostile whites outside the plantation, or attempts to travel, when any could be stolen and sold back into harsher servitude.

Jesse remained the Route contact. It was he who brought word from the Memphis people, he who told of times and places and changes.

In time, a few of the Talbot people did drift off, to Hernando and even to Memphis, accompanied by their former master, where there was a growing free Black community not far from the new Shelby Institute.

Everett Talbot tilled his acres that season of 1845, but his heart was not in the work. For him, a way of life had passed, and he withdrew from the society of the other planters, with their balls and political rallies and constant deal-making. He, the butler James, Jesse and Jesse's wife Blythe, the housekeeper, became the circle of his life.

The children and grandchildren came from Memphis, and urged Everett to move there, sell out the homeplace.

"No, I'll not consider that. Your mother's here, and I shall join her in a few years. This is Talbot ground, and it will remain so as long as I draw breath."

So that was that. And Memphis daughter-in-law Stella was secretly glad for the distance between her and the old man.

The Cotton Route continued its operations, accelerated now with more moderate weather. The organization recruited important members in a former slave couple on the Robert McRaven plantation near Byhalia, whose owners were those Sarah Talbot had heard of. Hettie and Sam Barnes became vital links in the information chain, for both the Holly Springs and Hernando routes.

The Blaine sisters worked their land as always, and managed an existence several levels above mere survival. Jenny still dreamed of romance, often with Tom Brannon in those dreams. Kate firmly and finally rebuffed earnest Shelby Coulter, he of the bulging eyes, the hungry children and the rare abolitionist views.

"Way I see it, I got a family of m'own t'care for," she stated. He eventually turned his attentions to a minister's spinster daughter.

Susan enjoyed attendance at dances and picnics in the community, and attracted the attentions of several young farmers. She was unmoved at their clumsy advances.

"Lookin' for free labor," she told her sisters. "Like I was livestock. Or breedin' stock, mebbe. All right for you, Jenny, t'dream about beaus an' frills an' bein' took care of by a man, but it just don't look t'me like much of a way t'live."

Kate agreed.

The women became used to the nighttime guiding of the runaways, and faced the trips with a matter-of-factness grown of familiarity. They found new hiding places, new and better routes, and traveled these paths with new confidence. None of them grew careless, but each knew she could handle any situation that arose, for the simple reason that she *had* to.

~ * ~

From time to time during the years that followed, slaves from local plantations escaped. This triggered intense manhunts by the slave catchers of the region, and the Route shut down till things calmed. Through the grapevine that somehow connected plantation Blacks, these runaways often knew of the Blaines' work, and eventually one came directly to them for shelter and help. It was June, the heat already high.

This would be suicidal, the sisters knew: hiding a local slave. But the hard choice would be to refuse to help, and that, as Susan said "sticks in my craw." The runaway was a teenage boy, with the scars from beatings on his back. His name was Jupiter, and he'd run from only about fifteen miles east in Marshall County. He'd known not to go north, but his appearance here could as easily get him caught, and the sisters jailed.

Or hanged.

It must have taken great courage—and luck—to locate this farm and knock at the darkened door of the farmhouse, with only the closely-guarded rumor that these women would help. But then it had taken equal courage to slip away from his masters too, right after roll-call at day's end. Jupiter had simply announced to his parents that he needed to go to the privy, and then kept on going. Now, in near daylight, with this house stirring early, his life was in these women's hands.

And that daylight was almost upon them, and very soon after that the catchers would be out. Probably with good dogs, and Jupiter's trail wasn't that cold. He either hadn't been near a stream to lose his scent in water or hadn't thought of it. A hasty conference around the table followed, with the lamp lit and one sister keeping watch with the last-season hunter's loaded rifle.

"No use blamin' th' boy," Kate said, "but we got t'do somethin', an' quick. They'll search ever' empty shack, send word all directions. Cain't hide him, an' that's a fact."

"Cain't turn him in, either," Jenny insisted, from her post at the window. She moved from one opening to another, alert for a light, or the sound of dogs.

"Jesse," Susan stated. "Jesse's headin' th' work at Talbot's now, an' mebbe he c'n slip th' boy in with th' field hands."

"Would that work?" from Kate. "Owners'd know him, if they came."

"Won't come, not west like this: they'll leave it to th' catchers. An' cain't search out ever' farm in th' country, 'thout knowin' which way t'go."

"But they'll trail him here, or at least this way, with dogs."

"Oh, that's right... Well then, boy, we gotta make a trail on past here. Git him somethin' t'eat, Jenny. I'll be back quick." And Susan was out the door.

In moments she was back, leading their one horse and a mule. Jupiter was finishing off a piece of cornbread.

"What're you up to?" Kate demanded.

"Gonna make a trail, like I said, t'wards Hernando, fast's we can. Then ride him on back t'Talbot's. That'll give us a bit of time, 'cause they'll try t'find him in town first. Hope Jesse'll know what t'do, then. Now, Jupiter, yer prob'ly tired, but y'got to run 'longside me long's you can." The boy nodded, eyes big in the light from the candle Kate held.

He was barefoot, in ragged clothes, and yes, he was tired, from his all-night running and hiding. But he set out, keeping up with Susan's horse as she led the mule toward town. She marveled that he'd known the way, and in the dark. *Must've got directions from mebbe a carriage or wagon driver'd been here.* Slaves knew a lot more than their masters ever suspected, she'd learned.

It was three miles to town, and the boy gave out after two of them. He stumbled and fell, and Susan jumped down to help him up.

"Couple hunderd yards on, there's a creek, Jupiter. Git to it, y'can wade in, lose yer trail. Put you on this mule then, and we're headed fer a place should be safe." *For now, at least.*

They reached the creek, she helping him along, leading their mounts, careful not to leave her tracks in the dust of the path. There, she helped him up on the mule a few yards downstream, standing both animals in the shallow water. They climbed a low bank well away from the path, and headed back for the Talbot plantation, mindful that daylight had come in earnest.

This was a perilous ride, with people out early, and Susan considered what excuse she could give for having the boy with her. None at all, she realized. So she had him follow a few paces behind, trusting that if she sighted anyone on the way ahead, she could have a few moments for him to hide. Mercifully, they encountered no one.

Once there, Susan hid the boy and their mounts in the woods and slipped up to Jesse's cabin, which fortunately was near the woods and a little off from the rest. She knocked. The door opened and Jesse pulled her inside.

"Whut's wrong, Miss Susie?" His face showed alarm. His wife Blythe had already gone to the Talbot house, and their children were grown and among those who had gone.

"Got a runaway, f'm close by, Marshall County. Left a trail on t'wards Hernando, then rode him back. Hopin' y'd know what we c'n do fer 'im."

"Oh, that's bad, close lak this. He come west, though; that'uz smart. Lessee, reckon I c'n slip him in 'th our han's, off from th' house. Won't none of us tell, but got to keep 'im away from Mass' Ever'tt."

"That should do, for t'day. Then what?"

"Umm. Somebody got t'git word t'Tom Brannon, an' fast, or we gon' lose us a boy. Mebbe git in trouble bad, too."

"It's all trouble, Jesse. One of us can go t'Memphis, I guess, an' just see what we c'n do. How long c'n you hide him here?"

"Reckon we c'n git him inside after dark, mebbe git th'u t'morrer. Be hard, after that, 'spesh'ly if th' catchers come."

"Let's hope we c'n move him quick, then. We'll git word to you soon's we kin. I'll drop him back at th' far corner, where th' schoolhouse path is, 'n leave him t'you."

"That's good, then. An' you be keerful, Miss Susie."

It was well into the day when Susan reached home again. All was quiet, but she knew the dogs and the slave catchers would be along soon. *This cain't keep happenin'. Put us all in danger.* Not that they weren't in almost constant danger, anyway.

"Well, girls, th' fat's in th' fire. Jesse says one of us got t'git t'Memphis quick, find Tom Brannon t'git us outta this'n."

"I'll go," Jenny volunteered. "I know th' way. It's Friday, an' time I git there, Tom'll likely be able t'leave school, an' git to whatever's gotta happen next."

"By y'self?" Kate asked. "Could be chancy." She wouldn't be that worried if it had been Susan.

"Well, I got a friend," her sister assured her, taking her gun from a drawer.

"Guess y'do, at that. Well, Susie, whatta you think?"

"Best way, I reckon. Gonna ride, er walk?"

"Got no saddle, so I reckon I'll walk. Be there 'round three, mebbe."

"Be wore out. Wal, no help fer it, I guess. Take some vittles."

It was more than fifteen miles to the Shelby Institute from the farm, which was farther than their hiding places, but Jenny set off confidently, even with the small worry that she might miss Tom Brannon for some reason. He had told them there was a new free Black teacher at the school who knew of the Route. This young woman would surely be there or nearby if Tom wasn't.

Let's see, her name's Anna ...Anna Blake, set free by her owners years back down in Hinds County, but come to live with them later, near to Byhalia. Jenny felt sure she could find one of the two.

~ * ~

It was still before the time their sister would be reaching the city that the catchers came. The dogs had been able to follow the cold trail, and it led by woods and fields right to their house. Susan and Kate were in the garden hoeing when the three men rode up, the hounds milling, barking.

"Got a runaway, ladies. M'name's Luddy Holtz, f'm Marshall County, an' this's Abner Shaw an' Bill Bates. Y'seen a boy 'bout fifteen? Run off las' night." The man's pig eyes shifted, taking in the barn, outbuildings, the house.

"Reckon not," Kate sized Holtz up. He was stout, stubbled red face, and not clean. Chewed tobacco. The other two were lean, hawkish men, bearded. All of them were heavily armed. "But them dogs say he's shore been by. Must've been 'fore we's out. Whyn't you look in th' barn; might've hid in th' hay, though ain't much there, now."

"An' Lord," Susan spoke up, affecting fright, "we'd oughta look under th' house, too, an' in it, case he slipped in on us." She even looked scared, which was a stretch for her.

"Reckon we will. What's y'all's name?"

"We're th' Blaines. Farm this place. I'm Kate an' this's Susie. Jenny's gone t'town. Boy ain't got a gun, has he?"

"Oh, no. Didn't 'pear t've took ennything, jist run. Figger he's lost, headin' west. Er jist too dumb t'know. Mebbe knew somebody in Hernando, try t'find help thar."

"Mebbe: some crazy folks there, fer sure. Wal, let's have a look," Kate propped her hoe, led two of them to the barn. "Susie, help Mr. Holtz search 'round th' house, now."

The hunt was brief, because the milling dogs struck Jupiter's trail on away from the house.

"They onto him!" Holtz yelled to his men as the pack raced off excitedly toward Hernando. The trio mounted and followed. The sisters watched them go.

"Hate t'have them three after me," Kate remarked.

"Fer shore. Heard of that Holtz. Lets his place run down, huntin' runaways. Acts like he tracks 'em fer fun, much as th' money."

"Reckon so. But he's seen us now, an' he'll remember, if he ever sees us agin."

"I c'n do without seein' that'n agin, ever." Susan picked up her hoe.

~ * ~

The two sisters were surprised next day by Jenny and Tom Brannon arriving in a hired buggy in midafternoon. She'd reached him in time with the news of Jupiter, and he'd acquired forged papers for the boy. She'd spent the night with Anna Blake, the new teacher at the institute, the striking Black girl.

"Smartest one woman I ever seen," Jenny reported to her sisters, "white *or* Black." Brannon grinned. He'd been much taken with this English teacher too, and had helped recruit her for the Route. It turned out also that she was from the very plantation in Marshall County Sarah Talbot had told them of, where the owners farmed broad holdings without slaves.

Susan rode to Talbot's with Tom, stopping him well short of the place. She slipped through the woods to the fields, where the hands were working. Seeing Jesse, but not Everett Talbot, she climbed the fence and went to him. Jupiter was nowhere to be seen.

"Slave catchers still lookin' in town," he told her, "but they be heah by t'morrer, sho'."

"Now how you know that, Jesse? You been t'town?"

"Naw, Miss Susie, th' news, it jis' got feets. You got a way for th' boy?"

"Tom Brannon's waitin'. When I didn't see Jupiter, I'se afraid Holtz'd been here already."

"Not yit, like I tol' you. Mass' Ever'tt come heah while ago, so I run th' boy off to th' woods. I git'm now. Where Mist' Tom at?"

"Off th' road where th' schoolhouse path comes in. Says he c'n take him in daylight if he moves fast. Got papers."

"That fine, now. Bes' git goin', then. Bad if he run on Holtz, papers er no."

The frightened Jupiter was soon in Brannon's buggy, headed toward Memphis. But not before the sisters had impressed on the young teacher how dangerous local unescorted runaways were. To all of them.

"We'll have our contact get that word around among the slaves," he'd promised. "We can take care of them if they can wait for a run, take them west or east, but it has to be done right."

Remembering the starved Celie, the slain Juno, Susan had replied that no, some of them just couldn't wait.

Seven

The runs were not all so successful. Once, in July, Tom Brannon ran into waiting slave catchers as he came south from Memphis. He heard their talk, hidden at a creek bridge, then doubled back to follow another obscure road. But there were men there, too. A field hand had escaped from a nearby plantation, and the catchers were out in force, watching every possible way north.

There was no way to send word, and Kate, with six runaways in the barn northeast of Hernando, waited through most of the night. In the group was a terrified girl of six, who'd had to be carried part of the way. She whimpered almost constantly, not from pain but from fear, deadly fear. The one older woman tried to hush the child, reassure her, but the sound wore on everyone's nerves.

And they were now out of food. Kate slipped away, back the way they'd come, with the bucket to bring stream water just before dawn, and literally almost ran into someone, moving as stealthily as she. A twig had broken, and she'd heard the brushing of cloth against leaves.

Kate drew her pistol, moving as quietly as she could to one side of the forest path. The other person stopped, and there was a long, eerie quiet as the two tensed in the standoff, each waiting for the other to move again.

Slowly the blackness grayed into predawn. Kate had no idea how long she'd waited, straining for any sight of what—whom—she faced. What could she say to anybody, here? That she was lost? This wasn't on the way to anywhere but the overgrown barn, falling in as it was. No woman would be out alone like this.

Well, nothin' t'do but wait for light. Probably only one man, since she'd heard no movement suggesting she was being flanked. *Hope t'see him 'fore he sees me. I'm in black, an' if he ain't, he'll show first.* She crouched, absolutely still, peering. But she needed sleep, and she was growing stiff from not being able to shift her weight, even. Strangely, she thought she smelled ham. *Must be that hungry,* she thought, *imaginin' things.*

Then she saw it: the slightest movement, dark against lighter leaves that were catching the rising trace of light. She inched her pistol around. So he was in black, too. She'd pulled her brimmed man's hat low, and had a black shawl to hide her face, and now searched for the man's face, which should show first. She reflected briefly on the fact that she would have to kill him, but pushed the thought away. If it came to that...well, it just would. *Watch for th' face, now: it'll show 'bout there...*

But it didn't. *Must be covered, too. Well, this's gonna be who's quicker I reckon, an' that's all there is to it. Unless...* She cautiously reached down with her free hand, felt for a stick, anything to throw. And her fingers found a hickory nut from the fall before. It was soft, with its shell half-decayed, but it came up soundlessly in her hand. Slowly she raised it, drew back, lobbed it across the path into brush. It made a sound.

And part of a face turned, its cover slipping. A face she knew. She couldn't help exclaiming.

"Susie?"

"Katy? I was sure a catcher had got all of you." Her sister came to her, putting her own gun away.

"Well, you 'bout got y'self shot, girl. Had me spooked in black thataway. Had t'be up t'no good, hidin' thar. What's that I smell?"

"Got food. Figgered y'missed Tom, or whoever. Runaways still in th' barn?"

"Are. Gittin' 'em some water. They'll be plumb scared by now, sure."

The sisters got the water, moved quickly back to the hiding place.

"It's me," Kate called softly as they neared. The gray structure loomed in the mist that had dampened them both. The sagging door opened, and they were inside. Nothing was visible. The girl was quiet, probably scared witless. "Got food an' water. This's m'sister Susie." She lighted the candle, and the dark faces materialized. Breaths exhaled.

"So what's t'do, Katy?" Susan asked, once the food had been distributed.

"Been study'n on jist that. No place t'move 'em, now it's come day. Jist hafta chance 'nother day here."

"I reckon. Twicet as likely t'be found, though. Ain't gonna rain, at least. Y'wanta go on home, let me stay?"

"No, reckon we c'n keep watch better, both of us. Choppin' time, so shouldn't be nobody along, but somethin's helt up our guide, an' I'm that worried."

"Well, Tom, er th' preacher, c'n come in th' day, but don't know if Tom'd chance movin' 'em now."

"No, he's had t'do that mebbe too many times of late. Folks sees him too much. An' when he talks funny like he does, they gits s'spicious."

"Jist hafta hide an' watch, then. Sorry 'bout this, folks: do what we kin fer you." Susan wasn't sure just what they'd be able to do if slave catchers came. Maybe have to shoot their way out. And yes, they could do that, if there weren't too many.

The day wore away slowly, with nothing to do but wait. The woman had finally won the child's confidence enough to keep her quiet, which helped. Others took turns keeping a double watch.

The sisters learned the surprising fact that all four men had slipped away in late daylight from a land-clearing crew when the overseer had passed out from too much whiskey. They'd had word of a contact at the edge of the nearest village, in Tishomingo County, and had reached the place in darkness.

This Route member, a doctor, had begun the run west with the woman, who was a housemaid, and the orphaned girl. The doctor often called on emergencies at night, so had hauled them in a two-horse spring wagon, supposedly to a clinic, all that night, while the men had walked cautiously alongside the road. He'd had to sedate the frightened girl.

Susan had often wished she could learn more about their charges: where they'd lived, what they were leaving, besides bondage. Often like these, leaving their families, she knew, friends, ties to home and all they'd known, usually from childhood. And what lay ahead for them? She couldn't forget the icy Hiram Hyde, so driven, so fiery in his devotion to this cause. *An' prob'ly don't really care what happens to 'em once they're North.*

But all the sisters sensed that the slaves would take anything, any deprivation over being owned, being just *things* to their masters, not people. They guessed that it was worth it even if they died up there: at least they'd die free.

The maid expressed it best when she told them:

"Ain' fooled, thinkin' life gon' be fine up Nawth. Reckon I'se gon' wu'k jis' as hard. Scrub floors, clean up after white folks, carry slops. But I do that, er ennything I got to. My kids all sol' off, dunno whar. My man daid. I got nuthin' in this life t'show I evah been heah 'cept this freedom. I gits Nawth, ain' nobody gon' be able take that away. Nobody." The four men nodded; the girl listened, her eyes large.

~ * ~

A double knock sounded after dark, and Kate opened the door to a nervous man of fifty, Eli Dobbins, the cotton merchant's clerk she'd seen only once before.

"Trouble?" she asked.

"Roads blocked last night. Runaway between here and Memphis. I've a wagon and team at the road on west. We must hurry, now." The man was sweating.

"Y'got papers?" Kate was worried whether this shaky man could handle this.

"Yes, the doctor in Tishomingo sent the names and descriptions. And Mr. Hyde prepared these. I pray they'll get me through. I'm supposed to be a slave trader this time, since I'm not as familiar here as the others."

"Sounds right," Susan put in. "But by th' roads it'll be a long trip. You dodge 'em on th' way down?"

"Well, no trouble there, me bein' just one man in a wagon. But they'll block the roads tonight, I'm certain. Shouldn't be looking for six people, though. I'll have to brazen my way through."

"You'll do all right," Kate patted his arm. "Catchers ain't dumb, but don't look nervous, an' they won't have no reason t'suspect you."

Once at the wagon, the women helped the clerk chain his charges together as part of the necessary ruse. He kept apologizing to the runaways, until Kate stopped him.

"They ain't stupid, Mr. Dobbins. Reckon they c'n stand a few hours in chains; you jis' make sure y'git 'em safe t'town, y'hear?"

~ * ~

Luck was with the clerk for most of the night, and he had to use the slave-trader story only twice, on the roads that way. But just before dawn, a wobbly wagon wheel splintered in a pot hole some distance from Memphis. With no one to send for help, Dobbins resigned himself to wait for daylight, and whatever he could manage then. He thought for the thousandth time how unfit he was for this work, and feared yet again that he'd fail, at the worst possible time. But thought of the three sisters and their resourcefulness, their apparent lack of fear, bolstered him. *If they can do it…*

At full light, a farmer rode by.

"Y'got trouble?"

"Afraid so. Trying to get these slaves to town early, broke a wheel. Cain't leave 'em to get help." Dobbins tried to sound like he thought a slave trader would.

"Reckon not. You a trader? Ain't seen you 'round here."

"Yessir. Got these off a place went broke down in th' Delta."

"Hmm. Little one ain't gonna be worth much fer a while. Others bring a price, though. Care t'sell me one them field han's?"

"Would, but I've got the lot sold already, in town. But next time, I'm sure. Is there a blacksmith shop close? Good long way to one I know in Memphis."

"Well, old Ben Shackelford, next t'me, has got a smithy on his place. Reckon I c'd stop in, have him ride out, see what he c'n do for you."

"I'd be much obliged, sir. Brought help, but my man wanted to visit folks in Hernando. Shouldna' let him."

"No. Well, keep me in mind fer a good buck next time. Got a big crop in, an' we're behind on choppin'. Name's Joel Barber."

"I will that, Mr. Barber. I'm Carson White from Jackson way. Don't usually come this far, but my helper knew of that sale." Dobbins had rehearsed all of this information, and hoped it sounded sincere. Playing it back in his mind, he decided he'd done the best he could.

~ * ~

In time, the other farmer, a smith and passable wheelwright, was able to replace the wheel, and Dobbins drove on into town. Now the problem was getting his runaways into the safe house in daylight. There was no place to hide them, and they needed food. The girl had begun to cry again.

Dobbins, desperate, drove to the Shelby Institute, stopping some distance away on a side street, where he locked the chained runaways to a wagon brace, and chained a wheel so it couldn't move.

"Tell anybody asks that you're on the way on through town, soon's I can get back," he cautioned them. "Tell the name I used: Carson White. I'll be back quick."

He found Tom Brannon just heading for a class. Drawing him aside, he explained the problem. But there didn't seem to be a solution.

Just then an attractive young Black woman walked by. Dobbins knew her: Anna Blake, the newest recruit for the Route.

"Anna, do you have a moment?" Brannon asked. She glanced at Dobbins.

"Of course. Let me put these books in the office, then let's go outside."

There, she soon learned the dilemma. She thought a moment.

"Bring them to the church," she said. Tell Reverend Ezra they're to paint the building, a gift from somebody. They'll have to work till dark, then we can go ahead as planned."

"Anna, you're a genius," Tom praised. "Now, I know you have to be back at work, Eli, or do you have more time off?"

"I don't now, Tom. I was due back this mornin', after yesterday."

"All right, then. Anna, can you go before your next class?"

"Maybe. Then you bring food, Tom, when you can get away. Yes, I'll meet you at the church, Mr. Dobbins."

Anna Blake spoke with no trace of the slave patois of the region. Her owners had schooled her and the rest of their slaves down in Hinds County in preparation for freeing them. The community of planters had nearly lynched these benefactors, who'd then sold out and come to near Byhalia as non-slaveholders. They'd farmed with hired hands and some who shared the crops. Successfully too, to the amazement of their neighbors.

Anna left the school, then walked to the neighborhood hardware store, still in the racially mixed edge of town. She bought paint and brushes, being careful to explain the supposed situation.

"Some kind people have loaned the church some of their help," she told the proprietor, an older man with a round face and glasses. His name was Ellis Cantwell, and he'd been warned that he'd starve, opening a store here among poor whites and poorer free blacks. The opposite had happened, his customers being so anxious for Cantwell to succeed in providing for their needs here in the midst of them.

"That's right neighborly, Miss Anna. Reckon bein's it's for th' church, I c'n take a bit off th' price."

"Why, thank you, sir. Reverend Ezra will be so grateful. We all are." The storekeeper beamed.

This striking woman in her early twenties had become a favorite since coming to Memphis. People—all people—liked being around her. Unfortunately, some of the white men assumed upon seeing her, that she was some slave owner's 'fancy gal', kept for his pleasure. Her perfect speech and obvious intelligence had always belied this misconception, and among those in the environs of the institute, she was considered almost a celebrity.

Her work with the Cotton Route was a secret to all but its members, of course, who kept her away from any actual guide work for the obvious reasons: there could, in 1840s Mississippi or Memphis, be absolutely no legal explanation for a Black woman to be out with a group of slaves at night.

She hurried to the church with her purchases. Eli was directing the runaways in picking up trash and pulling weeds in the yard. He was almost shaking with the strain, looking frequently over his shoulder. She started them on painting the walls that were within reach, wishing for ladders. She sent the relieved Eli on to his job. The girl complained of hunger.

"Just a little while. What's your name?"

"Clytie. What's yers?" *Clytemnestra: the imaginations of some of these slaveholders...*

"I'm Anna. And we'll have something to eat before long. You're doing a good job, Clytie." The girl smiled broadly and slapped on paint.

Then Anna began to fret: she should be back at the institute. *Have to think of an excuse. Someone sick? Held up some other way?* No, the other teachers had seen her there already. Maybe Tom had made some excuse for her. She fervently hoped so. But one thing sure: she couldn't leave these people here by themselves, not even for a short time.

Providentially, the Baptist minister John Kellog arrived a few minutes later, with ladders tied onto his buggy, and food for the runaways.

"Can you stay?" Anna asked him. It was well past time she returned to school, before some serious suspicions could arise.

"I can. Tom's given me a story that should hold up. We'll keep them here till dark, then get them to that other safe house on Second Street."

Eight

That run was successful, but it had the effect of frightening Eli Dobbins to the point he sickened with the tension, and had to stay home for a week. He regretfully told Hiram Hyde he could not continue the work; his nerves just wouldn't stand it.

Hyde was not sympathetic, but reasoned that a shaky guide was worse than none at all. This would leave them short, though. The Baptist minister was steadfast, a rock, and so was Tom Brannon. The others had their assignments elsewhere in the operation, and weren't really suited for guide duty. He *must* recruit others...

~ * ~

Hyde rode up to the plantation house he'd heard about, intent on impressing upon these enlightened non-slavers the need to join his efforts. He'd been unsuccessful with planter Robert McRaven near Byhalia, by coincidence the very planter who'd freed and raised Anna Blake. That man had pointed out that the first place slave catchers would search would be somewhere like his plantation. That had been a disappointment to the New Englander, but now he'd try these other people, hoping they'd be more sympathetic to his cause.

Why can't these provincial people see the need? Why do they cling to their evil ways, enslaving God's people, even while enjoying what culture there is here? Narrow minds, wallowing in ignorance, blind to the logic of equality? I will be more forceful this time, accuse, if necessary. Make these hypocritical, misguided half-serious planters squirm with God's accusations.

I shall not fail.

He was greeted by a black butler, who he knew was a freed servant. And he was pleasantly surprised to learn that this planter was originally from New York, a decade-past transplant. *Ah, thank you God, for leading me here.*

"And to what may I attribute your visit, sir?" this Evans Cardwell asked, after welcoming Hyde. The place was well-appointed, evidence of good taste everywhere.

"As you will have ascertained, sir, I am from the Northeast: western Massachusetts. I operate a commercial goods business in Memphis, supplying outlying stores in the region. I came South several years ago, drawn by the evident need to aid people of color. I find few other whites willing to help in this cause, but had heard of you and your wife, from associates who knew you were a non-slaveholder."

"I see. And just how do you find ways to aid them, Mr. Hyde, if I may ask?"

"We are active in providing employment for those who have been freed, first of all. And our efforts have helped establish a school for educating freed young people, in practical trades, plus the arts, language." Hyde hadn't been a part of that effort, but wanted to sound as philanthropic as he could.

"Admirable, sir. I know the Shelby Institute, and have contributed to it. I admire Headmaster Bancroft greatly."

"I, too. But despite our best efforts to aid, many thousands of Black people, God's people, remain enslaved, as I'm quite sure you are aware. We are, shall we say, seeking ways to aid in their …well, attaining freedom." Hyde wasn't sure how his host would react, so had been treading lightly so far.

"By legally purchasing any whose owners are willing to sell?"

"That would be ideal, yes. But alas, we are not funded to that extent. Such an undertaking is beyond our means."

"So you're aiding runaways, surely? Knowing that is illegal, indeed a hanging offense." It was a statement, not a question. Cardwell appeared to be considering this.

"Aiding, yes, but not soliciting, nor actively encouraging. We believe the difference is quite significant."

"A moot point, if you are caught."

"Yes. But speaking of points, we require the aid of clear-thinking participants such as you, sir, to further our work."

"In what way, Mr. Hyde?" The man had not warmed to this subject as he'd hoped. *Not another half-committed one, I hope.*

"We require additional guides, as well as more way stations for their charges, places for them to hide during the day on their way to freedom. Of necessity, they must travel by night, and of course have someplace providing concealment before dawn, at each stage of the journey."

"And you're asking if we can be guides, provide such concealment, or both." The planter rose, paced. "Or in other words, you're asking us to commit a crime against the laws of this state, a crime that would get us hanged if caught. Do I state this correctly?"

"We believe the risk is worth the end result, Mr. Cardwell. Our guides risk their lives every day, in this cause we believe in."

"Of course. But let me ask you a question, sir. Have you personally guided escaped slaves to freedom? Put your own life in danger to ensure the success of such a ...shall we call it a *run?*"

"Well, no, I haven't. But my role in organizing the effort is far more valuable to it than any individual guide's. We can replace guides, but no one else has come forward to head such a concerted effort."

"Then let me ask another question. Where would be the first place a slave catcher would search for a runaway?"

"Our experience is that they go north toward free states..."

"But the *first* place on that journey. The first hiding place, say the day after his escape? Would it be on the property of a cruel slave master?"

"Certainly not, since such a man would not hide a runaway."

"Ah, then it would follow that said slave catcher would come first to a place like ours, with no slaves, would you not agree? Making our active participation doomed to failure, exposure, even punishment by hanging."

"As I said, a risk one who believes in freeing God's people must take." Hyde was seeing failure. Again.

"By choice. The guide's choice. The person's choice who agrees to hide the slave. The person who chooses to participate in any way with your program. Make no mistake, sir, I appreciate your efforts. But they are yours, not mine. We've chosen to operate our plantation without slaves, to pay our help, and sharecrop with some of them. But that is our choice, Mr. Hyde, no one else's. And I'm afraid we here cannot substitute your choice for ours.

"Good day, sir."

~ * ~

Tom Brannon, as a single man, could and did go often on the runs, but ran the risk of being seen too often by too many people. He was a former Chicagoan, and had not made many close associations in Memphis. Therefore he knew no one else who could be recruited.

The safe-house owners were mostly old, unfit for escort work. They'd led Hyde to the minister, and to Eli Dobbins, he of the faint heart. But they knew of no more prospects. Memphis at this time was not exactly teeming with abolitionists anxious to risk their lives in the actual work. And of course as he'd stated, Mr. Hyde himself considered his leadership position too vital to risk on the routes themselves.

The obvious solution would have to be reduced traffic; that was all. But that was not an option the director of the operations was willing to consider. This was God's work, only He hadn't provided enough help. And His servant Hyde did not feel he could wait on divine intervention this time.

So he tried every other option. One, a merchant selling farm equipment, seemed possible. Abelard Gregory was familiar with the area south of Memphis, having traveled there often to demonstrate his wares. The new turning plows John Deere had perfected were eagerly bought, once they were demonstrated. So Gregory often left the running of his store to his wife, and with implements in his wagon, went regularly toward Hernando.

Perhaps Hyde just wanted too fervently for Gregory to be sympathetic to the mission, deluding himself into believing the man could be recruited. At any rate, he arranged a meeting late one day near closing, at the store, just as the merchant was about to lock up.

"Mr. Gregory, sir, could I have a few minutes of your time, please?"

"Are you a potential customer, sir?" He was assessing the black clothing, the stovepipe hat.

"Not at all, sir. I am actually a wholesale merchant, but not of farm implements. My name is Hiram Hyde, and I hear you are familiar with the territory between here and the Hernando area farms. Is that correct?"

"It is. Perhaps we could indeed discuss the possibility of your firm's branching out, supplying me, at a competitive cost of course."

"That is certainly possible, and bears further exploration. But what I want to ask you, sir, is this: You employ several free Blacks, do you not?"

"I do. I recognize that trained freed slaves are quite capable, given the opportunities, contrary to popular belief."

"Yes indeed. I too, am sympathetic to the difficulties free Blacks face. But to be frank, I am seeking, and actually finding, a way for more of the enslaved to become free. Does that idea possibly appeal to you?"

"Somewhat, and I actually know of half a dozen citizens of this town who have, shall we say, put their money where their mouths are. Buying slaves, helping them acclimate to survival, then freeing them. I approve of that, yes."

"Ah. Could we perhaps then continue this conversation at a more convenient time and place? I'm sure your wife must be waiting supper for you by now."

"Yes, actually. And if you've discovered another method by which this work may be done, legally of course, I should be glad to explore it further."

Hyde was elated. His instincts about this man were proving true. He took his leave of him, after agreeing on a time and meeting location.

For his part, Gregory had masked his instant distaste for the macabre Mr. Hyde upon first seeing him, as a sort of raven-like spectre. *No, more like a vulture, somehow. I know that's judgmental, but I don't think I could do business with that man, no matter a possible commercial connection. Or whatever he's dreamed up regarding freeing slaves. I think, Mr. Hyde, I must steer clear of you; I'm doing quite well without that ...entanglement.*

And so the Route's director was again deeply disappointed at Gregory's polite but firm declining to pursue a further relationship. *Damn the man: another lily-livered pretender at compassion. Put his money where his mouth is? You fail to live up to that level of sincerity, you coward.*

And so it went with others he might have recruited. Nobody, it seemed, wanted any part of his admittedly illegal dealings, no matter their righteousness.

But Hyde persevered. He called on several ministers, hoping for another rocklike Reverend Kellog. Only to be denied, even rebuffed by these men supposedly God's earthly representatives. *Hypocrites!*

One, who could only be described as a shirt-tail preacher, Brother Lester Jenkins, was known as a highly unconventional, Bible-thumping exhorter. Hyde theorized that his dogged adherence to Scripture might mean he'd recognize God's clear (to Hyde) message to, if necessary, slay the master and free the slave, His child.

He approached the good (self-styled) reverend one Sunday after a rousing outdoor service beneath a brush arbor, since Jenkins at present had no fitter venue.

"I say, Reverend, that was a sermon directly from our Maker. Congratulations, sir, on your insights." Hyde offered his pale hand.

"Why, thankee, suh. Yes, I see m'self as a sort of channel from God to these sinners, meanin' all of us. Ain't my words; they comes direct from Him, way it should be. Don't you agree? And what might yore name be, suh?"

"Hiram Hyde, Reverend. And I'd like the opportunity to learn more about your inspired interpretations of Scripture. Might we spend a bit of time on that subject? All of us need enlightening on the Word, and I sense you, sir, have gone further and deeper than some of the more …conventional pastors of this fair city."

"Why shore, Mr. Hyde. Allus like t'discuss God's Word, with ennybody'll listen." And Jenkins even invited this austere man, obviously of deep faith, to supper that very day. Of course the invitation was gladly accepted. Again, Hyde felt that here, at last, was a man who'd see the righteous path to God's desire to free His people from bondage.

Mrs. Gregory was obviously unlettered, a plain farm woman, which put Hyde off not at all: his target was the equally unlettered but forceful preacher, the kind of fearless man he needed. And was, he was certain, to become a useful cog in the Route's wheels—*gears—whatever.*

Except that the meal was served by a comely Black girl, as subservient, even timid, as he'd ever seen. *Well, she's another example of her race's members not being ready to acclimate...*

Then the girl, one Venus, sloshed the soup while setting it down inexpertly. Jenkins exploded.

"Was you raised in a barn, girl? I didn't buy you to shame us in front of comp'ny thataway! Want me t'sell you down th' river? Now, you git yerself back in th' kitchen, an' send that wuthless man of yore's t'do yer work. *Git!*

Well, this just wasn't going to work. Hyde left as politely as he could manage, given the disappointment—no, rage—churning inside him.

~ * ~

There *was* one person with the necessary zeal for the cause. One dedicated member of the organization who would not hesitate an instant, no matter the odds. Hiram Hyde waited a week more, while diligently seeking a new guide, praying in his stern way for another person--any other person--for this Godly work.

And at the end of the week, with no success, no other prospects, he went to call on Anna Blake.

~ * ~

"But she's Black," Tom Brannon argued. "She'll be hanged if she's caught."

"So will any of us," Hyde pointed out. "So none of us can allow ourselves to be caught."

"But she'd be treated like trash, outraged, violated..."

"Probably. So, I repeat, she simply cannot be caught."

"Mr. Hyde, we can't send Anna out. I'll do twice the runs; I can do it." He was pleading, his earnest face almost sweating.

"That would make you twice as likely to be caught, and we cannot risk that, sir. You are overexposed as it is. No, Miss Blake is intelligent, resourceful, and wholly committed to our cause. Now, I should like for you to guide her the first time, instruct her diligently, give her every aid, so she will succeed." Hyde was finished.

He knew this young man was enamored of Anna Blake, though she was of the different race. Hyde allowed himself to envision briefly the white flesh of the northerner pressed against the bare black of the desirable Anna Blake, and the image sent a thrill along his watery veins.

And yes, she might be apprehended, raped by slave catchers. They'd be certain she was some white man's plaything, and take crude delight in despoiling her. He felt another thrill. But—and he shook himself to bring his thoughts back to the mission—*our work is worth the risk. More than worth it.*

And any faint heart can do the work she's handling: scheduling, supplying—even Eli Dobson. Yes, Miss Blake must go onto the Hernando route. And soon, since our people have made all the necessary contacts.

Not a perfect solution, but the only one.

The only_one.

Hetty and Sam Barnes, while wholeheartedly committed to the cause of freedom for their race, were shocked to learn that this exceptional young woman was to be out on these perilous runs. She was the *last* person who should be sent; didn't that Yankee Hyde see that?

Hetty and all the others of the Route network, including the Blaine sisters, sent messages to Hiram Hyde, protesting this exploitation of one of their own.

He was unmoved. Like most fanatics, sincere in his devotion to his mission, he tolerated no other points of view. Anna Blake was needed. She was willing. She was able. Ergo, she was the new guide from north of Hernando to Memphis. And, he added as an afterthought, *may God have mercy on her.*

Nine

Anna's inauguration as a Route guide was to accompany Tom Brannon on an actual run. He instructed her again and again to watch for anyone out at night: hunters, farmers going home late, and of course, the slave catchers. He advised her to wait a few moments at each landmark before proceeding to the next, to better orient herself to the changing directions she must negotiate.

He'd told her he'd strongly opposed her being sent out, for the obvious reason that she could have no legitimate business being out anywhere alone at night, and certainly not with runaway slaves. She agreed, but her commitment to the cause they both served was strong enough to trump that rational objection. Not that the prospect didn't frighten her deeply.

They left at dark, skirting the lighted windows at the edge of town, where the Institute was located. Tom set a brisk pace in the autumn chill, pointing out dim landmarks under a scattering of stars. There was no moon, and Anna must learn the way entirely by what she could make out against the sky.

He made her repeat again and again the landmarks as they passed them.

"Count steps if you must. Now that we're past the outskirts of town, it's a quarter mile along this creek to the bridge. Stop and stay hidden until you're absolutely sure it's safe to cross, then back into the woods, to the left. Now repeat that."

"A quarter mile after I strike the creek, to the bridge. Stop to make certain it's safe. Cross. Then left."

"And through the woods due south by the compass all the way to the hayfield. You won't hit another field till then, even though it's several miles. That's the longest leg. Gate twenty paces to right. Cross field. West around farmhouse. Stay far back: dogs.

"Once past, due south again, two miles. No houses; lots of cotton fields. Watch for the road, diagonally from your left. Follow it as it curves, a half mile southwest to a fork. Left a quarter mile. Overgrown path at gate, long way. Abandoned barn. Come up from behind it. Knock twice at narrow door. Repeat."

"Through the woods..." She could see the route in her mind, a lonely, frightening way to the barn, and double that on the deadly return. "...Knock twice."

"Good. Now here's the bridge coming up. That's where patrollers will be, if they're out. There and on the road. Not a sound, now." They slipped close, then crouched, scanning the willows along the wide creek. An owl sounded across in the woods. Or was it really an owl? They waited.

Then Tom took a pebble from his pocket and tossed it onto the planks of the bridge. It clattered across and into the brush on the other side. Nothing stirred. They straightened, then moved across on silent feet. The dark woods waited. They slipped among the trees, Anna's heart thumping in her chest.

"Now it's safe to risk a match," he whispered, taking his compass out. In the brief flare he set their course south, and they moved among the trees. Too cool for snakes, she reasoned, but what did you do in summer? *Wear boots and pray, I guess.*

The hayfield was a long time coming, but finally there it was, a lighter shade ahead. The gate was where it should be, and she felt better, in the open. They moved quickly across it, wide of the distant farmhouse.

"I always toss something at the bridge," Tom told her. "Most folks can't stay still long, and if somebody's there, he'll almost always jump at a sudden noise."

"What then?"

"You wait. If someone's there, you wait. He'll get tired and leave eventually. If he doesn't, you have two choices: find a place to wade the creek and circle the bridge, or go home."

"And the people in the barn?"

"They know to hide another day. The creek's too wide for a log across anywhere, and too cold to swim, now. I've had to go back only once since summer. Smelled the tobacco smoke away off. Man, or men, apparently ready to wait all night. When you know there's no longer time for the complete trip, you go back." He reflected for a moment on the insanity of this.

"As I said, I've objected strenuously to Hyde's sending you out alone, Anna. And I wish there was some way to forbid it."

"You go alone."

"But if I'm caught on the way out, there's really no danger. What can they prove? But you..."

He need not finish. She remembered too well the ways of brutish men with helpless slave women, back in Hinds County, that one named John Moad and his man Lobo, those years earlier. A Black woman alone had no chance with slave catchers. No chance with coon hunters either, or with even that stray farmer on his way home after dark.

He's right: this won't work, she told herself. *I can't do this alone. Why are they sending me out like this? I'll do this once with Tom, then we'll have to find another job I can do.*

It seemed a very long time later when they slipped up to the rear door of the barn. Tom rapped twice and the door opened immediately. Anna smelled the close air, old hay and cows and sweat, and a very palpable fear.

There were five of them under the care of a white, muscular farm girl about her own age. A woman of thirty held a small boy with enormous eyes. A girl of twelve stood with two men, one perhaps her father, the other bent with age.

The farm girl spoke quietly with Tom Brannon. Anna watched her in the dim candle light. She'd brought these five from beyond Hernando by herself the night before. A white girl, alone. Her name was Susan Blaine.

"Aren't you afraid?" she asked Susan, "By yourself and ...all?"

"Some. But I c'n outrun most men. An' I got this." She showed the butt of a pistol. "An' this," and a long knife appeared from her waistband.

Susan could plainly take care of herself, Anna saw. But why did she take the risk? What moved her to...?

"You wanta know, don'tcha?"

"Yes. If you'll tell me."

"When I was little, I saw a drunk overseer beat a slave woman t'death. She fought when he tried to ... t' take her, y'know? Grown up, but she was little. I know they ain't all like that, but too many is, one way or t'other. So I do what I can, when I can. My sisters and me, we run our place. Got no man, none of us. We take turns on this part of th' trip. You got a gun?"

"No. Well, yes, but I didn't think to ...But I can shoot."

"Bring th'gun. Git two. And don't ever, *ever* git caught." Susan turned and hugged the woman, then the girl. She lifted the small boy and kissed him goodbye.

"Bye, Cecil, Ab." She laid a hardened hand on each man's shoulder. "Git movin', Tom." And she was gone.

From the beginning, the boy had trouble keeping up. His mother carried him. Then the younger man. The old man shuffled onward, never slacking, and the girl glided on newly shod feet. They moved along the road quickly, Tom out ahead, she bringing up the rear. They all knew to melt into the forest at the approach of anyone, and tension was high in the air.

Then it was due north, off the road, and the heaviness lifted somewhat. Anna took the boy for a distance. He reminded her of her brothers when they were small, growing up down in Hinds County. He went to sleep, head on her shoulder as she strode on. An ache began in her back.

Tom took the boy as they skirted the farmhouse. The hayfield stretched before them, the dark woods beyond.

Then the sound of distant dogs barking. Instinctively, the Blacks stopped, eyes wide in fear.

"Keep moving. They're too far to've caught our scent," Tom urged. And indeed, after a few seconds, the barking stopped. Anna felt hair on the back of her neck lie down again.

They stayed close in the woods, feeling their way literally from tree to tree. It seemed they should have come out near the bridge by now. No, there was a big forked sycamore she remembered, its upper limbs ghostly in starlight.

Tom stopped them, then went ahead. Time dragged while he was gone. Anna pictured him, crouched hidden at the bridge, his eyes growing accustomed to the shapes of bushes, the willows still with their leaves. She took the girl and the woman aside so they could relieve themselves.

Tom was back. They moved quickly across the bridge and onto the path up the creek. Not far, now. What time was it? *Stay dark, please God.* The old man, Cecil, moved steadily on. What awaited him up North? He could perhaps work, but only for a while. And could they—his family—were they even his family? Could they support him up there?

What kind of life could the girl expect? She should stay in Memphis, go to the institute. Who made the arrangements? Better not to know, Tom had said. You can't become involved. Absolutely not. Do your part. Get them safely to the next station. Try to forget them.

Forget the boy's huge eyes that were like her brother Wes' when he was four. Forget the slim girl, the old man. Remember stout Susan, if you like. It was the Susans who made the Route work. And the Toms. And yes, even the Hiram Hydes and the industrialists up North like that Obadiah Banks, the Route's primary recipient of these runaways.

Just do your part.

The safe house. Then home. There was an hour of sleep, then the day's teaching. Anna tried not to notice Tom, concentrated on the lessons, on the eager, free Black faces before her.

Do the job.

~ * ~

It was two weeks and a half later when word came. Anna did not hesitate. But she took from her drawer the pistol her former master had given her, and she loaded it and set a cap in place. Then she measured powder and shot, and took a keen knife from the kitchen.

It was cloudy, hiding a half-moon. If the clouds broke, it would be bright as day. She prayed for rain. A slow, misty rain to muffle footsteps and hide her and the runaways.

Alone, she moved faster, gliding along, reliving the barefoot years in Hinds County. The creek, the fishing holes, her brothers...

At the bridge, waiting, she smelled tobacco smoke and heard voices. Two men crossed, talking. Something had made her move across downwind to wait, and she was glad when she saw the dog with them. They passed from sound. *Good. No one else waiting then, or the men would have spoken to him.*

The woods were like an old friend now. *Deep shadows, black. The night is black; I am black. Hide me in your blackness.* The clouds broke, and shafts of light illuminated her way. The forked sycamore. More woods. And more. Then finally the bright hayfield. *Wait, then.* Clouds again. A pall of fog at the cotton fields. Compass.

The road, and now a heavy mist. Her hand rested on the butt of the pistol. She heard the clink of harness first, then the creaking sound. A wagon. She slipped into the trees on the downwind side. No dog. The mules plodded by, the farmer half asleep.

The gate: the barn. No children this time. Three men and a woman. Not Susan, but similar. One of the sisters, thinner, older.

"You're Anna."

"Yes."

"Watch the tall one. Got a mouth on him. I'm Jenny."

"Thanks. How's Susan?"

"Fine. Worried about you. Got a gun, I see. She was 'fraid you wouldn't wanta use it if y'had to."

"Tell Susan I can shoot the ears off a squirrel, Jenny. And any man lays a hand on me, dies."

"Tough. Stay tough. Stay alive." She hugged her. "Come see us in Hernando."

The tall young man eyed her too closely, Anna felt. The woman watched him too, as they slipped out of the barn. Anna set a brisk pace along the road, watching for cover if needed. The mist had intensified, and their clothes were soon soaked. They turned north.

The tall man moved up alongside Anna.

"Gon' be free," he murmured to her.

"No talking," she whispered, and stepped ahead.

"Ain' nobody hear us out heah…"

"Not if you don't talk, for sure."

"Gon' git me a free gal, lak you…"

The other two men moved up, caught the lad by each arm, mouthing him to be quiet. He started to shake them off. Angry. His voice snapped out.

Anna was suddenly enraged. She turned, leveled her pistol at the man. His eyes went wide.

"People can die to get you to freedom, boy. Now, you do your part, or I'll leave you for the crows to eat. Stay back, and not a sound!"

Where did that come from? From necessity, that was where. It was enough that danger waited at every turn of this perilous path, from the slave catchers, the planters, hunters, even the good law-abiding Christians of the region. Then for one of the runaways she—they—were risking all this for, to endanger them… She strode ahead, willing her anger away, focusing on landmarks, keen to possible danger.

Hours later, in the shielded lamplight of the safe house, the young slave's face was sullen. She raised an eyebrow and tilted her head toward him as the old couple pointed them toward cellar steps.

"We'll watch him," the woman whispered. "God bless you, Anna. You did it. Alone."

She had. Alone, and done right. She gave Tom Brannon a smile at school as they passed in the hall. He winked.

That initial run by herself was without incident then, and it served to convince her that she could indeed, do this: succeed, despite everyone's hand raised against her. That didn't mean she'd conquered her nerves, or quelled her fears. But the thought of just those few now-free people of her race, on their way to a meaningful life, buoyed her spirits, fortified her for the next run.

And she continued to succeed. In dark clothing, she was almost invisible as she slipped from brushy fields' edges to forest, from dense roadside brambles to high-banked streambeds. And on the return trips, she insisted on absolute silence, once more even having to threaten a talkative field hand with her pistol.

Most of her charges were appreciative of the efforts she and her colleagues were making on their behalf. But sometimes, imagining they were already free, a few rebellious runaways, usually teenage boys, gave her trouble. In each case, the others of the group had managed to subdue any outbursts. Anna imagined these individuals had been trouble, would be, anywhere, in any situation. *No different from whites, really.*

But what could these few misfits expect to find, up in mostly-white areas, where even the most deferential Blacks were barely tolerated? She shuddered to imagine the swift retribution they'd face.

~ * ~

The other Blaine sisters were still shocked at the Route people's sending Anna as a guide.

"Bad 'nuff, us out where we got no call t'be," Kate declared. "But that girl, no way in hell c'n she git away, if th' catchers git onto her."

"Said she's got a gun, an' knows how t'use it," from Susan.

"Mebbe so," Jenny put in, "But don't none of us know what it'd actually be t' hafta kill a man—or moren' one."

"Wal, she's got grit. Course she was with Tom that first time. Diff'runt now, out by herself."

The news had found its way to all the guides, and they were universally outraged. Hetty Barnes had all but raised that girl back on the Hinds County place, and after she and Sam had rejoined their former owners in Marshall County in 1841. And Hetty, who'd learned to read and been taught proper speech, had helped teach Anna and the others their owners had freed.

They and Anna's family had been among those who accepted land in Hinds County upon their owners, the McRavens, freeing them, instead of going with them to the new place. Sam, a blacksmith, had felt he could succeed as a free craftsman in that familiar territory. And Hetty had tried to explain their choice further to the planter's wife at the time.

"It just seems more like really bein' free," she'd told the woman to whom she'd been maid almost all her life. Most of the other former slaves had traveled with the white family, to work their new place for wages or a share of the crop, and the gift of some land of their own there.

These planters had taught all their slaves to read, write and handle business decisions prior to freeing them. But the hostility toward them from their white neighbors had been intense, and the McRavens had moved to the new territory, where they weren't known, to start over.

And the resentment toward the four families of freed Blacks in Hinds had mounted, with the arrival of a ruthless aspiring planter who drove his own slaves with the lash. John Moad's overseer had been a Texas outlaw, proficient with gun and knife. The pair had begun a systematic campaign to drive the free Blacks out of the country, or contrive to have them stolen.

The hitherto sympathetic sheriff, the Blacks' principal protection, had been vilified as that lowest epithet a slave owner could use, "nigger lover," by Moad and his ilk, who eventually got him voted out of office. Then the real intimidation had begun. The Black carpenter found he couldn't get work—any work. Neither could the blacksmith. All the families were harassed until they were fearful of even leaving their farms.

Then Moad and his men had caught Sam Barnes returning from a visit to another of the group. They tied him to a tree and lashed him with a bullwhip and left him still tied, for dead, his back a mass of open, bleeding wounds.

The Barnes had then, accompanied by the earlier sheriff's brother, fled to their former owners, and finally to real freedom.

A postscript to that story was Robert McRaven's riding back to Hinds to see to the welfare of the remaining families. As coincidence would have it, he rode onto another beating and attempted rape of another freed slave by Moad and his foreman. The victim had been then-fourteen-year-old Anna Blake.

He shot them both.

And Anna's parents, fearing for their beautiful child, had begged their former master to take her with him, knowing this would not be the last incident.

So Anna Blake, a name she'd chosen from her reading, had rejoined the houseful of McRaven children, in age between the eldest two daughters, who became best friends. Her education had continued, fed by the planter's extensive library, his gifted wife's teaching, and a natural thirst for learning the girl possessed.

Ten

Abel was fifteen, a bright, inquisitive boy whom the planter's wife was grooming to replace the aging slave butler Isaiah, there on the Carruthers' plantation out of Meridian. He and young Clinton Carruthers had been companions since they were five, and he'd always had more latitude than the other Black children. The two had managed all sorts of outrageous pranks for years, and were inseparable.

Clinton had developed a rebellious streak, although he was sharp enough to appear always in accord with his parents' traditional view of slavery. Which he uncharacteristically opposed, but kept quiet about. He would appear the model, bigoted planter's son, but work in a number of clandestine ways, one of which was teaching his best friend to read, in absolute secrecy.

"What's inevitable, Abel, is the end of slavery, but just when, nobody knows. You see, as more people in this country are educated, the glaring inequality of the system becomes more evident. Leaders like Washington and Jefferson, though both owned slaves, were idealistically against the system. But they realized the white population wasn't ready for your people's freedom. That was their rationalization, of course, and it was a dodge, but as time has passed, more enlightened whites are seeing the end of human bondage as inevitable."

Clinton, for an adolescent, was intelligent, and by association and his own keen mind, Abel also questioned, probed, dug into questions of the human condition far beyond his years. He was also wise enough to play the part of the helpful, obedient servant to his peer, and to the household in general. And of course he never, never let anyone else know of his reading. Clinton smuggled books to Abel, and they made a game of hiding their discussions and views from all eyes and ears.

This was easier than one would expect, since the idea of a mere slave's being able to learn, originate ideas, was unthinkable to their owners. And if any of the other slaves suspected Abel was acting uppity, they gleefully kept the secret. "Boy gonna be th' butler when he's growed," his mother Chessy knew. "Talkin' right, actin' smooth gon' help him all th' way."

This view was shared by Abigail Carruthers, the plantation chatelaine, who foresaw having the most polished major domo in Mississippi. Let the boy learn, yes, and the other pampered planters' wives could turn green with envy. Not that he could really aspire to any degree of wisdom, but yes again, he should be encouraged to go as far as the limitations of his race allowed.

Clinton had an eventual plan in mind for his friend, but he'd keep that surprise to himself. *No use gettin' the boy's hopes up, but there's only one conclusion to reach for him in the end, and I'll just save that for when the time's right.*

"What'er you grinnin' about?" Abel poked his companion as they sat side by side, cane poles out, baited hooks in the creek. "Share?"

"Nope, gonna keep this'n from you, old fellow. Hey, you got a bite!" The cork had indeed gone under, and the murky water churned. Abel hauled in a sizeable bass after a struggle, and gloated over his catch, since Clinton hadn't caught anything. And he forgot the other boy's evasiveness.

"That's all right, my man; I'll just catch a bigger one. Watch me." But he proceeded to land only two smaller ones, which he insisted outweighed the 20-inch bass. And the sun was getting low, mosquitoes coming out. They argued good-naturedly on the way back to the quarters, where Clinton insisted on donating his catch to Abel's mother.

"Aunt Chessy, it's an honor and a privilege to present you with these denizens of the deep," he bowed, presenting his gift. "Your intellectual son out-fished me, but not by much, and there'll be a next time, believe me." He gave her a gallant kiss on the cheek.

"You Mass' Clinton, you g'on now, with yo' fancy talk. You give my boy th' big head, yo' manners an' all. But I thankee, young suh, an' now yo' mama be wonderin' whar her boy be. Bes' light a shuck on home."

This was a Sunday, their day of rest, so Abel, having savored most of it with his best friend, now reflected, and not for the first time, on their relationship. This was fine, for now, but he knew when Clinton went off to college, maybe over in the village of Clinton, past Jackson, or Memphis, or at the new university in Oxford, everything would change. Just what the white boy's peers away from here would think of his association with a Black was all too predictable. Never mind their closeness since childhood, out in the world Black was Black and white would be most certainly white.

With his future here already planned for him, life wasn't as hard on Abel as the other slaves, certainly not the field hands. His duties consisted of helping around the big house, seeing to it the cookstove wood was adequate, carrying water for the kitchen and the family's baths. Anything that needed doing, and he'd always tried to anticipate his owners' needs.

He'd seen firsthand what happened to a servant who got out of line, was slow or grumbled. *This's my life for now, and I'd be a fool to jeapordize it. Master sell me in a flash if he had any idea what I'm planning. Just bide my time till I can make it happen, bow and scrape and yes, be thankful for what I have. Never let on what I really want, will have, in this existence.*

~ * ~

As time moved past, the Cotton Route people devised new strategies to foil their adversaries. Now runaways were actually taken south first, instead of laterally. But not every time. And eventually men from other regions were shifted to act as slave traders in places where no one would know them. Paths, hiding places were changed frequently to avoid discovery.

Sometimes a shipment would have to be halted or rerouted when the guides got messages from contacts that an ambush was planned: someone somewhere had let an unwise word slip.

Susan was guiding a group of five, gathered from different locations in Alabama, Mississippi and Arkansas in the fall of 1854. They spied a campfire ahead that hadn't been there on her outward trip. A lone man warmed his hands, his rifle leaned against a tree nearby.

They froze, waited to see if the man, obviously a hunter, was indeed not part of a group. Susan could see only a small game bag; this wasn't the camp of a slave-catching party, she felt sure.

Or was it? There could be others out scouting the very forest they were traveling through.

They circled wide through woods she knew, moving as quietly over dry, fallen leaves as they could. When she felt they'd skirted the danger, she led them by her match-lit compass back toward the trail. But her nerves were still on high alert, and she had her hand on the gun at her back.

They were near the path again when a sudden voice rang out ahead, stopping them dead.

"Don'tcha move!" A match flared from behind a big tree. A lantern was lighted. A man stepped out, shotgun aimed right at Susan in the lead.

She knew the man. He'd been with that Holtz at their farm years before: a slave catcher. Was he just out hunting? Doubtful. Either way, there was absolutely no time left. And yes, he was looking hard at her face, remembering.

He was about to exclaim, when Susan's hand whipped around and she shot him through the heart. His cocked shotgun blasted down into the ground as he fell. The lantern tumbled into the dry leaves as the woods echoed the gunfire. She snatched it up, stamped out flames.

"Git his gun," she snapped. "An' enny money, shot an' powder he's got."

She reloaded her pistol, scanning the forest, tumult raging inside, but outwardly cool.

The runaways were shaking, eyes wide, but they moved. Susan doused the light then, and led them quickly away, heedless of the leaves crackling underfoot. *Not as noisy as th' gunshots...*

They met no one else, and moved as fast as possible toward the hiding place.

No, she thought, coming to a halt. *Man at the fire had t've heard. Have th' whole country after us by daylight. None of th' places safe. An' jist what in hell c'n I do now? They'll search ever'where: ol' sheds, th' swamp... An' yeah, I jist killed me a man, too.*

Wait, now: th' other man didn't see us. Cain't know we're a bunch. Find that... Bates, that was his name—shot, his gun stole. Nuthin' t'tell 'em who we are... Oh, but they'll still search. Fer a robber mebbe, but that don't change a thing.

They couldn't go on north: daylight would come soon. *Got to hide 'em somewheres, git word t'Memphis. Oh, damn... But git aholt of yerself here, girl. Cain't panic... Man was a no-count slave catcher. An' yeah, y'did kill him, but it 'uz him or us. Think, now...*

All right: nuthin' fer it but t'head for home. Th' three of us'll hafta hide 'em someplace, send word. Don't like it, but ain't no other way I c'n see.

They angled away and moved out. Through a waning night peopled with imaginary menace: the hand of the world was against them. So many dangers, real, conjured up.

Going wide past Isaac Ingrum's place, they came at last to the sisters' farmhouse before dawn. Susan crept forward, motioning the runaways to stay back. *Don't wanta git shot by m'own sisters.*

"Katy, Jenny! It's me! Don'tcha shoot me now."

A light showed. Kate opened the door.

"Where are they, girl? You lose 'em?"

"No, but hadda shoot me a catcher. Bates was here 'th Holtz that time. Least one other out there, but he didn't see us. Didn't know him. Ennyway, they'll be all over, soon. Nuthin' fer it but t'bring 'em here. Wrong thing t'do, but only thing."

Jenny was with them, mouth open at the news.

"Th' swamp?" she asked.

"'Fraid not. Too close t'where I shot th' man."

"All right, then," from Kate. "Gotta go to Talbot's agin. F'm what you say, th' other man don't know what t'look for, so we jist chance it. Hope he don't know how many hands Talbot's got."

"Only way, I guess," Susan agreed. "I'll git on with 'em, then. Jesse'll hafta keep 'em outta Everett's sight."

"He's porely," Jenny told her. "Shouldn't be out in th' fields hisself."

Susan rejoined her charges, explained the plan. They set off then, mindful of the rising light. Once near, she had them hide again while she slipped up to Jesse's still-dark cabin. She knocked.

"Who's there?" he called.

"Susie. Got us a problem." A lamp was lighted, the door opened. Jesse's wife Blythe stood back. Susan hesitated.

"'S'all right," Jesse assured her. "She's knowed all along. Come on in an' set." Blythe went to build up the cookstove fire.

"Run into catchers, er at least one of 'em was. Coulda been jist out huntin', or mebbe somebody told. Ennyway, I hadda shoot one that knowed me. Other'n didn't see us, but sure heard. None of th' hidey places safe, ner th' swamp. Hate it, but wonder you c'd slip 'em in with yer hands."

"How many?"

"Five. Three men, growed, an' two women, mebbe thirty years old."

"That's a bunch. Mist' Ever'tt's sickly at th' house, but we ain't got but six left. Folks might know that."

"I c'n take th' wimmen to th' house," Blythe suggested. "Be puttin' up stuff f'm th' fields, after I look in on Mist' Ever'tt. Tell 'im these is frien's, helpin' me lak I help them."

"Right in th' Big House?"

"Don't b'lieve Mist' Ever'tt know th' diff'runce. Don' nevah come out to th' kitchen. Besides, he porely with a fever."

"Might work," Jesse reasoned. "Three mo' in th' fiels, could be on loan. Y'say th' one man didn' see how many?"

"Didn' see nuthin'. Had a fire, so we went wide."

"All right. Sorry y'had to shoot one. Be hard 'round heah fer while. Harder on you, though. Killin' ain't easy." Jesse reached, put a sympathetic hand on Susan's shoulder.

"Ain't had time t'study on it yet, but it don't set easy, no."

~ * ~

This time Susan was the one who set out for Memphis on their one horse with a secondhand saddle they'd traded Ingrum for. She rode astride in a divided skirt, armed, confident, and the sisters had no misgivings about her traveling alone with the catchers out searching.

"Don't fergit," Jenny reminded her worried older sister, "I done it on foot that time."

"You was lucky."

"We all been lucky, so far. Or mebbe th' Lord's jist lookin' out for us."

"Hope He keeps on doin' jist that."

And apparently He did, since Susan made the trip uneventfully. It was early enough in the day that she didn't have to hurry, and she took time to appreciate the color of dogwood and black gum leaves, flaming red as the season moved toward winter. She remembered the trips in the wagon with her father and sisters, heading to Memphis to sell the produce, those years ago. *Never woulda thought it: takin' th' same road, only this time helpin' runaways git free. Gotta be th' Lord's work, like Jenny said, er we'd sure been caught 'fore this. Don't mean we c'n let up, though: gotta keep bein' careful, with so many out after us.*

The miles slid past, and she was surprised to note landmarks that told her she was nearing the city. *Guess I been daydreamin' th' day away, an' I'm gittin' close.*

While in Memphis, she made it a point to go alert Anna Blake, a young woman she'd come to admire greatly, instead of one of the other contacts.

"That Hyde's a born fool, girl, to be sendin' you out on th' routes thataway. Got a notion to go shake some sense into him."

"It's all right, Susan. I'm so very careful, and yes, if we're caught, any of us, we'll hang or worse. But I have to agree with Mr. Hyde that our work is more important than the risks we take. And I'm so glad you and your sisters are doing this work with us. You're rocks we can build on, tie to. We couldn't do this without you, and we thank you so much." She took the white girl's hands, then hugged her warmly.

"Well, it ain't easy. I gotta tell you, I had to kill a man was about to shoot me last night, an' it's eatin' at me. But I wasn't about to let him take us after all th' work an' trouble ever'body'd gone to t'get th' bunch that far. He knew me, was a slave catcher, one of them does it more outta hate than fer th' money."

"Oh, I'm so sorry you had to do that, Susan! I've wrestled with whether I could do that myself, and I honestly don't know, if it came to that. Though I know I wouldn't give up my charges either... so yes, I guess I'd have to."

Arrangements were soon made for the reverend Kellog to bring the runaways to Memphis, and Susan accepted this extraordinary young woman's invitation to stay overnight. They talked about everything, from the children Anna was teaching to the hardships of farming, which the Black girl remembered well.

Then it was goodbye, with Susie's repeated invitation to Anna to come visit the sisters at their farm out of Hernando.

"Jist don't try t'come by yerself, girl—too risky. Course I guess y'could slip on down at night, th' way you been doin'... No, don't wanta be th' cause of you gittin' caught. One of us'll come for you, an' ain't a man alive'd dare t' give us trouble."

No, and this courageous girl has proven that, in the most forceful way.

~ * ~

It was not easy for Susan, getting the killing off her mind. *Sure, th' man was a snake, him an' Holtz an' th' rest, scum of th' earth. An' I know he'd a shot me first, 'less I'da gone along t'be hung. But killin's bad. Man had a wife 'n young uns, too.*

Later she made discreet inquiries. Bates had lived over near Red Banks, and teamed often with Luddy Holtz, the most active of the catchers. She got word to Hetty Barnes, asking what she might do for the widow and children. Wasn't their fault the man needed killing.

The reply was meant to reassure her: Hetty reported that Mrs. Bates had been on the point of leaving her violent husband. Had, in fact, done so before, but returned after he'd promised to stop drinking, abusing her and the family. That hadn't happened, unfortunately. But now they'd gone back to the widow's parents, who were apparently better off financially.

So, man needed gittin' rid of, reckon. Could jist be I done ever'body a favor then, doin' what I done. Mebbe so: mebbe git t'where I c'n live with it, in time.

So it was a troubled young woman who rode from Memphis that day, with conflicting thoughts churning around inside her, guilt at killing Bates weighing her down, and of course the danger, even if imagined. That, the real part, would continue to threaten the sisters, from every righteous citizen in the land.

But she was warmed too, from her time with Anna, clearly the most intelligent woman she'd ever met. *Shows what a Black woman c'n accomplish, give her th' chance.*

After Susan's notifying the Route people of the incident, the Hernando branch had to be shut down until things quieted. This frustrated Hiram Hyde, but even he saw the necessity of the suspension. A killing, even in self-defense, would and did put the authorities on double their watchfulness; wouldn't do to play into that trap.

The respite did delay Anna Blake's having to guide again, much to the relief of everyone except Hyde. Tom Brannon kept up his search for sympathetic prospects, as did others in the region. The problem was, of course, that most reputable men, those who could pose as traders or owners moving their slaves, just didn't believe in freeing slaves at all. And wouldn't risk their lives even if they did.

It was a near-hopeless task, Brannon feared. He was no favorite in Memphis, he of the Chicago accent and the intense manner. And just as many were put off by him as by the officious Hiram Hyde.

The Baptist minister had also tried without success to enlist a chosen few of his fellow clergy, posing strictly theoretical scenarios to feel out their views. He had to be very careful in this, a subject that no one was neutral about. Not surprisingly, the responses proved to be universally negative, as they had been with Hyde, despite the congregation's supposed compassion for God's people.

His *white* people, it seemed.

~ * ~

One man, an astute thinker and now wealthy despite his lack of formal education, began adding odd bits of information, events, together. He traveled often in Mississippi, in Tennessee and eastern Arkansas on his business, a business closely linked to the slave/cotton economy of the prewar South.

Nathan Bedford Forrest was a trader. In horses, cattle, cotton.

And slaves.

Over the years he had become the man to contact when an aspiring planter sought to clear land and establish or expand his holdings. He had developed an eye for productive field hands, efficient household help, craftsmen such as blacksmiths and carpenters, all of whom would be credits to their owners.

Forrest considered his work more as an employment agency than traffic in human beings. Match the right worker to the job, with that eye to the temperaments of both master and slave. Place good workers in the care of 'good' masters, whatever that might mean. Find secure homes for families whose bankrupt owners might otherwise sell them into worse conditions.

Of course there were un-placeable Blacks, even in the most carefully-planned excuted deals. Sometimes a moody or even rebellious slave had to go to the auction block, to be bought for little by an exploiting, often cruel master who could or would not afford better. And who might well starve his workers, work them to death. Bad business, but sometimes unavoidable.

Bedford Forrest was no saint, and admittedly placed profit above all else. But he also aimed to please: it was the essence of good business, after all. And his customers came back for more, to the man who knew his Blacks, and knew his planters too.

Now, the very white gentry who required his services also paradoxically looked down upon this entrepreneur, whose business was nevertheless entirely legal, if not at all moral. Despite their dependence on the slaves he provided, many in the drawing rooms of the South viewed this—and indeed all such traders—with disdain.

This amused Forrest, who was frank in his dealings and in his profession. *Call a spade a damn spade: don't make it any prettier to call it 'n earth-moving implement, or whatever. But if these planters need t'keep space 'tween themselves an' th' hands that keep 'em in their white-pillared houses, why, just let 'em. They wanta play blind that way, it's their call, not mine. They wanta treat 'em like cattle, doesn't matter what I think: their business, though it's a damn shortsighted owner that'll put his work force at risk. But nobody ever said a planter's gotta be smart. Just lucky, maybe. An' I ain't about t'judge 'em. They pay me good, an' by God, I work m'ass off for every greenback.*

But Forrest's keen eyes saw the steady, if scattered, successful escape of regional slaves as a phenomenon. *Average field hand too dumb t'get away without help. Catchers not about t'lose their income, so work, hunt 'em harder.* And it used to be just about no slave really got away. Had to show himself, sooner or later, and everybody was on the watch.

No, somethin' goin' on here. Lot like what I hear of back East, the abolitionists puttin' together 'n organization, that Underground Railroad thing, with money an' reg'lar guides, schedules. Never heard of such 'round here, though. Course if anybody had *heard, nothin' like that could operate: get busted up quick.*

But somebody's gotta be helpin' them dumb hands git North, I'm that certain. An' that catcher gettin' himself killed: coulda been just a robber, but mightn't been, either. 'Nuther piece of th' puzzle.

Of course he knew it could be the work of just some few do-gooders here and there, hardly making a dent in the system. *Lotta slaves all over, even if you leave out th' big planters. Farmer got a couple: field hand, an' wife t'help in th' house, that's where most of 'em are. Abolitionists think we're a buncha kings down here, with armies of hands choppin' cotton. Ain't but maybe a dozen big uns to a county, even in th' Delta.*

But it didn't bother him a bit if a few slaves ran off. *Don't matter none just how: th' thing is, for ever' one gone, that's one more place I c'n fill. One more chance t'find 'nuther good hand 'nuther good home. An' yeah, you Yankees up North got t'deal with th' runaways now, damn your sanctimonious souls.*

So whoever y'are, jist y'keep on keepin' on out there. Nathan Bedford Forrest ain't gonna hinder you one bit. Yer really helpin' ever'body. Slaves git free, I make more money, abolitionists git t'feel holy. Owners lose all right, but a lot of them proud bastards need t'git brought down a notch, now'n then.

Bedford Forrest's wife did not like his profession, however. She urged him to go into some other business with his sharp mind. Railroads, maybe—that new line down through Hernando from Memphis to Jackson. Or he'd make a fine army officer, she suggested. Of course, if he'd been down in Mexico in '48 she'd have worried every day. Could've got shot; that's what happened in war.

Maybe so, he mused. Maybe she was right. *Any fool with foresight c'n see th' slave system's full of holes. Free labor ain't free. There's folks hirin' hands, some sharecroppin', like that*

McRaven feller raises horses near Byhalia. Doin' better'n most owners, that'n. Law of nature: man'll work harder for pay, chance to git ahead. Blacks no different: known some smart uns. An' th' dumbest slave in this white man's world knows a heap more'n his master thinks he does.

But no, I couldn't go nowhere in th' army 'thout West Point er VMI. Be takin' orders f'm dumb-asses their daddies got appointed officers. Gall me t'death. But this damn business in Washin'ton, now... wanta tell us how t'run our states, shove stuff down our throats. Whar's Jefferson an' Jackson when we need 'em? Federalists—call themselves Republicans now—aimin' t'take over ever'thing.

Push us too far, I might just hafta throw in with these highborn planters, whup their Northern asses.

Eleven

Abel was a year older now, and taking on more responsibility around the Big House. He knew it'd still be several years before he would become the new butler: the folks wouldn't want anyone too young in that responsible post. No, their plans for him meant more time in this holding pattern, more time to plan.

And that plan was freedom. No, he wouldn't be here to fill that coveted slot in the plantation's hierarchy, not be the gracious, bowing head of the household slaves. Abel would take a last name, get up North, and be his own man. He'd heard of freed slaves working in the factories up there, and the very thought appalled him: underpaid, charged outrageously for everything, chained to a system designed to keep them in bondage as surely as if they were still slaves.

Abel would find a way to get into some school somewhere, study hard, learn, excel in some field. He'd heard there were Black doctors, Black lawyers, Black professors north of the Mason Dixon Line, and he swore to become one of them.

But first to plan his escape. And he'd also heard, via that mysterious grapevine among slaves, of an organization out of Memphis helping escaped slaves. He didn't know even a name, but the more trust he could build here, the more he'd be allowed the privileges of a soon-to-be elevated Black man, he felt he'd learn more, and soon.

And he was able to. His father Moses was the plantation carriage driver, and had taken Hamilton Carruthers' elder son Mason and his body servant along with him to Oxford, to the university there, to enroll the young man. And on his return, Moses regaled the other Blacks with tales of the white boys, most of whom also had their servants with them, some even with their dogs.

"Boys thaink that college, it's gon' be lak some picnic," he laughed. "Reckon a bunch gon' go back home, they fin' out they gotta study over there. An' I'se sure them young gals in Oxford's daddies gon' lock 'em up at night, them wild boys gits to runnin' 'round." That got a knowing chuckle from his listeners, including Abel.

"What's the college look like, Pa?" The boy had imagined it to be all grand buildings, like maybe a sort of park. He'd seen engravings of such places in books Clinton had slipped him.

"Oh, ain't but th' one big buildin' now, but they's more goin' up all over. Big one all brick, got white columns all 'cross th' front, big high steps on up. Lotsa board houses 'round now, but I heah it's all gon' be brick when they gits to it."

"You have a good time up there?" his wife Chessy asked, her eyes big at the imagined sights of the place.

"Oh, so-so. Lotta Blacks 'round, workin' on th' buildin's, helpin' tendin' th' white folks, makin' like they's better'n most of us. Was one other carriage driver, he got to tellin' it 'round 'mongst us 'bout..." Here Moses looked around to be sure these slaves weren't being watched.

"About what, Pa?" Abel knew he wanted to hear what his father thought must be kept quiet.

"Well, sho'ly ain't nuthin' to it, but he say they's some folks in Memphis as helps enny hand gittin' treated bad, they c'n help him git away. Now, don't none of you breathe a word, or we all in trouble, but he tell us they's a school up there fo' Black kids, couple teachers slips 'round, works in th' dark, t'git ennybody away he wants t'run." Moses sat back, knowing this tantalizing news, whether true or not, would give his people here something to talk among themselves about forever. *Freedom, it's a scary thaing, but nothin' wrong 'ith givin' us all somethin' t'dream 'bout, even if it ain't evah gon' happen.*

"Don't suppose he'd heard any names, or wouldn't tell, did he, Pa?"

"Well, not d'rect, but he did tell of a Black woman teaches at th' school, she know fo' sure whut it's all 'bout. Name of Anna Blake, freed b'her folks on back in Hinds County, 'fore her white folks, they gone up to Byhalia."

That was all his father could impart, but for Abel, it constituted a start, if tenuous. Could be this woman knew nothing useful. Or that the other carriage driver had her name wrong. But he remembered a rumor, and small talk of a family running their plantation near Byhalia that had freed their slaves, were now paying them, or operating on shares. This was so rare, this oddity had made its way across the state in bits, to the ears of the Carruthers hands.

Not likely the same people, but if true, there's that woman who's pulled herself up, must've studied, to become a teacher. And yes, there was that word that some Englishman was going to start such a school. Clinton says there are such places up North, but in Memphis? Maybe what he says about slavery on its way out has already started with that sort of thing. And the woman was freed, maybe even taught by her owners first? Hardly believable.

~ * ~

It took months for the furor over Bill Bates' killing to die down, during which Hiram Hyde chafed, sulked, berated, and generally made his organization's members feel helpless. Surely there was *some* way to reactivate the Hernando route. Surely *someone* was brave enough to start the runs again. It was *summer*, for the merciful God's sake. Couldn't they...

Tom Brannon finally sent word along the branch grapevine: set up a run. So contacts down in Mississippi diverted a band of escapees from the Holly Springs route to the south, then west, then north, the guides in place. He'd had to abandon the role as trader, with too many legal ones around. That entrenched one, Bedford Forrest, knew all his competition, and probably knew too that he, Tom, was a teacher at the institute. Best not push that role, then. Trust to darkness, luck, and God.

It worked. Things had returned to normal it seemed, and yes, everyone agreed that operations could resume. Just be extra careful out there, Brannon cautioned: wasn't an accident the catcher Bates had been out that night last fall.

And so the Cotton Route, never discovered, continued its operation: a handful of escaped slaves at a time going North, to whatever fate awaited them.

~ * ~

Hetty Barnes, while wholly committed to the cause of freedom for her race, was further outraged that this exceptional young woman Anna was to be out on these perilous runs again after this hiatus. She was the *last* person who should be sent, after the Bates killing; that Yankee Hyde must be blind not to see that.

She and others of the Route network, including the Blaine sisters, sent messages to Hiram Hyde again, protesting this doubly dangerous decision in the face of this more intense danger.

He was deaf to all their arguments as before: she was to continue being one of the guides from north of Hernando to Memphis. And he secretly imagined her inevitable capture, to be violated by barely-human slave catchers, and again the picture lingered.

~ * ~

Enoch was a field hand on a plantation known as Land's End, in a curve of the Mississippi River some miles from Clarksdale. His master, Marshall Calloway, drove his slaves hard, in his plan to have the finest plantation in the state. He employed no overseer, riding daily among the workers in his fields, personally seeing to it that each slave worked without slacking.

Calloway was of that planter belief that Blacks were inherently lazy, and surely needed constant discipline to do their best. He used a whip, backed up by a pair of pistols, whenever he deemed it necessary, which was often.

Enoch often dreamed of freedom, those nights he couldn't sleep well there in the bed he'd shared with his wife Reenie. *Had* shared. She'd dared talk about freedom to one of the household help, who'd whispered it to another. Reenie was almost a model wife, servant, but she loved to talk. About anything that came into her head. The other slaves liked her, but shook their heads at her constant stream of confidences. *No harm; gal jist laks t'run her mouf.*

But Calloway's wife had eventually heard just enough to imagine, then suspect a possible planned uprising, that constant threat feared especially by harsh slave owners. And when she'd told her husband, her fear had produced a magnified version. No slave, man or woman, could be allowed to foment rebellion.

Reenie had been sold downriver, literally torn from Enoch's arms by the slave trader's helpers, muscular men who enjoyed bullying Blacks. Calloway had held a pistol on his field hand as these men hustled his wife away.

Enoch never saw her again.

The bitterness grew inside him, the raw injustice, the mounting hatred for his master. He debated fashioning a knife from scraps of iron at the blacksmith shop, slipping into the big house at night to slash the man's throat. Of course he'd be caught, hanged, but how much worse would that be than living this hell with no possible reprieve.

The only restraining force for Enoch was his son, five-year-old Seth, already helping in the fields, a boy without his mother, to grow also without hope. Enoch's plotting against the planter, his bloody plans for revenge, justice, were always abandoned at thought of his sure separation from his son. Seth had been in a state of shock at losing his mother, and only lately was beginning to accept life without her. Enoch would not, could not, risk losing Seth.

The boy slept in a rope trundle bed that was shoved back under his father's every morning. During the sleepless hours, Enoch could reach down and touch the sleeping boy, assure himself that his only family was there, safe.

As Seth grew older, his father thought more and more about freedom. Not so much for himself, but so that his son might have a real life ahead of him. There were, of course, whispers among the slaves about the supposed Promised Land up north, where Blacks were treated like kings, but Enoch knew enough about human nature to doubt this. *Maybe jis' a job, 'nuff pay t'buy us a place, send th' boy t'school.*

But how? Clarksdale, the nearest town, was still many, many miles from free states like Illinois, Indiana. There was no way a field hand could slip off, evade slave catchers for weeks of foot travel, with no way to get food or shelter. And certainly not with a young boy along.

Enoch toiled on, seemingly accepting his fate, but his mind worked constantly: *Gotta be some way t'git free. Talk 'mongst th' house slaves 'bout some white folks he'ps us, sometimes. Git m'self in trouble, askin' 'round, but I take th' chancet, if there's somethin' to it.*

Chauncey, the master Calloway's butler and personal servant, traveled with him everywhere. This ancient slave served also as valet, groomsman, when at home. He was the one Black the planter grudgingly admitted was mostly human, having shown a quick grasp of everything required of him.

Over the years, Calloway had gradually, without being aware of it, deferred to Chauncey a little, even asking the man constantly at his elbow his opinions on rare occasions. Those opinions proved almost never to be wrong. Chauncey had observed much of life, and had learned a great deal about the human condition.

So it was that one of the Cotton Route's recruiters had heard of the Calloway plantation's man-of-all-work, as a possible influential, to-be-desired contact. He could be, this man, a vital link in the organization's chain, far enough away from operations in Memphis.

~ * ~

Clermont Stevens was a free black, a peddler driving his worn mule and cart the length of Middle Mississippi, a fixture now tolerated, from long if bare existence in the region. And he pretended to be so crippled with arthritis that no one bothered to try to steal him. His wares never failed to excite the women, from slaves, farm wives, even to plantation mistresses: the colorful bolts of cloth, the laces, kitchen wares, the scents and spices.

Stevens somehow found access to these exotic offerings, and made them available to the remotest holdings. And he was shrewd enough to stock necessities for the men, too. There were always gunpowder, lead, hunting knives, leather, buckles, even bits and bridles stowed away in the layers of treasures in his rattly cart.

By the 1850s, Clermont Stevens was welcome at virtually every homestead around the Clarksdale territory, and could come and go at will. And he'd become a regular customer of Hiram Hyde's mercantile business, with its wholesale customers at steamboat landings along the Big River.

So, personally sought out and paid a little by the Route's director himself, the peddler was as a result the northerner's eyes and ears in the region. And as such, he contrived to contact Marshall Calloway's butler and everyman Chauncey, in the interests of the Cotton Route.

All this took time, as had everything about the organization's formation, growth, operation. But, impatient as Hyde had always been, he realized they must not hurry into possible discovery, with its obviously dire consequences. So recruiting this man of Calloway's took many months of the peddler's guarded approach.

Chauncey made it his business to monitor every slave on the plantation. Partly to further ingratiate himself with his master, but mostly because, despite his elevated position, he chafed under the same inhuman system of owner and owned.

Like any possession.

He could visit any field hand's cabin, converse with all the servants, share with them the burdens of their existence, without his master's suspicions. It was Chauncey who acted as a sort of go-between, often smoothing the friction between master and slaves, often spotting and handling emerging unrest, quelling resentment, envy, gossip that would mar the evenness of plantation industries, relationships.

So he knew of Enoch's despair. And he felt for this field hand, a man who'd lost the little joy his station in life had afforded him. More so since Reenie had been one of Chauncey's favorites, with her bright, talkative nature, her smile for everyone she met, her acceptance of things as they were, as they had to be. She'd asked little, received little, and in the end, suffered far more than a little, just for an unintended comment, a careless word.

"Boy Seth growin' like a weed, Enoch; know you'se proud of him."

"Am that, Chauncey. He stay cheerful, like his ma. Ever'body like my boy." They were watching the lad and two others driving the cows in from pasture. Neighbors had reported a panther loose in the region, and Calloway had decreed that all the stock be penned and guarded until the feared creature could be hunted and shot.

The boys chattered, laughed, teased as they herded the cattle through the gate, closed and latched it. Then, without being told, little Seth took two buckets to the well behind the separate kitchen, drew water, carried it to the wooden tanks for the cows. The other boys had evaporated with the closing of the gate.

That Enoch's boy doin' good: gon' be a good han', he keep on like that. Be sure t'let th' Massa know, keep eye on that un. Mebbe even grow up, take ovah when I'se too ole.

Chauncey maintained a dual role at the Calloway place, that of efficient right-hand to the master, with his eye constantly on the welfare of the plantation, and also now having been recruited, that of being the secret link that allowed the rare runaway in the region to succeed in escaping.

It was a dangerous game Chauncey played, but he did it well. He'd avoided aiding any runaway Black from Calloway's holdings in the past, letting it be known however, along the slave grapevine among other plantations, that he just might know something that could help others.

And over the months and years, several runaways from surrounding places had escaped, never to be caught. That Calloway had never lost a slave, the master attributed to his constant harsh overseeing of his people, along with the help of his trusted Chauncey.

That was about to change. While the servant half of this man saw in young Seth and his father the necessary units in the plantation system, the compassionate half knew that nothing but despair lay ahead for them. *An' that jis' wa'nt right, that sellin' Reenie down th' river. Reckon I'll jis' he'p make that right.*

Enoch brooded more and more, and it was Chauncey who urged him to keep working hard, not draw attention to his plight.

"Don' want th' Massa down on you, boy. You evah gon' git ovah losin' Reenie?" He was along on a wood-cutting expedition, and had drawn Enoch aside, out of hearing of the others. "Know you still grievin' 'bout losin' her, but you gotta keep doin' good, boy, or Massa, he git down on you."

"Ain't nevah gon' git ovah that, man. Gits wuss, more I thinks 'bout her bein' gone. Don't want nothin' t'do with no other gal; worry 'bout my boy 'thout no mama."

"Reckon so. So tell me, Enoch, whut you really want, fo' you an' th' boy, iff'n you could?" It was a bold overture, but Chauncey knew the answer.

"Iff'n I could? You knows, Chauncey, whut ever' one us wants. Some kinda life, that's whut. Don' wanta think 'bout Seth jis' bein' a fiel' han' ever' day, till he git ole, die, like th' res' us." The slave's eyes were far away, beyond the trees, the firewood stacked on the wagon. The Mississippi fall air held a tint of amber, of approaching cold.

"Thought that was it. Now, you knows I'se close to th' Massa, do ever'thing he want. But I'm same's you, boy: wanta be free m'se'f, but ain't gonna happen, ole's I be."

"Now, you ain' 'bout t'git me talkin' 'bout no freedom, Chauncey, so you go to th' Massa, tell him, git me sol', lose m'boy. Git on wid yo' talk, now; I ain' sed nothin', y'hear?"

"Ain' gon' tell that man nothin', Enoch. I knows when t'open my mouf an' when t'keep it shut. Ain' nevah got none us in trouble, has I? Evah?"

"Oh, reckon not. Jis' don' wanta even think 'bout ennything might make thaings wuss, y'know?" The last of the seasoned oak firewood was stacked on the wagons, and the other hands were converging. Chauncey leaned close.

"Wal, I jis' might know sum'pin he'p, boy, you wanta know mo'. Jis' you think 'bout it, y'hear?"

Enoch's eyes bored into his companion's. *What's he mean, heah? Is he gonna git me in trouble? Sho' not; I been good hand. He really know sumpin'? But th' other boys, they close. Think 'bout this, I will...*

And think he did, riding the wagon load of firewood, going about his chores, trying to sleep at weary day's end. He'd alternately shove this temptation out of his mind, but then let it in again. If there were really a way, he should—would—risk anything to take it.

Except losing Seth.

~ * ~

Susan Blaine eventually reached a point in her dealing with having killed the man Bates that let her stop worrying about it. She could not forget it, ever. She did ask God for forgiveness, praying silently at the little evangelical church near the farm. Didn't know exactly how He handled such as that, but well, she *was* sorry.

She tried to imagine her life—anybody's life—just being cut off that way, with nothing more to happen, no future, no hopes. A lot different from dying naturally. But then, she reasoned, maybe a man like that had cut off any future he himself might have had, with his meanness and all. Or maybe not. Too deep to figure, she guessed.

Meanwhile, Jenny had caught the eye, at a local church supper, of a newcomer to the region. He was Jethro Bennett, late of Nashville, a blacksmith. Gangly, with colorless hair and one blue eye and one brown, he was shy and awkward. And he stuttered badly. This was more pronounced when in the presence of women, it appeared. To Jenny he was no prize, and certainly not a ticket out of the grueling farm life. But he was an available man, and the supply was severely limited.

They tried to talk, she of the books she'd read, and the places she wanted to go. He haltingly, of Nashville and the demands of city life when you weren't of the leisure class. He'd wanted away from the always-behind work under a short-tempered master smith. Wanted to set up on his own somewhere, being now a journeyman, and could do about any work folks needed. A chance encounter with a wagoner led him eventually to the Delta and Hernando, just far enough from Memphis he didn't feel stifled. But there was a major obstacle to his pursuing a bride in this part of the country, one he'd keep hidden inside, for the present.

Both Kate and Susan rolled their eyes at their sister's newest scarecrow-like attraction. They alternately predicted to each other that she'd get past this, or convince herself Jethro was really her knight.

"She's got her sights set a mite higher, I'll wager," Susan insisted.

"Mebbe. But she ain't young's she was, an' that's gotta figger in. Might jist up an' leave us, Susie."

"Wal, if she does, she jist does. Dunno she'd be happy though, no better off'n she'd be: blacksmith's wife."

"An' Jethro's so bashful, he mightn't ever work up his nerve to ask her, lot like Darrell was."

"He's tall 'nuff fer you, Katy. Jenny gives up on him, you'd oughta have a go at th' feller." Susan's eyes were merry, down in the stovepipe-looking sunbonnet she wore where the two were hoeing in the garden.

"Lord, no. Had to 'bout raise you two; don't wanta hafta raise 'nuther half-growed boy."

Susan often wondered if her stern sister really were that impatient with men. She herself could envision perhaps a future relationship if the right man should appear. But Kate... well Kate was always going to be just Kate, and that picture didn't include a man in her life, she reckoned. Ever. *But things change,* she reflected. Who'd ever have figured the three of them, ordinary as dirt, to turn contraband agents? With ties to that secret bunch in Memphis, abolitionists, about the worst thing a southerner could call a body?

The two sisters would never discover the one obsession Kate had been disappointed with, on back in her teenage years. Lurvy Kessel was a transplanted Pennsylvanian, from a rural German settlement he'd fled to see more of the world. And that world had, for a brief interval, included Hernando, where his strange speech, his quick ways, set him apart.

And Lurvy was a handsome young man, by any standards. Blond hair, chiseled features, powerful build, not appearing conscious of the tittering tongues and fluttering hearts of the young ladies of the town and surrounding county. But as with so many handsome men and pretty girls, things had come easily for him, and he was accustomed to being in charge, leaving the weeping girls behind.

Kate was swept up in hopeless infatuation, even near-worship of this comparatively civilized Godsend, as she termed Kessel. She had contrived to be available at country dances, twice actually being swept up in those strong arms, almost swooning in joy. Not choosing to see his roving eye as their feet moved in perfect concert.

Somehow this severe sister had been able to mask her admiration, with her unchanging face, her secret safe from even the family. She dared not hope for a union with this catch of the county, but she fantasized, thought constantly of him.

And yes, was torn inside when she saw him go off with first one, then another of the shallow, pretty faces always around. She realized that she was to him, almost invisible.

Then he'd moved on, in his quest for new experiences. But she still had memories, albeit mostly those fantasies, of that brief, bright, heady non-relationship.

~ * ~

Yes, things did change. Perhaps not inside stoic Kate, but all around. *This crazy secession talk, now. Bunch of fire-eaters, whipped up by loudmouth politicians;* no telling what this nonsense would lead to. Change for sure, and who knew whether for better or worse?

No, it'd be for worse, the three sisters concluded. Jenny's reading and the commonsense they shared had taught them that runaway politics often led to war, and that seemed a strong possibility now. Get touchy people riled up enough, something always seemed to set it off: cuss-fights slid into fistfights, then on to gunfights, and enough people on both sides, that was war.

So no matter how things were apt to get out of control, it'd change things a lot. They tried to envision what a war would be like for them. Try to stay out of it, of course, but the way folks were talking, that might not be possible. And if by some miracle a war reached this far, they couldn't imagine how bad that would surely be.

But that was in the future: thing to do now was keep on keeping on. Plow, plant, weed, harvest, cut wood, spin, weave, scrub. It was what a woman did, no matter what else went on around her.

And yes, Kate speculated, maybe her mooning sister Jenny would end up leaving them. Maybe not. Maybe marriage would be to her like being a fish out of water, once it got to be a real possibility. *Well, just hide an' watch, I guess.*

Twelve

Anna Blake continued to guide runaway slaves on the last leg of the journey into Memphis. Every time Tom Brannon or another of the Route personnel argued that the danger to her was too great, given her race and gender, Hiram Hyde demurred. He pointed to her successful completion of every single run, contrasting it to others that had been compromised: Susan's Blaine's killing of the slave catcher Bates, Jenny's clubbing of the hunter. Eli Dobbins' failure to get through on schedule. The times even Tom Brannon, hitherto their most effective operative, had elected to turn back.

By contrast, Anna had eluded all discovery, and her guiding had been without flaw, if it had indeed experienced one close almost-brush with hunters. Hyde regularly held her up as the example of efficiency, and against the very odds the others cited.

"She cannot pose as a slave trader. She cannot pretend to be a farmer transporting his field hands. Even the Blaine sisters, since they are white, could conceivably have a reason for being in the company of Blacks, armed and guarding them. But our Miss Blake has no protection, no recourse. Yet she delivers her charges without fail. She is, in short, indispensable to our efforts." There was no arguing with flinty Hiram Hyde.

For his own part, the director of the Cotton Route observed with fascination Anna's repeated successes. But this was tinged with another, darker reaction. Over and over in his mind he pictured this extremely attractive young woman, educated, even refined, being caught by brutish white men. In his imagination they would rip the clothes off her perfectly formed body, beat her, degrade her, force themselves on her in an orgy of lust and violence. And Hiram Hyde, that pious, dedicated instrument of God's mercy, would shudder with excitement at the picture.

In his saner moments, Hyde would repudiate such fantasies, jerking himself back to focus on his vital work, driving from his mind such weaknesses. But he continued to send Anna out, even knowing that with each trip the odds against her were lengthening. She could not go on forever defying the law of averages, he knew. *But meantime, just look at the number of slaves she's shepherded to freedom.* And so he was justified, in his own mind, in risking this one individual for the benefit of the many.

And of course, God would continue to protect her. Surely.

So it was on a fall Friday Anna set out to travel the now-familiar but tortuous path south to the current hiding place. By chance she had left Memphis before dark, in the company of another teacher going to visit her parents. Anna had told her she would spend the night with Black friends south of the creek bridge, and bade farewell to her white counterpart where the road forked. *Well, that's true, in essence: I'll surely be out all night, and friends? Possible, I suppose, if short-term ones.*

"Will you be safe, alone?"

"Oh, yes. It's just a bit farther. They're expecting me." She did feel safe with her pistol and knife hidden on her.

Crossing the bridge in fading light, she entered the woods to wait for dark. It came soon, and she was on her way, over one of the faint paths she knew well. The miles seemed to melt away, landmark after landmark, and she reflected on how familiar all this had become. But she cautioned herself to be careful; there was always the danger.

Later, tall Kate Blaine turned the band over to her at the shelter, a fallen barn roof of cypress shingles canted upon one half-height wall. Hunters had supported the precarious tilt with stout posts to provide some shelter from rain.

There was a tall, muscular field hand named Ned, a middle-age cook, Lily, two teenage brothers, Jack and Zack, and Aphrodite, a ten-year-old girl. Anna smiled at the names, no doubt mixtures given by a combination of Black parents and plantation masters.

She could not know as they began the trip north, that the slave catcher Ludwig Holtz had learned of the group's existence from a farmer's son. The boy had glimpsed their lookout while hunting a lost cow that day and heard the murmur of voices from under the fallen roof. By sheer chance, the slave catcher had been on the way from Byhalia and met the farmer in the road. Recognizing Holtz, the man had told him what his son had seen. And had given him directions to the place.

Holtz was alone, and knew he needed help. He knew the runaways, if they were that, would move north at dark. He had time. Turning back, he reached his frequent partner Abner Shaw's farm by late afternoon, and the two recruited a neighbor of Shaw's for the hunt. Jake Wessel was a hungry-looking, stoop-shouldered specimen whose eyes lighted up at the prospect of a slave hunt. But they were far east now, and it would be dark before they could return and find the place, in overgrown brush and woods as it was.

Shaw, living closer to the Hernando area than Holtz, said he knew the roads. He scratched a rough map on the ground.

"If'n they go on nawth, they gotta cross th' road past Pete Osborne's place. Stay back, 'cause he's got thet pack of dawgs. We set up 'long here, we c'n head 'em off. Jist far 'nuff f'm Len Styles' farm, 'bout here, fer 'em t'git th'u 'thout nobody seein' 'em. We stay close, one of us'll shore git 'em."

"Whut if they cut wide west?" Holtz asked.

"Don't thaink they will. Prob'ly try t'make it t'Memp'is 'fore mawnin', so hafta go mostly straight up thar, way I see it. An' they's farms close together west thataway. Must have some a them abolitionists he'pin' 'em f'm somewhar. Somebody's bin gittin' 'em away, y'know, fer a long time."

"Have, fer shore. Like t'trap 'em at thet shed, though, mebbe git whoever's he'pin' 'em."

"'Fraid we'll miss 'em, we try that, late's it is."

"Wal, we'll go on whar y'say, then. Dunno whar these come frum; ain't heard nuthin' around. But if there is nigger lovers guidin' 'em, could've started out on south a ways."

So the men, heavily armed, headed for the road they were sure the runaways would have to cross. The farmer had declined to join them, fearing a shooting encounter. Holtz would have liked more men, but then that'd mean dividing whatever payment there would be too many ways. Besides, he felt the three of them would be more then able to corral a few ignorant slaves.

He and his men were only a few minutes behind Anna's first reaching the road, her short walk down it, and her leaving it to go on south. They'd managed to get lost for half an hour, despite Abner Shaw's assurances that he knew the way well. Now, stationing themselves at even intervals along the road near the likely route, they could hear each other if they called out.

While they waited, Holtz speculated on this group. *Must've come f'm a long way south, us not t've heard nothin'. Thet means somebody's shore he'pin' 'em, all right. Damn abolitionists, thet's who. But who'd know th' way? An' in th' dark? Hafta be frum 'round here. An' Billy Bates, gittin' shot thet time. Prob'ly a robber, but not fer shore. Could be a reg'lar operation goin' on here, right 'mongst us. Shore ain't caught all thet's run, of late...*

His conjectures were cut short by a sound in the road. Or maybe not a sound: just a certainty that someone was moving cautiously along it. There it was: a faint shuffle. Could be the runaways. Or a deer, or some other wild animal. A panther? The hair on his neck stood up. He eased back into brush on the north side of the road, making a sound. The shuffling stopped.

Damn, it could be a panther. C'n see in th' dark, 'n I cain't. That decided him, and he struck a match to the lantern he'd brought from Shaw's place.

A sudden stampede of feet burst right in front of him. He almost dropped the lantern, but saw black shapes turning, running back away from him.

"*Halt!*" he roared. "Ab! They's here!" And he ran after the dark-clothed figures. "Stop, I say, er I'll shoot!"

They did not stop. He crouched, set the lantern aside, leveled his revolver at where he thought the bunch were, and fired. Heard a cry. *Yeah, mebbe winged me one've them boys, scare th' rest of 'em.*

"Now jist stay whar y'ar! *Ab!*"

"I hear yuh!" came faintly from down the road beyond the fleeing shapes. Holtz could not see beyond the weak circle of light, but advanced, holding his second gun out. Then he heard a crash in the brush at the north edge of the road. *Damn, they gittin' acrost!* He ran forward to see low limbs still shaking, the road empty.

"This way, Ab, Jake! They's done got acrost!" Running feet, as the two others raced to him. They lunged into the woods, a second lantern helping light the way.

Holtz's bullet had hit no one, but Anna had lunged aside instinctively at the shot, stumbled on a limb where high wind had torn it off a tree, fell on a jagged edge of it. It had cut a gash in the flesh of her lower left leg. She'd managed to shove her charges back off the road the way they'd come. The shock and pain made her unsure if she'd been shot. *Shooting blind: could've hit any of us, killed someone.* Then strong arms had swept her up and they were in the trees. Big Ned had her. She reached, clamped her hands above the wound, which had now registered as intense pain.

Then Ned had suddenly laid her down. He picked up another fallen section of limb and hurled it back across the road north into brush, then scooped her up as it crashed, and slipped quickly with the others through the woods they'd just left. She was thankful for his quick thinking.

"Where to, Miss Anna?" he asked after they'd put distance between themselves and the road.

Where, indeed? Anna had willed her mind to work despite the pain, but nothing had come. The shelter was not an option, with the catchers out. Nor were the other two...

All right: the swamp. She'd heard Holtz say they'd crossed the road, so there should be time...

"Back to that stream, Ned. We'll wade in it, lose our trail if they bring... dogs." The pain was blinding: the cut must be deep. "Follow it into a swamp I know. Get word to... Kate again, somehow." Just *how* would be the hard part.

The stream became boggy. They all knew there would be snakes there, even cool as it was, and Anna heard sharp intakes of breath around her at each faint sound. Then there was finally a hummock, with big trees.

"Here. We'll wait for light to go deeper. Dogs... will backtrack us across the stream to the shed." Ned laid her against the trunk of a big water oak, hardly breathing heavily.

"Now, les' see that laig," the cook Lily insisted. "Come close, y'all; block th' light." Anna submitted to a match-lit examination of her leg. "Good," from the woman. "Clean cut, girl, mos' like a knife. Bleedin' good, too. Di'n't break nuthin', Miss Anna. Heah, we tie it up tight, stop th' bleedin'.'"

Anna was fairly sure she hadn't left a blood trail, clamping the wound as she had, though there was some inside her skirt. The sharp edge had made an angry furrow, which looked deep, and oh, how it hurt! But she thanked God it wasn't worse. And she thanked Lily, and big Ned.

Holtz and his men found nothing beyond the road, and guessed the slaves had moved fast, on what must be to their guide a familiar trail. And who'd been the guide? He'd seen only Blacks in that brief scramble. And the jumble of tracks told him nothing.

Well, didn't matter. They were now on the way to Pete Osborne's place and his pack of hounds. They'd pick up the hot scent for sure. *An' we got our hosses; they cain't outrun us.*

Osborne joined the chase, his mixed dogs excited, ready for the night's hunt.

"But these ain't no bloodhounds," he pointed out. "They'll tree a coon er a 'possum, but dunno 'bout niggers."

"Fresh trail: they'd oughta do," Holtz said. He led them back to the site of the skirmish.

"Got past me here, musta been a buncha young bucks, run hard; couldn't ketch up to 'em." The men pushed into the woods on the north side, the dogs sniffing, milling. But no scent reached them.

"Damn," Shaw lamented. "They shore *ain't* bloodhounds."

Back in the road, the dogs kept leading the men off south.

"No, that ain't it," Holtz argued. "Seen 'em bustin' th'u th' brush jist thar. Durn dawgs backtrackin' 'em."

Finally, on the off chance the runaways had indeed doubled back, the men followed the dogs. They eventually crossed the stream, still on what the slave catcher was sure was the back trail. And sure enough, they finally reached the fallen roof.

"This's where th' feller's boy saw 'em," Holtz announced. "I tol' yuh, they's halfway t' Memp'is by now."

The scent beyond the shed was long cold, so the men turned back north. Osborne took the dogs home, while the other three rode fruitlessly north, having no idea which way to go.

At first light Anna, who had not slept, gave Ned directions to the Blaine farm. She'd visited the sisters twice in the years of their work, and knew the long way from the swamp.

"There's a road going south that joins the one we were on, about here," she drew a map in the dirt. "Stay in the woods alongside both roads. This will be a turnoff to the left to their neighbor Isaac Ingrum's' place. Dogs there. Stay on ahead about a quarter mile to the sisters' lane. Road goes on past to the Talbot plantation about here, another mile. The sisters' house is part log, part board, no paint. No dogs. You'll recognize Kate if she's out, and she will be, in the fields.

"I hate to send you, but I can't travel yet, on this."

"Carry you," Ned offered.

"Too far, and slow you too much. Just stay hidden now on the way, and pray the catchers have given up. We'll move deeper into this swamp, now. The sisters know it; they'll find us."

She debated giving him her pistol, but could envision discovery and a battle with the slave catchers. That would undoubtedly end in his death. No, better to count on staying hidden, moving fast.

"And Ned," she squeezed his big hand, "go with God."

~ * ~

Enoch kept turning over in his mind what the planter's right-hand man had told him. *Might know sumpin' he'p you.* But every time he saw a glimmer of hope in the possibility of following up on this hint, he also remembered how close Chauncey was to the master, how he'd wormed his way into the slave owner's confidence. No way would the man risk that position of trust, power.

Would he?

No, he'd best not say another word to him, get himself and his boy too, in trouble. Old saying was 'better th' debbil you knows dan de one you don't'.

But Calloway was clearly the devil himself, the slave reasoned, and how much worse could it be to see just what Chauncey might've learned? Every field hand knew that slaves had run away, and while most were caught, some were not. Some believed God protected those who believed in Him, and maybe that power guided those few successful escapes.

Or maybe those they never heard from again had just been lucky, following the Drinking Gourd's north star toward freedom, long states away. Enoch didn't know. He'd about lost faith in a God that'd let his sweet wife be sold away, left him with raising his boy. Yes, to a life that was no life.

But to escape? Through white man's territory? That loomed as a simple impossibility, as it had in every hopeful individual slave's mind. The odds were just too unsurmountable: a friendless, hunted fugitive, running, hiding, with no guide, no way to find which way to go. And no one to trust, the long, long miles he'd have to travel, with every one of those white people eager to catch him, sell him, or keep him a slave in a worse place than the one he'd left.

No, he'd be a fool to try something like that, even alone. And give up his son? Worse than foolish. Best to just keep on here, hoping that things would change. Which of course, they wouldn't.

But this thought of freedom wouldn't leave him. It kept him awake at night, hearing Seth's regular breathing, there on his pallet. Enoch knew there had to be a way out of this endless misery, and here Chauncey had let just enough drop for him to grasp at, to try to make something out of.

~ * ~

The Blaines were indeed out scything hay when they heard the low call from the woods at field's edge.

"Miss Kate." Ned had lost the way only once, but had then found the roads, and from then on it had been a matter of stealing along parallel to them. It was nearing midmorning.

"Who's there?" Kate called.

"Ned. F'm las' night."

"All right. Stay hid; I'll come." She moved, the others scanning the surrounding woods. Susan retrieved a shotgun from a fence.

"Now what happened, Ned?" Kate stood nearly as tall as he.

"Catchers at th' road. Shot at us, an' Miss Anna, she fell, cut her laig bad on a sharp limb. Carried her to th' swamp. Lost th' men, but don't reckon it safe t' go on, an' she cain't walk."

Oh, Anna. "How bad is it?"

"Don' seem that bad, but deep. Cut a place b'low her knee, back side. Wind-throwed limb, side th' road, all splintery I reckon. Says it bad hurt, throbbin'."

"Thank God. All right, then. Got t'be sure t'clean it, mebbe put some whiskey on it. Bleed good?" Kate was realizing almost her worst fears for their friend. *At least she wasn't shot, but coulda been, fer sure.*

"Yas'm. Tied tight, but bus' loose if'n she walk, sho'."

Kate called the sisters over from their vigil.

"They're in th' swamp, girls. This here's Ned. Catchers almost got 'em, an' Anna's cut bad in th' laig. Now, we got t'git her outta there, an' th' others on north. Means 'nuther trip to Memphis, I guess. My turn fer that. But one of you take food, an' see to Anna. Prob'ly git her to th' road, hide her in hay in th' wagon."

"I'll go to th' swamp," Susan volunteered. "Whyn't you take th' wagon, Jenny, on up an' over t'where th' path comes out on th' road. Show her, Ned. Then we gotta git her t'there…"

"I carried her in," Ned said. "I c'n carry her out."

"Good. It'll be some dangerous in day, but that's th' only way we c'n make th' hay wagon work. Women jist ain't out at night."

Ned rode with Jenny, hidden in the hay. Kate rode too, to shorten her walk, their horse having died that winter. Susan went with them partway, with food, bandages, and a flask of Ingrum's medicinal whiskey. She'd cut across woods to reach the swamp a closer way. Everyone was armed: Ned had a long knife from the kitchen.

"If y'run into th' catchers, Jenny, they might know Ned f'm last night, so keep him hid. Take him with me, somebody might see him. An' ennybody gits t'pokin' in th' hay, y'll hafta shoot 'im."

"He hollered to two mo' men," Ned supplied.

"Three then." Kate nodded. "We c'n handle three, if need be. I won't go on till yer in th' woods good, Ned." From the look of her, Ned imagined this stern woman could handle three by herself.

They eyed the sun: this would put Kate into Memphis in time, she hoped, but everything depended on her reaching Tom Brannon at the Institute. Or perhaps the minister Kellog; she knew where he lived. After that, the Route people would just have to take over.

She planned ahead. They couldn't keep Anna at the house long without someone seeing her: nosy Annie Ingrum would be over, for sure. *That'n always just achin' fer company.* So yes, they'd have to hide her till Tom or someone could come for her with a legitimate story.

And Holtz: how'd he know? Well, always a chance somebody'll let a loose word out, no more'n there is for folks to talk about. Jist hope nobody's figgered out how we run things.

But Anna hurt, now. All right, this crazy business of sendin' her out's gotta stop: she coulda got killed. Th' Blaine sisters'll just hafta tell Mr. Yankee Hyde she ain't t'be sent any more, er we'll all quit. Hetty Barnes'll back us too, on that. Hard-nosed Hyde'll just hafta find 'nuther hand for th' Memphis part. An' gotta be a man fer sure, this time.

They reached the head of the path, though nothing showed. The guides always varied their route by just enough to avoid trampling the ground. Ned set off quickly, gliding silently through the woods, sure by now of the way. Kate waited, then walked on down the road and disappeared north of it at her brisk stride, leaving Jenny with the wagon. She'd tell the Route contact, then they'd have to come up with a story to cover Anna's absence from school.

This place was a danger point: anyone happening along would stop to see why a lone woman was waiting in a wagon at the side of the road. It was far enough from home that Jenny didn't know the farmers here, but that wouldn't help, anyway.

All right, she thought: *I'll hafta jist play th' faintin' female. Tell 'em I got a spell, an' hadda stop fer a minnit. Won't work fer long if they's too helpful, but mebbe Susie an' Ned c'n git here quick. She'll have Anna up an' mebbe goin' 'fore he gits there: she er Ned c'n carry her a ways, er two of 'em c'n brace her up on one leg part th' way, I hope.*

Sure enough, a farmer on a horse approached from ahead. Jenny fanned herself with a leafy branch. Then she had another idea. There was a woman they did know...

"Y'got trouble, miss?" he asked, reining.

"Nossir, jis'...waitin' fer m'sister. Hadda run to th' brush fer a minnit. Et somethin' didn't sit good."

"Oh, well then. Whar y'all frum?"

"Down t'wards Hernando, but I'm thinkin' we're on th' wrong road, here. This th' way t' Miz Ed Wallace's place?"

"Oh, no. That's back th' way y'come. Must've took th' wrong turn whar th' Hernando road comes in."

"Say so? Now, I tol' that sister of mine we's goin' wrong. But no, she was so sure she had it right. Wal, she'll be back in a minnit, 'n we'll git straightened out."

"I'd shore be keerful. Was a buncha nigger boys out las' night, musta run off. Fellers tried t'foller 'em with m'dawgs, but lost 'em."

"Don't say? Niggers out? We didn' hear nothin' down home." She tried to look alarmed.

"Ain't had time, I reckon. Feller name of Holtz, he shot into 'em, says he might've hit one, but they got away."

"Where to, you s'pose?"

"Hadda be Memphis. Prob'ly some a them abolitionists he'p'n 'em, way Holtz figgers it. He's a catcher, but he shore didn't ketch this bunch."

"Y'say it 'uz a *bunch* of 'em? Lawd, what'll come of it, niggers runnin' all over?"

Just then Susan appeared, alone, warned by the talk.

"'Bout time, girl. We's on th' wrong road, like I tol' you. Miz Ed's back t'other way, an' there's niggers loose, 'roun. An' no tellin' whut they's liable t'do, ketch us out by ourselfs."

"Howdy, ma'am," the farmer touched his hat. "I'm Pete Osborne. An' what's yore names?"

"We're th' Blaine sisters," Susan took over. "I'm Susie an' she's Jenny. An' I'se jist 'bout t'figger we made th' wrong turn, back a ways. We got our pa's ol' place down t'wards Hernando. You go ahead now, Jenny, an' I'll hold them ornery mules till y'git back."

"Wal, like I tol' yer sister, best watch out fer them runaways. But I speck them's long gone b'now." He rode off.

Thirteen

Jenny spotted Ned and Anna. She went to support the girl on one side while he took the other. They swung her along the few yards to the road.

"Quick, now," Susan was eyeing the road, her hand on her pistol. "Git in th' hay, Anna. An' Ned, you git back in th' swamp quick's you kin, to that other hidey place I tol' you about. Git th' others there. Prob'ly have somebody there t'git you by late. Gonna be close timin', an' might jist be tomorrer night."

"Yas'm, Miss Susie, Miss Jenny. An' God bless you bofe." He was gone with the food, a dark shadow amid the trees.

Susan backed, turned the wagon.

"Now Anna girl, we got to hide you up close till Tom or whoever c'n git you back home. Reckon he c'n work somethin', if he don't run into Holtz."

"That farmer said Holtz jist shot in amongst 'em," Jenny told them. "Didn't keer a whit. Jist glad he didn't hit you, girl, er ennybody else."

"Thank th' Lord this ain't a gunshot then," Susan stated. "Be hard t'explain, ennybody wanted t'know. Accident, but we'd hafta answer a lotta questions, you bein' at our place an' all. An' that Holtz, he'd mebbe figger somethin'. You hurtin' bad, Anna?"

"I can stand it. That alcohol was like fire, though."

"Good, though I know it hurt a sight. Means no infection. You'll be back up in a few days. Got a story for th' folks back home?"

"Just tell them the truth: stumbled in the dark, fell on a splintery limb, I guess, had to stay with friends. I was supposed to be with a family out of Memphis for the weekend."

"Should do it," Susan said. "If it heals right, shouldn't enny doctor be needed. But you'll be out a few days, with us er in Memphis."

Anna endured the jolting of the wagon hidden from passersby in the newly-cut late hay. Its smell was a pleasant reminder of days in the fields as a child, first on the McRaven plantation in Hinds County, then the years on their own place as freed slaves. She reflected that her brothers were grown now, working the acres with their father. Maybe she'd be able to visit them soon, if she could get Sarah or Rosanah McRaven to go with her. Even the new railroad cars weren't safe for a Black woman alone, but she could pose as anyone's maid.

But that gunshot, now: the violence, the fear, the reality of it. This was almost as bad as it could get, assuming they could still complete the run. The old apprehension was back, the imagined lurking of slave catchers in the dark. Depraved men who'd shoot into a group of people indiscriminately. Perhaps she should have killed the man, lighted as he'd been by the lantern, but her first instinct had been to get her charges away. And he'd called to the other men: no chance in a gun battle.

Thank You, God, for Ned's quick thinking: throwing that limb to put them on the wrong trail. Now, what will become of that good man, a field hand, up North? Be with him, dear God, and all of them.

They put Anna in the loft, in a cramped makeshift bedroom, half-carrying her, where no visitor was likely to discover her. Jenny made up some willow bark tea for the pain, and her special broth. Susan satisfied herself the bandage was clean and tight. Anna felt a surge of gratitude toward these stalwart sisters, engaged in this work, caring for her as another sister. She felt much as she had at the McRavens' place, with Sarah and Rosie so close to her, the inseparable trio of them. *Long since...*

~ * ~

Clinton Carruthers told Abel he had a surprise for him. It was another year later, and he was to go visit his brother Mason at the university. The double purpose was to show the boy where he'd go in another two years, get to know the place. The parents reasoned that their sons would have a grand time of it, there in the college town.

And Clinton had convinced them he needed his servant Abel along. Certainly they would agree that this son also should present himself as a gentleman, future prospective student, properly attended. And they'd agreed, after cautioning their son to keep an eye on both Abel and his father Moses. He assured them that, armed with his pistol, there'd be no trouble.

Now it was time for Clinton to tell his friend what he'd planned for two years and kept secret from him. From everyone, actually.

Abel was somehow to escape, many miles on the way to Oxford, slip away at night at a predetermined inn and join a group of fleeing slaves passing near the town, guided by a Route operative. This was west of Tupelo, at the limit of the organization's forays.

And yes, Clinton would mount a hunt for the boy as soon as daylight showed he was gone. A fruitless search, north the way the runaway had surely fled. Clinton knew his parents would be outraged at the escape, would give him hell, and he didn't care. But, his opposition to slavery still hidden, he'd make every effort to decry this betrayal, commiserate with the family over the loss of this promising but ungrateful traitor. And savor the thought of his clever companion succeeding somewhere safe, with a real life ahead of him. He'd even slip Abel a little money, but depended on the Route people to handle the rest.

Clinton had learned of the Cotton Route from relatives the family had visited up toward Grenada earlier. Some northern abolitionists, it was reported, but nobody knew where they were located. Too many slaves escaping for it to be just the few displaced Yankees, down here causing trouble. These folks had heard the Underground Railroad rumor, allegedly operating in the eastern states, and feared there was a similar effort closer to home.

Actually, one of the kin, a daughter, had scandalized the family by brazenly marrying one of these emigrants, down from Illinois. A likable cotton merchant, the newcomer was a successful businessman, whose knack for making money impressed the otherwise suspicious Mississippians. They'd reluctantly accepted him, and would never discover his anti-slave sympathies.

It was this man who'd taken Clinton aside and actually asked him if the Meridian folks mistreated their slaves. Assured that only rebellious ones were punished, the in-law eventually discerned Clinton's distaste for the system, in guarded conversations with him. And mentioned the existence of the Route, which must be kept absolutely secret, of course.

Subsequent letters between the two, coded to appear innocuous, established the time and place for the planned escape. Enough later that there should be no connections suspected.

It was a daring plan, and it had to be kept from everyone, even the boy's father Moses, right there with the carriage, who'd be as surprised at the escape as anyone. But it would succeed; Clinton Carruthers was certain of that.

"Here's what I've got for you, old friend," he'd told Abel as they tramped the autumn woods well away from the plantation house. "I'm about to shock you with a bold undertaking, one that'll change your life."

"Man of mystery. What, you're running away from home to join a circus?"

"No, *you* are. But not, I hope to a circus. To a *life*." His grin was huge as he watched Abel's eyes widen.

"You don't mean... no, you're funnin' me, you nasty old tease. Not funny."

"Not funny at all. You're going with me to Oxford, only you won't get there, you see. You'll escape and never be heard from again. I want a life for you, Abel my friend, and you'll never have one here." He put his arm around the Black's shoulder. "And I'll miss you like the devil, but I've been planning this for two years, and it's about to happen. Just promise me you'll make something of yourself, once free."

"You mean this? You're serious?" This was too much to take in: just what he'd set his sights on, but not somewhere in the future, here and now.

"Serious as death, which might not be the best choice of words. Yes, and even your father can't know, nor anyone else. You'll be painted as the ungrateful, traitorous, spiteful runaway, throwing away your chance to be the exalted butler of the realm, after all we've done for you here. And of course I'll be the outraged, vengeful former master, cheated of his lifelong companion, his *property*. You know how I've felt all along, Abel, and here's our chance to get a start on that eventual wearing-out of this ugly system. So, what do you think of that?" He poked Abel in the ribs.

"I think you're out of your idealistic mind, that's what. You'll never make it happen, first of all, and you'll be disowned for letting it succeed. Aiding and abetting, it's called. But oh, God, I thank you, Clint! You can't know how much freedom means to all of us who can only dream of it."

"Got a pretty good idea. I've seen your people herded, beaten, deprived, sold like cattle at the first sign of unrest, and it sickens me. And I'll tell you another thing: if I do go to the university here, or somewhere else, I'm leaving this state, this region, and going someplace civilized. Maybe take the grand tour in Europe and just stay there."

"Well, you're right. I'll miss you, noble friend. But say, as a free man, I can get word to you later, and we can meet up north somewhere. No need to disappear forever from each other."

"And you damn well better do that, or I'll hunt you down and kick your ass. Use another name, mail a letter from another town, and we'll make it work, whenever. What an adventure! This'll be better than our putting the whiskey in the punchbowl at that ball, when old Mrs. Hundley got drunk and rubbed herself all over Mason."

"Or the time we put a burr under Judge Chester's saddle. Yes, I'll miss you, old friend, but surely not for long, if we work it right. Let's make that vow now, that we'll meet again, say just after you graduate college." So they did that, solemnly.

~ * ~

Kate's long stride had banished the miles to Memphis, and while she had not found Tom Brannon, she had reached Reverend John Kellog, the Baptist minister. It seemed Tom had gone to visit another Northern family downtown, and the reverend didn't know where.

"We can go in my buggy," he conjectured, "but this is only the next night. Catchers may well reason the runaways are holed up somewhere till dark, and be out watching. I've my Sunday service tomorrow, too. I'm afraid we must wait another day or two for the run, Miss Blaine."

"Be hard on 'em there in th' swamp, but Susie an' Jenny c'n feed 'em. No help for it, I guess. Well, I'll leave it to y'all here then, an' be goin..."

"Oh, you mustn't think of going back tonight," the minister's wife Miriam insisted. "You'll stay with us, of course. And why not ride the cars back after church tomorrow? You're near Hernando, I know."

"Wal, I..." She *had* brought along a little money...

"We insist, don't we, John? I know what vital work you and your sisters are doing—God's work—and we can certainly do more to help."

"Well ma'am, I didn't bring enny clothes to wear t'church..."

"If it won't insult you Kate, we've a trove of donated dresses here for the needy. Why don't you and I go try some on? John, tell Cook we'll be half an hour?" And Miriam bustled a bemused Kate off to a back room in the parsonage.

"Now, don't be offended, please. These are from a lady uptown who's quite tall—doesn't go to our church, so she won't see—and I'll wager they'll fit."

So stern Kate Blaine, who almost never went anywhere, indulged herself in trying on various donated hoop-skirted dresses with the delighted Miriam Kellog, for all the world like two schoolgirls. She could almost understand her sister Jenny's fantasizing over that other life she was so sure was out there, somewhere.

And next morning at church, Kate tried to act like the sophisticated woman she'd come to resemble. She'd resolved to go through with this, and to maintain an aloof silence, so as not to give away her country speech and mannerisms. *Smile an' nod.* For her part, Miriam thought Kate's composed, angular face and her height gave her an air of secure authority.

Miriam introduced her as Miss Catherine Blaine, a friend from the Delta, hinting at plantation connections. "Their place is close to the Everett Talbots'". Kate almost laughed. But she remembered the gracious Sarah Talbot, and resolved to act like her. Mercifully, they'd arrived just before the service began, shortening the act.

"We'll slip out quietly," the minister's wife whispered. "I know you must be nervous, but isn't this fun?"

Well, maybe that was the word for it. After a few flustered moments, Kate found she enjoyed the covert glances, the whispers, and she knew for the first time in her life she was creating a stir. So this was what a lady was s'posed to do, s'posed to look like. *Git old quick, I reckon. No wonder society wimmen's always havin' cases of th' nerves.*

They left before the final hymn ended, only partly to reach the train in time. As they rolled away in the Kellog buggy, Kate had to laugh out loud.

"Don't never tell a soul please, ma'am," she implored. "I jist loved it when y'told that white-haired lady I'se f'm a plantation. We got us 160 acres, an' nobody but us three t'run it. We're dirt farmers, plain 'n simple."

"You may not realize it Miss Kate Blaine," Miriam told her soberly, "but you and your sisters are among the finest ladies in this world. Don't ever forget that." And she hugged the astonished Kate warmly.

~ * ~

Enoch could stand the doubt no longer. Today he'd find a way to get Chauncey alone, find out whether the man really did have a way for slaves to escape. He'd keep his inquiry vague, so that if the butler did report his questions to Calloway, that wouldn't result in his being sold away. He hoped.

No opportunity presented itself until late, after the field hands had trudged back to their cabins and Chauncey was talking with the carriage driver as he unharnessed the horses at the big barn. Enoch, glancing around to be sure they were alone, stepped up as the butler turned away toward the big house, pointing to his hoe as if to show the other man something about it, in case of prying eyes.

"Hey you, Chauncey. You doin' good?"

"Some good, yeah. You?" He also cast his eyes about, then seeing they were alone: "You got sump'in say t'me, boy?"

"Hopin' you'se th' one talkin'."

"Mebbe." He took the hoe, pointed to the nicked edge. "You's sho'?"

"'Pends on iff'n you c'n make it happ'n." He forced himself not to look about him, draw attention.

"I c'n do that, boy. Gon' be hard, bofe you, but jis' you wait. Gits late, I come t'yo cabin, tell you 'bout whut's gotta happ'n." He handed the hoe back, turned away. Enoch headed for his cabin.

Big Mattie, the blacksmith Caleb's wife, always shared her family's meals with Enoch and Seth, and had left their supper for them. The boy ran from the last of his friends, took his father's hand as they entered the cabin. *Boy wore out, lak me, but he still full of life. Gotta keep it that way.*

After Seth was asleep, Enoch sat up, watching the embers from his dying fire flicker, hearing the quiet whisper of the flames, feeling the warmth of the bricks against the winter chill. *Be col' tryin' t'travel, this time th' year. Mebbe oughta wait fo' warm time...*

The tap on the door was faint, but he jumped up, opened it a crack. Chauncey eased inside, noted Seth asleep, closed it. The two moved closer to the fireplace, sat.

"I be quick, boy. An' you don' say no word t'nobody, an' don't let even yo' Seth know." It was a hoarse whisper. Enoch nodded. "Now, you knows Clermont Stevens, th' peddler, he come th'u ever' couple months er so." Again the other nodded, eyeing his sleeping son.

"I'se thought 'bout him, some. He th' way?"

"Not hese'f. No, they's white folks down f'm Memp'is, be heah t'he'p us. An' po' folks name of Brady, live up t'ord Clarksdale, ain't got no slaves. Stevens, he git th' word t'Brady, enny of us wanta run. I tells th' peddler who-all's ready, an' he send Brady. All you gotta do is, when I tells you, you'n Seth, you slips out to th' woods south, when it good dark. Don' go nawth, 'cause that's whar they looks fust. Brady meet you soon's you gits 'mongst th' trees, an' he take you on down, then 'cross east, fore daylight. Hide you'n enny mo' he got, someplace till dark agin.

"Then, 'nuther guide, they calls theyselves, he take you on way east, clear outten heah, till it safe t'turn nawth. Take a long time, but they's got it all set up, on thru' Tenn'see, then on up t'whar ain't no slave state."

Enoch heard this whispered confidence with growing alarm. How could anybody hope to stay hidden from the catchers for what would surely be weeks, many, many miles on foot?

"Dis gonna wu'k, Chauncey, or does enny us really git free?" His eyes were hard on the butler.

"Wu'k ever' time. Ain' nobody runs bin caught. You be th' fust f'm heah, an' that some rough on me, but th' Massa, he trus' me. I make it up lak you'n th' boy, you be stole, some trader I seen askin' 'roun', he grab you bof."

"When this happen? Be col', hard t'travel."

"We waits till spring, now. Mebbe las' of Feb'rary, fust warm spell. You jis' keep on doin' whut you s'posed to, 'bout two months, an' you'n yo' Seth, you be on yo' way, sho'." The butler rose, looked long at the sleeping boy, then squeezed Enoch's shoulder, turned, slipped out the door.

~ * ~

It actually had been a simple matter for Tom Brannon to ride the railroad cars to Hernando the next weekend after Anna's injury and hire a buggy to drive out to the Blaine sisters' place.

He'd reported her injury to his employer at the school, so no one expected her back there soon. Anna was up and cautiously about, though the wound, healing, still tightened the flesh in her leg. She was fearful of breaking it loose. Tom had brought crutches, and she was able to move well enough on them.

The minister had completed the run, finding the runaways safe in the swamp as per Kate's directions. John Kellog had about him a steely air of certainty that few questioned, in any situation. His wife supposed it came from his absolute conviction that he was doing the right thing, or trying his best to, before God and all His people. The characteristic served him well, whether in the pulpit or out on an illegal slave-guiding expedition.

Taking her leave from the sisters, Anna had hugged each one. She felt closer to them than to anyone outside her own family. She'd laughed with them over Kate's stylish outfit, but also assured the tall woman she did indeed qualify as a lady.

"It's not clothes, Kate, or money or social position: it's honesty, honor, kindness, and you have them all. Every one of you has them. I couldn't want for finer friends."

For their part, the sisters had enjoyed the company of this educated and equally kind young woman. Just Susan's age, the two had grown close in these few days. Jenny also was captivated by the idea that this Black girl who'd so impressed her could move so freely about in her part of Memphis, be on equal footing with the other teachers, those in her mixed-race community. Kate took it for granted: *girl's earned her place, an' no more'n right.*

Anna was the recipient of bold glances from men in the Memphis-bound railroad car, who assumed she was Brannon's 'fancy gal', his personal plaything. Only his almost defiant demeanor kept at least one of them from offering to buy the girl. Tom was not tall or intimidating, but his brusqueness did not invite familiarity. *And yes, that bulge in his jacket is surely a pistol.*

Once home, Anna sent word she'd be back at school on Monday, even if still on the crutches. And she was visited by the austere Mr. Hyde, who was solicitous, almost apologetic.

"We've decided it is no longer safe for you to be out on the Hernando route, Miss Blake, after your... unfortunate accident. You will be in charge of safe houses and supplies again, and we will suspend the said route until we find a replacement for you. By that time things should have quieted down there. My condolences." He rose and left.

And of course you've received a number of ultimata from my counterparts, demanding just this action, I know, after the bullets flying. But admit he'd been forced to change his mind? Never. She smiled a tight smile. The remembered terror had dimmed, but not left her.

~ * ~

The Carruthers carriage left the Big House, with Clinton and his servant Abel, to travel north, not on horseback, since Clinton's mother was sending requested packages to her son at the university, and to friends and family on the way. The plan was to pass well east of Grenada until the return trip, to visit family friends before turning west toward Oxford. It was on this last leg of travel that Abel was to disappear, at the designated inn, away from any town.

So the routine of the trip was firmly established as the carriage wound its way north, stopping once to have the horses shod, the wheel bearings greased, and stops at inns on the way. There Abel and his father Moses slept in makeshift quarters in the stables, while Clinton enjoyed the offerings of the table and bed for whites, the custom of the times.

At last the remote inn was reached, and though still early in the afternoon, Clinton told the carriage driver they'd stop over here, let the horses rest. Besides, he told him, he was feeling ill, no doubt from something they'd eaten earlier.

155

There was a note for him there, delivered just moments before, the innkeeper told him, by a messenger on horseback. He read it, and his face hardened. *This will change everything: must handle it, though.*

~ * ~

Jenny Blaine was now experiencing *déjà vu* regarding her beau, Jethro. He came to call, and squired her to dances and picnics, but made no effort to further his suit. And truth be told, she began noticing, reacting to, more his rather obvious shortcomings: his appearance, which was that of a homely young man apparently uncertain just where to place the next foot when walking. His painful shyness, evidenced in the reddening of his long face whenever she spoke to him. She'd come to overlook his stuttering, knowing he couldn't help that. But that he was a competent blacksmith amazed her, he seemed so fumbling, so awkward.

Prob'ly thinks of me 'bout like one of his anvils, she concluded. His seemed to be a world of tangible objects, not one of the subtleties of romance. He could read and write, and calculate the worth of jobs he did, but had absolutely no curiosity about books, ideas, or anything else much beyond beaten iron. She became more uncertain that she could ever make a life with such a specimen.

And of course she constantly compared him with the intense Tom Brannon, whom she had come to set up as the ideal: the urbane, the dedicated, the committed. She knew by now that Tom was smitten with the beautiful Anna. They had touched on that subject while she had been here in the sisters' care, and the girl had confided that even with the obvious strictures of race aside, she just didn't have feelings for Tom, beyond their working relationship.

So, end of that story.

Jenny told herself she still could hope, although it wasn't hard to see she'd never find a place in Tom's life. Dream stuff, that was what Tom Brannon was, and would remain. *Well, waitin' on Jethro's tedious, but prob'ly th' only way fer me.*

Fourteen

Clinton Carruthers had been at a loss after reading the note, but realized he must act decisively, and not in the way he'd planned. As the daylight waned and the time approached for Abel's imminent escape, he determined just how he had to handle the situation. Because the note he'd received from his father Hamilton Carruthers, at this inn the family often used, told him that somehow an unguarded word must have slipped out, or perhaps it was just idle speculation by one of the field hands. That Abel, his closest companion, was to seize on this trip to escape, to run away from the young master, in a desperate bid for freedom.

At any rate, Clinton's father warned him of the supposed attempt, and charged him with making certain the slave remained the planter's property, even if the boy had to be chained the entire way. Too bad he'd become the son's companion all these years, the ungrateful, traitorous boy would be whipped at least, or even sold away. And would in no way ever be trusted: forget any idea of becoming the plantation butler. Couldn't take the chance he'd poison the others, spark a rebellion.

And Clinton was to recruit the innkeeper, and watch the boy's father Moses the carriage driver, to make certain Abel remained a captive there and on the road afterward. And, if it came to violence, the boy might even have to be killed. Also, if Moses tried to intervene, he had to go also. Better to set an example, nip any idea of a dreaded slave uprising.

So Clinton told the innkeeper he'd need his help, and to find a chain and locks to keep Abel captive, also telling him of Hamilton's note.

"I'll need you to watch the boy's father, the carriage driver, Mr. Cleary, while I restrain him tonight. And I'll have to keep him chained the rest of the trip: can't give him the chance to slip away."

"That boy's been yore shadow since botha you was little, Clinton, an' now he's gonna try to bust loose? Ungrateful little bastard. Oughta jist shoot him."

"Too valuable to kill, unless I have to. No, I can handle him till we get back home, then my father will deal with him. Guess he's been planning this a long time, never let on about it at all. Just goes to show you can't trust a one of them, doesn't it?"

"Does, fer a fact. Don't s'pose th' ole man was plannin' t'run, too?"

"I certainly hope not. Neither of them would get far anyway, no idea which way to go, catchers out. Foolish idea, and the boy had it so good, with plans to make him the new butler. Ungrateful is right."

So with the chain and two locks and keys, Cleary and Clinton, both armed, slipped out to the stables. It was now completely dark, with just a candle lantern burning inside. The slaves, father and son, had made pallets in the hay, were preparing to sleep. Clinton pointed his pistol at the boy.

"You, Abel, get over here by this post. Now!"

Abel's eyes went wide. What was this? Was this his best friend, threatening him with a *gun*, holding a *chain*...? He stood, unable to move, taking in the innkeeper, also holding him and his father at gunpoint.

"Wh... what *is* this? Why're you...?"

"I said *now!* Up against this post. I'm going to have to chain you to it. Try to escape, would you? After all we've done for you, ingrate! Traitor! Is this the way you show your loyalty? I'm sorry I ever wasted time with you."

Finally realizing that his plan, his trusting the white boy, all they'd shared, the future he'd longed for, all this was crashing down around and through him, Abel moved dumbly to the post. Stood with his back to it. Cleary kept his gun on him, also threatening Moses, who'd stood, dumbfounded, disbelieving this... treachery, that's what this was. His boy... And where'd the master's son get the idea his Abel was about to run off? *No such thing...* They were soon to learn.

"I got this note from Father, that somebody at the plantation learned of your plans to run, Abel. He didn't say how he heard, but that doesn't matter. I'll keep you chained, and I'll have my gun on you every minute of this trip, you hear? You're not getting free, boy, not now, not ever! And I'm quite sure you'll be sold, once we reach home." Clinton's face was grim, determined.

He looped the chain around Abel's neck, locked it, then locked the other end of it around the post. The boy could move, lie down, but that was all. The sometime future butler of the Carruthers plantation house was now and would forever be at best just a field hand, surely to be sold, perhaps to a cruel master who wouldn't be impressed a whit by his intelligence, his proper speech. *Hoe cotton, pick cotton, bend yo back, boy: you ain't no better'n th' next hand.* Clinton pocketed the keys. Then he forced the bewildered Moses to precede him and Cleary to the inn proper, where he was locked in a storage room.

Abel, betrayed this way, searched for a way, any way, to escape. His friend, companion, trusted ally turning on him this way... *But don't waste time in self-pity. There's got to be a way to get away. Cheap locks, maybe able to pick this one, slip away. I was to meet the runaway's guide about two hours from now. So, use this time trying, hard.*

But there was no nail, no piece of wire, nothing to try to open the lock with. The post was heart cedar, set deep in the ground, holding up part of the stable itself. No way to cut it, break it, even if he'd had a saw, hatchet.

No, I'm stuck here: no hope, no remedy, condemned, betrayed, and no help for it. He sank down, sat dejectedly on the straw pallet, his head in his hands. *And I was so close to freedom, the way we had it all planned out: join the other runaways, get to Memphis, then on north, be on that railroad to a real life. This will kill Mama, Papa too...*

An hour went by, glacier-like, with images of the life he'd had on the plantation. Chosen early on to serve the big house, spared the hardest tasks, clearly to take the old butler's place. He now guessed he should've been content, never been taken in by the false promises Clinton had come up with, to tantalize him, build empty hopes. *When it all comes down to it, I'm just property, and Clinton had a choice: help me, or put his family first, the place. Blood's sure thicker than water. Why'd I ever trust him? Fool, blind fool. Set me up this way, give me hope, dreams.*

Should've run on my own, take my chances with the catchers, every man's hand raised against me. But I know I couldn't have made it, be caught, taken back, sold. Same outcome, then. But the betrayal, the lies, the way he's treating me like dirt now...

There was a sound, and Abel raised his head in the darkened stable, trying to separate a form from the blackness. The hair on his neck and arms raised, his eyes widened to catch sight of whatever was slipping toward him. Some demon? A robber? Wild animal? What...

"Keep quiet, Abel. Not a whisper from you. I've got just a short minute for this, or I'll be missed. Hold the neck lock out, let me get the key in..." Stunned, the boy did as told, and felt Clinton's fingers as he fitted the lock, turned the key, freed the chain. "Now, I'll leave this bent nail here by the open lock, and that'll be how you escaped. You've got time to meet the runaway's guide, just as we planned." He clutched the astonished Abel to him in a quick bearhug. "Goodbye, my friend, and go with God."

And Clinton was gone. To enter the inn by the back door he'd come through, innocent of any duplicity. He bade Cleary a goodnight, checked to find that Moses had fashioned a sort of bed of empty jute fiber sacks, relocked the door. Climbed to his own bed, lay down, his heart thumping in excitement.

Abel slipped away, downwind from the inn. He didn't remember whether there was a dog, but he didn't arouse it, or anyone, moving in the starlight into the forest, orienting himself by the tree limbs against the sky. *Past this big oak, then east a bit of the north star, two miles straight on. Snakes, stay asleep, let me pass.* He focused on the way, finally letting the reality of Clinton's freeing him into his mind.

Boy had to wipe out suspicion then, so the innkeeper and yes, even Papa wouldn't know. Don't reckon he'll ever tell a soul, be just as outraged as the family. Clinton, friend, I should've known I could depend on you, though you had me in hell there for a while.

~ * ~

Robert and Tranquilla McRaven had returned from a trip north, having left the care of the plantation in the hands of the older children, all of whom worked responsibly with the hired hands in the fields.

They decided to visit Anna on the way out of Memphis. It was mid-afternoon when they arrived at the institute, to learn that she'd met with an accident a few days before, and was at home.

"What kind of accident? Is she all right?"

"I believe Mr. Bancroft said it was just a cut," the receptionist told them. "She stumbled and fell on a sharp limb where it'd been torn off a tree in the wind, cut her leg badly. We were quite worried, but the doctor said it wasn't serious. We're quite fond of Miss Blake."

Anna hobbled to the door on crutches. She opened it hesitantly, now being wary of potential enemies. Seeing her friends/former adoptive parents, she was delighted. She dismissed her injury lightly, insisting that accidents happened to everyone.

Robert was suspicious: he'd seen the momentary expression of fear in the girl's face. He didn't doubt for a moment that this devoted young woman was somehow helping members of her race, and that could possibly include her even aiding runaway slaves. He remembered the visit by the austere Hiram Hyde, when he'd explained that he and his wife could not risk aiding the effort.

"First place the catchers would search," he'd pointed out, which exact sentiment Hyde had later encountered with the planter Cardwell.

Now, could a vague reference Hyde had made to a 'contact' in Memphis that'd led him to their plantation actually have been Anna? *Surely not, yet... And that could actually be a gunshot wound.*

After the visit, he confided in Tranquilla, who had her own concerns about the leg wound. *The very kind of thing that could happen if...*

"We'd suspected she'd become somehow involved, and I was proud of her, thinking she was perhaps gathering clothing, arranging food or shelter for escaped slaves. But she seemed really apprehensive, didn't she? At first?"

"She did, yes. And all right, everybody has accidents. But I suspect that wasn't just a cut: never heard of that kind of thing from a fallen limb."

"No, and it could well have happened if she'd been out at night, running from danger. If that zealot Hyde is actually sending her out to guide runaways, he's a blind fool! Why, if she were caught, she'd be subjected to every kind of vile outrage..."

"And be hanged. I remember he said their organization's ends justified any and all means. A fanatic, despite whatever noble aims."

"What can we do to help? We can't let Anna continue in this, not after what must've been the narrowest of escapes."

"Nothing we can do. She's a grown woman, must make her own choices, do what she can. We can't imagine what inhuman treatment drives a slave to run, but despite her freedom, I'm sure *she* can. We'll never understand the situation from their viewpoint, no matter we sympathize." He thought a long moment more. "And no, there's nothing we can do to help her."

"We can continue to pray for her."

"Yes, pray."

~ * ~

The Clarksdale winter wore itself out, in those damp, not-really-bitter days of hiding Mississippi sun. Enoch's hopes rose with the warming weather, the fantasy of escape he'd nursed through the dark days.

He'd managed to trade for shoes for Seth, imagining that when they ran, it'd be through snaky woods and brush. The blacksmith at the plantation was also the shoemaker, and had made a sturdy pair for the boy, just a little loose so he could grow

164

into them. And his wife had also knitted socks for him, who was after all a favorite of everyone.

The field hand waited for word from Chauncey, but dared not mention the planned escape to him. *Man coulda changed his mind, waitin' fo' me t'say sumpin', git me sol' away, 'thout m'boy.*

But one night with no moon, Enoch again heard the soft tap at his cabin door. He glanced at sleeping Seth, opened to the butler.

"You ready, boy?"

"I be ready fo' ennythaing, Chauncey. Whut you got in min'?"

"You knows whut. T'morry night, jist soon's everthaing quiet. Straight south, now. Brady, he ready, an' I gits th' word t'him. Jis' you acts lak ever'thaing goin' good, then you'n th' boy, you slips out." That was all; the butler turned to go.

"Chauncey, you ain' gonna git us in trouble, are you?" The dark eyes were hard on the other's face, glinting in the coals of the fire. Enoch's big hands flexed, and Chauncey reflected that the field hand could snuff out his life at will.

"I be on yo' side, boy. Gonna he'p you fin' a life fo' yo'se'f an' that boy." A pause as the old man looked at the sleeping child. Then he gripped Enoch's hand. "An' th' Lawd bless you, son, an' be with you all th' way." Tears stood in the faded eyes as Chauncey slipped out the door soundlessly.

There would be repercussions, accusations, punishment surely, when it was discovered that Enoch and his son had disappeared. Chauncey knew this, knew he'd put his head figuratively on the block, waiting for the axe. *Don't matter: I done wha's right. Mebbe not git th' chance to do it agin, but it's done, an' done right. So, white master, you c'n do your worst t'me, an' I'll take it, swaller it. Ain't much, just two more gone t'freedom, but it'uz all I c'd do.*

And the system of white owner and Black slave would endure, he knew, until maybe that merciful God would set His people free, as He'd done with Moses in the Good Book. Surely wouldn't come in this lifetime, but the butler believed completely that the time would come, in that same God's good time. *He don't figger things th' way we do, got His own timin' fo' sho. An' mebbe this's th' way it's to be, just one, two at a time. With th' work th' Route people doin', gotta add up.*

Chauncey pictured a moving, invisible train of Black figures slipping stealthily through the forests, the fields, hidden but always in motion, guided by those improbable whites. Risking their own lives to help his people, defying the system, the evil catchers, the proud planters, their work forever undiscovered. He looked up at the stars, those mysterious watchers of all the earth, and knew that one, that north one, would guide the trickles, streams of escaped slaves to their dreams.

~ * ~

During these years of their work with the runaways, Susan Blaine often speculated on just how this all was to turn out. Would they continue this till they died? Or would this increasing talk of division, even war, change things, halt their efforts, shut them down? She didn't know; no one knew. But time was slipping by, she and her sisters growing older, just surviving, working the soil, the days, seasons passing.

And she, a little like moody Jenny, sometimes imagined another life for herself, an end to things as they were. She'd surely get too old ever to imagine a life with a good man, even if one should appear somehow. She figured the years till she'd be beyond childbearing age, and there weren't that many ahead of her. *Well, mebbe th' Lord, He's not got my life planned thataway. Guess I don't really need a man, really, but like Jenny says, it'd be nice, th' right one.*

But I don't fool myself I'd be better off, still diggin' in th' ground, still workin' from kin see to cain't see. She thinks ever'thing'd change for her, be better, some way. Wouldn't, I know that, but have somebody to share with, that'd be nice, I reckon. Folks say wasn't none of us meant t'go through this life alone, but we're sure doin' it. Got each other, but that just ain't right, not fer all of us.

Susan had her dreams too, which the others probably didn't imagine, her being so set on the work, whether guiding runaways or the toil of the farm. Well, Kate might: no telling what went on in that'n's head. But no, not to talk about things like that, get all stirred up, hoping for things that wouldn't come about.

But she read too, everything she could get her hands on. Not caught up like Jenny and her fantasies, but to learn, to get her head into as much of the world out there as possible. The sisters traded books with any neighbors who had any, now and then bought one in Hernando. Doc Marion Rossel was always a good source of reading matter, and the women visited with him and his family often. His wife Mary Ann was the daughter of the lady over near Byhalia and her husband, who'd freed their slaves years before, and that whole family was educated.

Susan figured she had it better than most farmers, as she'd said back after their father had died. They were thrifty to a fault, could afford a few things like dyed cloth, enough cookware, make time for those visits to folks they liked. Not chained to the soil like so many, mostly because they worked hard, tried to stay ahead of calamities, setbacks. Take some time for themselves, despite the grind of farming. No need to pine, like her star-struck sister. Live this life the best she could, grab every chance for joy, whether in a friend's new baby, a dance or a church supper.

Life could be a lot worse, but there was more out there, for sure. And maybe, if it was God's will, that good man might just show up. And who knew, there'd maybe be time for a little one or two, if that happened. *If it's s'posed to, it will, I reckon. Just keep on keepin' on. An' mebbe throw in a little hope too. Can't hurt.*

Fifteen

The tall young minister viewed his shrinking congregation this morning with the realization that this church he'd labored in, sacrificed for, would at last be forced to close its doors. Despite his intensive calling on families here in Boston, despite his explaining the need for solidarity, support from them, the congregants just hadn't come, hadn't contributed.

And there weren't that many free Black people in that section of the city, nor in the rural areas close. Or sympathetic whites, even among the abolitionists who cried out against the evils of slavery in the South. They just did not want to share the pews with those they sought to free.

The reverend Harlan Sewell was also Black, the only son of the butler to Mr. Bartlett Dodge, recently deceased. That benefactor had contributed heavily over the years to Harvard College, with one stipulation: that this boy be educated for the ministry, however that must come about.

Unheard of, the college administration had insisted. Not remotely possible. So Mr. Dodge had explained patiently that he would withdraw his very considerable support forever from that institution, and contribute it elsewhere, unless his terms were met.

And they were, with much private grumbling, out of this wealthy patron's hearing. Classes of one were arranged, and young Sewell eventually graduated from that august bastion of higher learning.

But now the one church he'd been able to establish was failing. Most of its founding members had been elderly, those contemplating the proximity of their hoped-for salvation, many of whom were now dead. Sewell's wife Julia sewed, worked part-time as domestic help, created and sold quilts and children's clothing to help support them, but they were losing ground.

And now she was pregnant with their first child.

Harlan had considered another profession, had taken additional odd jobs, even considering moving to another location where there were surely churches he could serve. The only occupation he would not take was as butler. *And I'll do that too, if it proves the only recourse. But I'm certain God will find the right way for us: we must continue to trust in Him.*

And with practicing painful frugality, taking every handyman job he could find, Harlan and his Julia survived on his meager salary. Barely.

But then she went into labor. The midwife was summoned, a cheerful woman who reassured them that this birth would be without danger. Harlan nevertheless fidgeted, paced, tried to be of help, prayed, was banished from the tiny bedroom. He tried to work on his next sermon, could not concentrate. The love of his life was struggling, enduring unimaginable pain, laboring indeed, to bring this child of theirs into the world.

And then something unforeseen happened. The midwife was shocked, helpless as both mother and child stilled, died under her hands before any doctor could be summoned.

Nobody knew why.

Harlan Sewell was devastated. Repeatedly he asked his God why this had happened, why he must be struck with this double tragedy, why, as a man of God, that same God had seen fit to destroy all he held dear. He grieved deeply, retreated into himself, except for that brief time Sundays that he felt he must continue to minister to others at his dying church.

Dying, yes, everything's dying all around me, Lord. I'm dying inside, and I can't even seem to help those around me, so many of whom are losing, have lost even more than I. Strengthen me, dear God, against the bitterness, the evil I know comes from Satan. You've humbled me, Father, and now I ask you to raise me again, as You raised Your holy Son, as He promised, when we keep the faith, do our best to live by it.

It was a scarce six months later that the tiny congregation voted to close the doors to the church, no longer being able to support it, or its stricken pastor. And Harlan Sewell looked out upon a world grown gray and lifeless, a world in which he no longer felt he could fit, endure, survive.

He had grown gaunt, his tall frame bowed as if by weights of stone, iron, his face prematurely lined in grief. He came close, he later realized, to losing the faith he knew was all that could sustain, salvage him.

He continued to write to any and all contacts, searching for a viable church, wherever one might be found. Finally he accepted the fact that there was no place for him here in the North, which was the only home he knew. And considered for the first time traveling to that strange and forbidding region south of the Mason Dixon line, that place of the enslavement of his people, of reportedly cruel among masters and haughty, disdainful plantation mistresses.

But, they won't all be like that: abolitionist propaganda. Surely writers like Harriet Stowe exaggerate, to make their points. And even if most are, my people there need God's word, hope in Christ, and I can give them that—must give them that. And really, what do I have to lose, with such a move? Consider it missionary work, among those who need me—no, God—the most.

And while I may well starve there, I doubt if I'll freeze.

~ * ~

The mid-1850s passed. Jenny Blaine's Jethro Bennett sort of hovered near, but made no move toward matrimony. She had all but given up on him, and was constantly on the lookout for a more suitable beau. None hove into view, so she countered the smith's lukewarm attentions with her own. Which was to say, while not harboring any illusions, she didn't completely give up on him.

But she also recognized the passage of time, and thought bleakly of other spinsters, then of other women who'd married late, and this gave her hope. Faint hope.

Fifteen miles to the east, the McRavens' second daughter Rosanah, at the advanced age of twenty-six, had married a courtly Virginia lawyer, Malcolm Johnson, in Memphis. Then the third, Mary Ann, married Hernando doctor Marion Rossell. The eldest son John had attended the University of Mississippi and was also a practicing physician. Anna Blake's other family confidante, sister Sarah, had also married Lewis Benson, of Holly Springs. Yes, another doctor.

"Lot of doctors hereabouts," folks would observe. And in future years, the youngest daughter Ophelia would attempt to go into medicine also, but be rebuffed at the institutions of the time. She was a female, after all.

Then, after a brief three years of marriage, Rosanah had died in childbirth. And Tranquilla's father, Sanders Taylor, weakened by a stroke, had also died. That year was a devastating one for that family, and it was about to get worse.

By then, 1857, the talk of Northern arrogance and the divisiveness between Richmond and Washington was growing more pointed. The strong rivalry between the all-powerful Federal government faction and the local and states' rights one heightened. New states wanted to come into the Union as slave states or free states, and the issue was hot. Unfortunately for the South, the old balance: Jefferson versus Hamilton, Andrew Jackson versus Henry Clay, was no longer in place. Without a national champion for their rights to self-government, those in the South were in a losing contest.

Some farsighted individuals could foresee an inevitable conflict coming. And the issue of slavery, seen as only a peripheral one at first, would no doubt become a political bombshell, if the abolitionists had their way.

~ * ~

It was suddenly time. Enoch had tried hard to appear normal all that day, a seasonal, cool one in early March. The weather was dry, and plowing had begun, with his following the mule from daylight till the shadows were long. He was tired to the bone, but the prospect of escape buoyed him, gave him strength.

Gradually, the sounds of the plantation's slaves lessened. Enoch returned the dishes to Big Mattie at the blacksmith's cabin. He thanked her as usual, noting that this would be the last time he'd see this family. He turned quickly away.

And as quiet came like a soft blanket, he roused his son, got him dressed with only a whispered word of caution. The lad's eyes were big with question, but Enoch shushed him, led him to the door. He cracked it, peered out.

Nothing and no one.

They slipped out, well away from the big house dogs, and on soundless feet, headed with the slight breeze for the forest south of the row of slave cabins. Reaching it, they melted into the woods, clutching their coats tighter against the spring chill.

Enoch sensed the presence before he saw the man, leaning against a big oak. He stopped, his heart thumping wildly. The man moved.

"You, boy. You Enoch?" It was a hoarse whisper.

"Yeah, an' m'boy Seth. You Brady?"

"Am that. C'mon now, we gotta move long way t'night. Ennybody see you?"

"Naw, ever'thaing quiet." They struck out behind the guide, a lean, slightly stooped farmer, who apparently knew every twist of the non-path, every patch of briars to avoid. They made good time, Enoch holding Seth's hand, guiding him. The way led farther south, then a sharp turn east as the first hints of dawn lightened and the stars paled.

They proceeded cautiously to an abandoned barn, just a darker shape against dense trees. Brady left his charges concealed, while he crept up to a sagging door, knocked. It opened a crack, then a white woman emerged, looked beyond him. He motioned Enoch and Seth forward.

Inside, now lit by a single candle, were four other Black faces, eyes large in the flickering light. The woman was lean, middle-age, with a brusque manner.

"Just got here ourselves. Enny trouble?"

"No. This here's Enoch, an' his boy Seth. I'll run, now. God bless you, Sadie, an' you folks too." The farmer melted back into the brush.

"These is from on down Louisiana, Enoch. We'll stay hid till dark, then head on out. Go east a far piece b'fore we turn nawth, throw th' catchers off. Eat now, an' rest up. Be hard goin', fifteen, twenty mile on, come night. I'll stand th' first watch, then Chester, th' big un, he'll take over. Then mebbe you, next." With that the woman slipped out, closed the weathered door.

There was one other child, a girl perhaps seven, whose name was Venus. She regarded Seth with enormous eyes as the group of them divided ham and biscuits Sadie had provided. A bucket held water, with a communal dipper.

After they ate, Chester blew out the candle, and the slaves settled on straw to sleep. The girl curled up against a woman surely her mother. Seth closed his eyes, his father's arm around him, and slept. Enoch felt danger in the air, but he'd imagined that ever since stepping out his door. He'd noticed Sadie had two pistols on her, and a long knife in her belt.

He wondered at white people like her, and Brady, who'd risk their lives to help slaves escape. He'd heard via the grapevine, of abolitionists, crazy folks up North who speechified about evil slave owners, ranted and wrote pamphlets and worried government people about the canker of owning human beings. But if these two were of that label, they sure weren't crazy, the way other whites had always referred to them.

Lawd, bless these folks, an' he'p 'em git us on nawth, an' to whutevah You got fer us.

~ * ~

Anna Blake's world, her whole life, had been shattered.

It had been a year after Hyde had taken her off the route, but finding himself without another dependable guide, he'd then asked her to guide just this one run. And after long consideration, her loyalty to the cause had worked on her, and she'd conquered her reservations and consented. That she would again be out and in danger had been kept from the other guides, although of course they'd soon know. Hyde had pursed his thin lips, again convincing himself that the cause was worth every risk, to every one of those involved.

The crisis of this scheduled run arose from its having been reported somehow to the slave catcher Holtz. And before he could learn of Anna's being assigned to it, Tom Brannon had been called to his dying father's bedside in Chicago. A further complication developed when the McRaven son Harvey heard a brag from Holtz's son at school, that his father was about to catch a band of runaways.

He had in turn told Robert.

And not only had the McRavens suspected that Anna might just be the guide on this doomed venture, Hetty Barnes hesitantly admitted to her former owner that this might be possible.

"She's not supposed to be out on the routes anymore, since she…"

"Got hurt that time," Tranquilla finished for her. "But if maybe no one else could go, she might?" There was real worry in her eyes.

"There shoulda been others, but I heard th' regular guides aren't available. Some other last-minute emergency." Now the former maid twisted her hands in her apron, envisioning their favorite friend out, certainly to be caught, violated, hanged.

Robert had then ridden to send a telegram to Anna, warning her of the raid, but was afraid it'd been too late. Now Tranquilla decided to ride for the Blaine sisters' place herself, directed by Hetty, to warn them also.

What had happened was a collision of six slave catchers, some just along for the fun of it, with Robert, who'd located and trailed them. Tranquilla and Susan and Kate Blaine had ridden to warn the guide, who was indeed yes, Anna, who was still with the guide Jenny, at another tumbledown barn.

Holtz had discovered, then threatened the women, and Robert had shot him from cover. The spilled lantern-oil fire had then illuminated a savage gunfight, in which all the catchers had been killed. Two of those had been the targets of the plantation mistress, a deer hunter and skilled rifle shot.

But also shot through the heart was Robert McRaven, Tranquilla's husband, the love of her life, after having saved Anna's life, the second time.

The Black girl was devastated, only held together by Jenny's sure hand the rest of that fateful night on the way to Memphis. Then, the two of them having deposited their charges in the safe house, they went to Anna's cottage.

To find the belated telegram slipped under the door.

Anna collapsed.

Susan had insisted on riding with Tranquilla back to her plantation, helping tie Robert's body across his horse. There she did what she could to console the children, who were told only that their father had been accidentally shot in a hunting mishap. It had been all their mother could do to tell this lie without breaking down, but it was a necessary evil she managed. Barely, with the four still at home stricken, as was she.

Eventually Jenny had ridden the train back to Hernando, and after some days in which she helped any way she could; Susan rode her mule back to the sisters' place.

~ * ~

Enoch had never imagined the kinds of people who were helping the band of escaped slaves toward freedom. Brady was a small farmer, as was the woman Sadie. But the next guide was a doctor, who actually transported the group of them in broad daylight, having forged papers proving he'd bought these Blacks. It was known that he lived on an inherited plantation, and no one he should meet would question his intentions.

This man passed his charges on to the next guide, and continued his limited cultivation of his land, with just a hired man. Later questioned about the absence of his newly-acquired slaves, he affected disgust, saying he'd had to sell the worthless bunch. So he had brazened out this part of the run, and would in future employ other tactics to help in the cause.

The next guide was Kate Blaine, at yet another abandoned shed south of their farm. She delivered these charges to Reverend Kellog, who turned them over to the old couple at the southernmost Memphis safe house. Finally, weeks after their escape, Enoch and his son were with the others as they crossed the Ohio River one night in a boat guided by a minister and his daughter. After several more days' travel, they were lodged in three separate houses while their benefactors went about locating work for them.

Young Seth had kept his usual good cheer throughout their travels, becoming close to the others, especially Venus and her mother. He hoped to be able to see them, once settled, but it seemed work was scarce just then, and his father explained that they'd have to go no telling how far to find a home.

Eventually a kindly Quaker miller with one arm from a machinery accident, and his wife took them in, over in the next county. Enoch went to work carrying bags of grain and meal, and gradually learned the secrets of this craft. Seth played with their young children, and with those who came with their parents to the mill, some white, a few Black.

The worship of God these people practiced, and their speech was strange to Enoch, but he recognized His hand in his and his son's delivery from bondage, so accepted it gladly.

~ * ~

The escape of Enoch and his son enraged the planter Calloway. Chauncey's carefully planted story of a slave trader's having seen them and surely stolen them just wasn't believed. And the slave owner held his butler and right-hand man personally responsible for his loss.

"It was your job to watch the hands, Chauncey, and you've failed. Enoch was one of my best workers, and that boy showed promise. I'd even planned to start training him for a house job. But now you've lost favor with me, and I've a mind to sell you." The slave stood, head bowed, awaiting whatever punishment his master had in store for him. *Don't matter none: nobody buy me, old's I be. An' it'uz worth it, t'see that man an' his boy free. Do yo' wust, white man; this nigger don't care no mo'.*

"But you've been a great help here, up to now. And I'm sure you can see I can't trust you any longer. Now, I realize nobody will want to buy you at your age, and with no strength for the fields. So I'm left with the only discipline available: I'll whip you."

The words cut like the slave knew the whip itself would: he'd seen the master use it too often on recalcitrant Blacks. But he remained standing, still deferential, after Calloway had left.

"I heard that, Marshall," his wife Beatrice accused as the man searched for his bullwhip. "And you're not *about* to whip that old man." Her hands were on her hips, her voice icy.

"I certainly am. He let two valuable hands escape."

"No civilized man would whip a trusted servant, let alone one of his age."

"Now, weren't you the one who urged me to sell Reenie, just on account of a rumor about freedom? What's the difference?"

"The difference is, Chauncey's served us well for many years. Reenie we could and did replace, and you were the one who wanted to sell her, not I. And you've noted how morale among the servants has gone down since."

"Nevertheless, discipline must be maintained. Where's my whip? Have you hidden it?" He was stalking around, pulling open drawers.

"It's in the kitchen, and I've chopped it into pieces with a meat cleaver. Now come to your senses, Marshall! If the community hears of what you were planning on doing, we'll be ostracized out of the country. This is a civilized place, and not another planter here would consider whipping a frail old man."

He knew she was right. But what was he supposed to do, given that she'd won this one? Back down? Lose all the respect he'd built with his harsh management?

No. All right then: he *would* sell the butler. Easy enough to replace him. Or was it? Beatrice insisted that their columned mansion be kept in perfect order, with house servants trained as to every detail, and Chauncey had been the man who'd made it all work. No smudge or spot escaped his eye, not the slightest maid's omission got past him. And entertaining the cream of Clarksdale planter society, setting the standard, was what his wife lived for, and he too enjoyed the respect and admiration of his peers.

With Chauncey sold away, where *would* he find another so well versed, so dedicated to the perfection the couple demanded. Certainly none of the other slaves could handle that chore. He'd have to contact a slave trader, maybe that fellow Forrest, with whom he'd dealt before. Which made him remember his butler's story: *had* a disreputable trader perhaps seen that bright boy, actually stolen him and his father? Surely not: Chauncey had made that tale up of whole cloth.

Or had he? Calloway got his hat, strode out of the house to the blacksmith shop, that center of information among the slaves, that gathering-place of their gossip and news. Big Caleb was at the forge, shaping chain links, that ever-present need on every farming operation. His helper worked the bellows, and a plume of charcoal smoke rose from the glowing fire.

"Caleb, Chauncey tells me there was a slave trader poking around here the other day while I was out in the fields. Did you or anybody else see him?"

The butler had hinted to the field hands that a passing stranger just might be a trader, and for the Land's End slaves to be on their best behavior. So of course the word had run like fire among them. Hard as life was under Calloway, being sold to perhaps a worse master, as Reenie had surely been, was to be avoided at all costs.

"Wuz a feller sorta hangin' 'roun', yessir. Now, I dunno jis' whut his bizness wuz, but seem t'be lookin' us ovah, heah. I figgered he wuz heah t'see you, Massa, so I don' say nothin' 'bout him. Don' know nothin' mo'.

Is he lying? Can't trust a one of them. But Beatrice would know if anyone asked to see me, and she hasn't mentioned it. I do know of dishonest traders who steal slaves so sales are all profit. Forrest isn't one of those of course: man's fair, even if his occupation is tainted.

So I guess I must just eat this one, this time. But if it ever happens again...

Sixteen

The aftermath of the shootout near Hernando changed everything. For the Blaine sisters there was a complete halt to the Route activities. Six slave catchers killed was indeed a massacre, and one not soon forgotten in the region. Naturally, given the men's occupations, abolitionists were suspected, and hunted, to no avail. But in the increased watchfulness and hostility, the entire operation was suspended indefinitely.

For the McRavens, the devastation was almost complete. That their father had been killed, even supposedly in an accident, left the children numb, unable to get their minds around it. The doctor son refused to believe the explanation, but there was no other. Tranquilla, having suffered the loss of her first husband many years before in a brutal axe murder by a deranged slave, then her father earlier this same year, *and* her daughter Rosanah, found this new death staggering. But there was nothing to do but go on, blindly.

Anna Blake, conscience-stricken at the death of her former master and rescuer, suffered a period of such deep remorse that her associates feared for her. She seemed in a sort of daze, going through her duties at the institute mechanically, keeping to her tiny house, avoiding all other outside contact. Eventually, after a letter from Miriam Kellog to the sisters, Susan Blaine visited Tranquilla McRaven again, seeking a remedy for her—their—friend.

"She's grievin', an' that's t'be expected, Miss 'Quilla, but there's no help for it. Way I figger it, we all done what we saw's nec'sary. We're all jist so sorry you lost your good man 'count of it. An' I ain't happy 'bout killin' those men, but t'was a case of shoot er be shot."

"It *was* necessary, Susan. I killed two men, and I can't be sorry for it. At least not yet. Perhaps in time I can ask forgiveness, but just now it seems almost as if we were guided to remove those beasts from the earth."

"What I been tellin' myself. Well, it's all shut down now, an' with this secession talk startin' t'go 'round, don't know jist what'll happen. But Anna's down bad, an' there oughta be somethin' we c'n do for her."

Anna had written Tranquilla a letter tear-stained, full of self-abasement, and a hint of hysteria between the lines. She had written back, assuring the young woman that there could be absolutely no blame due, that they had all acted out of their collective conscience, and sad as it was, even Robert would have—indeed had—agreed to the necessity of their actions.

"I'll go visit her. I haven't wanted to leave the children before now. Would you please come too?"

"Reckon I could go, yes. Harvest's in; th' girls kin manage. Never liked that big town, but I guess I c'd put up with it fer a while. When'd we go?"

"Tomorrow's Saturday; she'll have the day off. I'll have the carriage readied." Tranquilla knew the trip would be good for her, too. Hard as it was, it was simply time for her to put the painful past away, again, at least in company, and move ahead to whatever lay there.

"Good. That means I'll git time t'visit my man Harvey here some, an' th' others. Never seen planters' kids out choppin' an' hoein' like yers. You're sure raisin' 'em right."

Susan was good for the family that night, with her pithy observations and sense of humor. She regaled them with tales of her and her sisters' coping with the community's confused and often gossipy opinion of them, their crafty neighbor Ingrum, and even the intermittent intrusions of prospective suitors, including the present Jethro the blacksmith.

"Jenny cain't decide whether to 'dopt him er shoot him," she observed. "He 'bout shrinks up an' disappears ever' time she looks at him. Good blacksmith, though, clumsy's he is. Shouldn't be talkin' bad about him, but I am: man's jist funny."

"Will does most of the smithing around here," his younger sister Ophelia told her. "Mama taught him."

"I heard you did ironwork, Miss 'Quilla. Now, there's something' I wisht I c'd do. Allus wearin' stuff out aroun' our place, an' havin' t'trade out enny way we can. Don't reckon there's 'nuther lady blacksmith in th' country."

"She's the best shot in Mississippi, too," Will boasted. "Won shooting matches." Their visitor could attest to that skill, having seen her in action.

So by drawing the children and their mother out, Susan managed to lighten the mood of this stricken household. She also promised to spend some time with them after they returned from Memphis, helping with the last of harvest, maybe in exchange for a few lessons at the forge from Will or his mother.

The trip was less than a day's drive, but they left well before sunup. Her hostess insisted on driving the carriage herself, another bit of independence Susan noted and approved. But just what their strategy would be with Anna, they couldn't yet decide.

They reached her house past midday, and found her nervously trying to sew. The stitches were erratic, a total departure from the work her former mistress knew she could do and had done many times at her home with the daughters.

Her hesitant greeting was swept away in the prolonged hug Tranquilla gave her, and the tears flowed from both. Susan stood quietly, noting the dishevelment and chaos in the little house, which she remembered as being immaculate before. *Girl is hurtin' for sure, an' here's Miss 'Quilla, just up from more'n a full-time job gittin' her young uns past this, doin' th' same fer Anna.*

"Miss 'Quilla, I..." the voice broke again.

"Now you just hush, Anna. There's nothing to say, and don't you go on blaming yourself for anything. We did what we had to do, all of us. And no, we don't know why it had to happen as it did, but we must not lose faith here, any of us. Now, Susan and I want to stay, and do what we can."

"F'm th' looks of thaings, y'could use a little help 'roun' here," that lady offered. "No offense, girl, but 'pears it's got some outta hand."

"It's such a mess. I just haven't felt like..."

"Didn't reckon y'had. But fer me, gittin' stuff done always helps th' moodies. So whattya say, Miss 'Quilla, we tear this place apart 'n put it back t'gether, fer starters?"

"Oh, you don't have to..."

"Want to. I been meaner'n a bear with a sore paw m'self, thinkin' about killin' those slave-catchin' snakes, an' I either got t'start a fight with somebody er jump into gittin' somethin' done, an' yer house here won't fight back." She peered behind a messy table. "Er maybe it will." That drew a part of a smile from both other women.

Two hours later, over mild protests from Anna, who had become much more active, the place shone.

"Now," announced Tranquilla, "We're going to indulge in the woman's cure-all, girls. We're going shopping." She was dressed in widow's black, but her determination to lift all their spirits belied her mourning garb and her inner ache. The three piled into the carriage and proceeded toward Memphis' center.

The teeming port city offered almost any necessity, luxury, entertainment. In the twenty-odd years since the McRavens had come to the Coldwater River country, the plantation mistress had come to know her way around the town. Anna, by necessity limited to her neighborhood in South Memphis, and Susan, who'd seldom visited the city, were enthralled. Doormen bowed, salespersons deferred, suggested, flattered. It was a whirlwind of shops and stores, and the carriage was soon laden with clothes and gifts.

Susan had brought along what money she had, expecting the trip, and Anna had savings, which she found herself spending happily. So this was not so much a charitable spree by Tranquilla, who nevertheless plunged in also. There were gifts for her many children, samples of town delights, minor extravagances. It all added up to a grand afternoon.

Finally, having bought food, since Anna would not be admitted to a restaurant with them, the trio repaired to a park in the still-mild late light over the river for a picnic. Gaslights illuminated the place, peopled with strolling couples gazing dreamily out over the Mississippi, and occasional groups of late-playing children attended by nannies. As usual, those they met assumed Anna was the ladies' servant, and this provided sly, humorous exchanges among them. All in all, spirits rose wonderfully.

Back in Anna's house, the three opened packages again, tried on clothes, waltzed around showing off. Susan had never in her rural life had such an experience, nor had Anna, always careful of her money, always restrained in purchases. It might be said their mutual friend opened their eyes to another life, one that had always been just beyond their reach.

And both younger women again reminded themselves that this friend did not exploit plantation slaves in order to enjoy this lifestyle: her callused hands attested to the fact that she still worked the fields, along with her children and their paid field hands.

Sunday morning they attended the tiny South Memphis AME church, the neighborhood sanctuary the citizens had built years before, and that the runaways had painted that time. The minister, aging Brother Ezra Timmons, welcomed the white women graciously, referring in his sermon to God's welcoming all His children, all the time.

Afterwards, Mrs. Colby, the church secretary, invited them to dinner, which they accepted. Hers was a small, neat house just near the church, where she and her husband lived alone, since their children had grown and moved North. Late coreopsis and chrysanthemums bloomed in orderly borders and plots, and red berries clung to shrubs.

The white women were treated exactly the same as Anna Blake, for which they were grateful. And both experienced a feeling of warmth and security, stemming from being welcomed by virtual strangers and finding this friendly place in the huge, essentially business-oriented town. The conversation never lagged, and Anna's spirits rose perceptibly.

"I am so pleased," the plantation mistress told them later, "that there is such *community* here, such examples of good citizens, living, working, being respected. This is what it could be all over the country if people weren't so blind."

"Well, the respect is limited just to around here," Anna replied. "Outside this neighborhood, we're still treated like something between people and mules, a little closer to mules. I try not to be bitter, but I face it every day unless I stay closeted here."

"Know what y'mean, girl," Susan agreed. "Seen it too much. But I figger we hadda start somewheres, an' gittin' as many as we could t'freedom, that's th' first step. Rest of it'll come, but who knows when?"

"When may be sooner than we think," Tranquilla warned. "This talk going around, about how we in the South are being ignored in Washington, treated as mindless tyrants, has divided the country, I'm afraid. Coupled with the disdain people in both regions seem to have for their opposites, it could become a powder keg. The issue of slavery is right in the middle of it all, and could just be the spark that sets off a war."

"Now, that'd be a real *stupid* way t'settle things," Susan declared. "Way I see it, nobody comes out ahead in a war, 'cept th' merchants an' factory owners supplyin' th' troops. If we c'd learn ennything f'm history, we'd see both sides er gen'rally worse off after every war than b'fore."

"Susan, you're an intellectual; do you realize that?" Anna exclaimed. "I've come to the same conclusion, but only after years of reading and study. You must be a keen observer of life and politics."

"Jist hide an' watch, all I do: don't git t'read near as much as I'd like to. But I've found out y'can study real hard 'bout a few ideas, an' come out close t'where somebody else has, after a bunch of schoolin', travelin', talkin' t'smart people. "

"If we ever get to vote, Susan, it's women like you who'll change this world, and for the better." Tranquilla was truly amazed at this farm girl's understanding. Anna, who'd known her for years, was not really that surprised.

"Wal, th' men'll keep us down long's they can I reckon, but 't'won't be forever. They'll keep on messin' things up so bad we'll hafta take over, sooner er later."

The upshot of this conversation was to get the women's minds off the recent tragedy, and to get them delving deeply into social questions, politics, religion, and whatever else came up. None of them could remember ever having such a wonderful weekend, despite the shadows that hung over them.

After leaving a much-improved Anna on Monday, the two other women continued their discussion on the road to Byhalia. Tranquilla wanted this woman to stay, help her alleviate her children's grief over the loss of their father, and she herself needed her, perhaps most. A deep and lasting friendship was taking root, and both were grateful.

Susan had known a social equality with the late Sarah Talbot, rare between dirt farmers and the plantation gentry, and here her new friend was even more on a level footing with her. A woman who was a fine shot, a blacksmith, a mother and now the working sole mistress of her non-slave plantation was a phenomenon, and she wanted to spend more time with her.

And there were the children, so out of the ordinary among planters' spoiled offspring. She suspected that young Harvey was normally a hell-raiser, and she'd liked him instantly. *Guess a woman's just meant t'be around young uns, after all...*

So the visit stretched out over several days, with Susan's energy, humor and wry commentary communicating themselves to this family. She worked with Will at the forge, learning the basics of heating and hammering iron. She closeted herself with the sisters 'Quilla and Ophelia, poring over dress designs in the magazines of the time, choosing patterns, trying fabrics, sewing. She entered into long discussions with their mother. and sometimes Hetty Barnes, on the state of the country, economics, even literature, of which she was surprisingly read, mostly from Jenny's books.

And she formed what would be a lasting closeness with young Harvey, whose interest ran mostly to farming, horses, any and all outdoor activities, from hunting to exploring. He and his best friend Dan McGraw from near Red Banks, were an irrepressible duo, wearing out even the stout Susan the days Dan visited. She realized that her own childhood had largely slipped past her, in the work of the farm and the demands of survival.

These boys were always coming up with delightful and often dangerous adventures, some of which they managed to pull off. At thirty, she couldn't quite identify with them and the girls, but there wasn't much she couldn't match them in. Whether that involved breaking a young horse or putting up hay or preserves or dressmaking.

And everyone's spirits lifted, with all the activity, the visits from neighbors, the bustle of post-harvest details. Until Susan realized she'd neglected her sisters. There'd be time for more visits here, certainly during the winter when things slowed down to mending, tending stock and wood-cutting.

She invited them all to the Blaine place as she mounted her mule for the ride home, and promised Harvey they'd hunt turkeys in the scrublands out from Hernando. She'd come to know this territory so well guiding runaways, she knew all the game trails.

~ * ~

"Well now, ain't you th' fancy one," Kate Blaine exclaimed, opening packages with her sister Jenny, treasures from the big town. "Done spent all yer money an' prob'ly borrowed, too." But her eyes shone at the clothes and the few trinkets. Jenny held a dress to her and waltzed about the room, laughing, then hugged her sister.

"Knew you'd been hoardin' yer cash fer a while, girl, but this's like Chris'mus at some Big House. Now tell us 'bout Anna, an' Miss 'Quilla. They gittin' over th' shootin' enny better?"

"Some. We hadda good time, spite of that. McRaven kids hurtin' th' worst, but Lord, that place don't never slow down, so reckon th' bad will wear off soon 'nuff. Anna blamin' herself, which we flat tole her wuz plumb stupid. Jollied her up some, an' she'll be all right, give her time." And she related the details of the Memphis visit. Then she had to expound on the activities at the plantation, mentioning young Harvey the most.

Kate smiled at her sister. Young enough, could maybe still find herself a man, have some little uns of her own. *Head ain't in th' clouds like Jenny's, an' jist might happen, someday. Sounds like she'd like to adopt that little feller she's set on. Well, hope they do come visit: liven things up 'roun' here. Three ole maids rustin' away, we know there's a lot more t'life, but don't seem bound t' happen enny time soon...*

~ * ~

Abel had indeed found the way to the hiding place Clinton Carruthers had learned of. The guide was one Carson Blevins, an affable, round little man who owned a store back toward Tupelo at a crossroads. Abel had waited there until he was afraid daylight would come, but then the man had slipped up to the abandoned, falling little cabin. Abel was on high alert, till he heard the low call.

"Abel, you here?" *He knows my name, so yes, this's him.*

"I am, sir. You the storekeeper?" He was poised to run, if this went bad.

"Yes, and the rest are right behind me." Blevins lighted a candle, motioned for five indistinct figures to enter quietly. "Get settled, now. I've food, and there's a bucket of water covered up back in that corner. Welcome, Abel, glad you could find us." Actually shook the boy's hand.

"Not as glad as I am, sir. Now, I'm certain we need to keep quiet, unless you're sure nobody can hear us."

"Oh, we're far from any house, and it's not huntin' season. If we keep it low, it'll be all right. Y'all will be travelin' together a far piece, an' 'twon't hurt to get t'know one 'nuther." He distributed food to the six, and though he'd eaten at the inn earlier, Abel reasoned that the next meal might be a long way off, so he took a portion of the cornbread, ham and collard greens.

He learned that these people, a young mother, her ten-year-old son, two field hands and a shoemaker, had somehow found out the way from their separate homes and gathered north of Tupelo. Abel marveled that the plan had come together so well, with no maps, nothing but remembered word to go by, in the necessary darkness. And he was astounded that Blevins was risking his livelihood, even his life, to help free these people. What motivated him?

Well, what motivated Clinton? He's gonna catch hell for letting me escape, even if he can convince the family he did all he could to keep me captive. He's smart, and I guess he'll get away with it. But I know this is just the first step. From what I hear, we'll hide here all day, then another guide will come, lead us another 15 miles or so, toward Memphis. But I hope these guides know enough not to take us north, the way the catchers will figure we're headed.

He needn't have worried: the next guide, a wiry old farmer, took them west to the next hiding place. Then another took them farther. They wouldn't turn north till near Hernando, he learned, be clear away from where they'd disappeared.

And so they were finally met by the Baptist minister Kellog, at a remote shed Susan Blaine had guided them to. Abel was impressed with this woman's evident knowledge, and they talked in low tones part of that day of hiding. For her part, this woman sensed that this boy had potential, and she took a few minutes with Kellog to urge him to try to get Abel into the Institute.

"He'd be far enough from that plantation they'd never find him, Reverend, with another name, and he's bright. I'm thinkin' what Anna and Tom an' the others c'd teach him, set him up for a real life. He goes north to a fact'ry job, I'm 'fraid he'll be worse off than where he was."

"That's troubled me, Susan, the fate of those we help free. I know enough about business to realize they'll not be treated as more than cheap labor. Yes, I'll sound out Tom or Anna about just what you suggest." Kellog had always been impressed not only with Susan's forcible dedication to the cause they served, but he appreciated her sharp mind. She too, had on one occasion stayed the night in Memphis with him and his wife, and they'd talked about a wide range of subjects.

So yes, he'd see if this could work out. Boy might make a Memphis lawyer, or a banker, if the narrow-minded people there would allow it. He bade Susan goodbye, led the six runaways off into the night, totally certain they'd arrive in good order at the safe house. God would protect them, on that he could rely.

~ * ~

Tom Brannon's experiences as guide on the last legs of the runs up from Olive Branch and Hernando had been the most successful, despite the feared overexposure. He could pose as a slave trader, slave purchaser, seller of slaves, or simply one who was transporting his property, if challenged.

He had never encountered slave catchers in all the years he'd been active in the Cotton Route. At first, he often moved his charges in broad daylight, with papers to prove his false ownership. He'd done this as often as he dared, though, knowing that being seen too often would arouse suspicion.

So like the others, he most often made his runs into Memphis at night, varying the route just enough to elude any watchers. He never let overconfidence lull him into carelessness, and his record was one of almost no failures.

But looking back on it, there was one confrontation that left its mark upon this dedicated member of the movement, for the rest of his life. And he would never forget the violence, the blood of it.

The way down from Memphis had been clear that night in 1855, and the little group of five runaways and Tom were returning quickly up the obscure path that would lead eventually to the safe house at the edge of town. There were three field hands, one of whom was well over six feet tall, a powerful Black named Artie. Two women, former house help, had joined the group, coming west first from the Columbus area.

Brannon had warned the band, as always, that they might meet hunters out, or farmers returning home late, or simply other nighttime travelers. Or the hated slave catchers, perhaps the only probable men out this late. Artie, quiet, thoughtful, had confided to Brannon that he was a peaceable man, but this freedom would be worth fighting for if need be.

"We hope that won't be necessary, but we must be prepared," their guide had replied, indicating his pistol. He also carried a long knife in a sheath inside his boot.

But he was mindful of the time Susan Blaine had killed the one catcher who'd confronted them, recognizing her. And back at the first of the runs, supposedly timid Jenny Blaine had clubbed that hunter. Then there was the more recent time Anna Blake had been shot at. The future massacre would wipe out six of the catchers, but also her benefactor, Robert McRaven.

No, there were no guarantees of safety in this business.

~ * ~

At first, Abel worried he might be discovered this close to the feared Carruthers plantation, but the attraction of the Institute with its advantages was strong. And he was encouraged by Anna Blake and Tom Brannon to enroll. These two also pointed out that life for those they'd educated had not often worked out well for them up North.

"Of course you're free, and would be up there," Tom pointed out, "but we hear back from some who've gone to safe locations who have been taken advantage of, used, treated almost as badly as when they were enslaved. With what you can learn here, you'll have a much better chance at a good life wherever you go."

"And if you change your name, it'll be impossible for your former owners to find you here," Anna encouraged." It's a bad joke that whites say they can't tell one Black from another." Abel had heard that one too.

"Besides," headmaster Bancroft assured him, "we've managed to hide more than one former slave when they've been tracked down, and we've become adept at it."

So he decided, and chose the name Horatio Barber. As far as anyone else at the Institute knew, that was his name and it would be on all his records.

Horatio noticed the slender girl first thing, because she always seemed to have the right answers when called upon. And she also had a book with her wherever she went. Her name was Samantha Echols, and she was attractive, even in the donated clothing the Institute 's students wore. The two of them had one of their classes together, and Horatio contrived to sit next to her as often as he could. At first he could think of nothing to say except hello, but gradually one or the other of them began to open up a little, and she would smile when she saw him.

Samantha was part of a family of slaves from a doctor's elaborate household in Natchez. He had left instructions for them to be freed upon his death, which had occurred in 1850. The parents and a son had moved north to St. Louis, but having heard of the Institute, enrolled Samantha there.

Anna Blake had been impressed with the girl's intelligence and had taken a personal interest in her. She knew a child of eleven separated from her family must feel abandoned, and spent time with her outside of classes. Tom also spent extra time with her, and she was often included at Anna's little house, as was Horatio, six years her senior.

The two students made an awkward pair, he a bit gangly in teenage, she still tiny and somewhat fearful at first. That wore off soon, as she came to realize that she could more than hold her own among the other students.

The shortage of teachers at the institute meant mixing the age groups, so she found herself in class with other younger children as well as older ones like Horatio. But being taught the same material, the age differences came to mean less and less.

When Horatio graduated from the Institute to go north to Chicago, it was with some misgivings. He felt prepared, and was eager to move into the world Tom described to him, but south Memphis had become home to him, and he'd miss the instructors, the neighbors and yes, his classmates. *Even that little sprite Samantha. Well, we're destined to part ways, and I wish her well.* Her smile for him was a little forlorn, he imagined.

~ * ~

Hiram Hyde tallied the number of runaway slaves the Cotton Route had led to safety over the ten years of its activities at that time. The Holly Springs and Hernando routes averaged nearly two runs a month each, or 48 in a year total. Multiply that by, say eight years, with the times out for having to shut down the operation, and that was 384 trips. Average four slaves per run, and the total came to 1536 freed bondsmen and women.

Unbelievable that their efforts had reached that number. And still undetected, despite the traffic, the slave catchers, the immoral slave-owning society of this degenerate South. He allowed himself a grim smile.

But it wasn't enough. They'd barely made a scratch on the system. Fifteen hundred of God's children safely up North, free, but many more thousands still in bondage. They must do more, somehow.

But effective guides like Anna Blake and Tom Brannon continued to be almost impossible to find. So were the more local agents, those willing to make actual contact with slaves willing to take the risk of running away. That meant going against the law, one's neighbors and often family, to make the Route's first step work.

No, the system was just too entrenched, the abolitionist realized, for any real inroads into it. The only solution might lie in this spreading talk of supposed infringement of the Southern states' rights by Washington that was gaining momentum in the region.

If this discord finally led to open confrontation between North and South, then the slaves themselves might rise up and defy their masters, walk off the plantations in the confusion, in such numbers as to be unstoppable. He envisioned such an exodus with growing excitement.

It might mean actual war in the end, but it would in his view be a justifiable war, with the hordes of the enslaved at last free. Yes, it all might end in blood. But if that were to be God's will, then so be it. The proud slavers brought to their knees, the Blacks forever free.

Yes! Let it come. And Hiram Hyde experienced an almost sexual anticipation at such a prospect.

Seventeen

As Tom's fugitive band reached a road they must cross, a match flared and a lantern was lighted. He and the slaves froze.

"Reckon y'd best stop right thar," a gravelly voice commanded, as a second lantern cast its light. Three men armed with shotguns spread out to cut off the stunned group.

Brannon thought fast: *catchers, surely, and too many of them, unless we can somehow smash their lanterns and run for it.* He looked to Artie, indicated with a tilt of his head that they should run. The runaway shook his head slightly. *All right then, I'll just have to brazen our way past them.*

"Jist whut we got here?" the obvious leader of the three stepped closer, peering. "Damned 'f 'tain't a buncha niggers. Whatcha doin' out late lak this?" to their guide.

"Got a late start. Need to get to Memphis by morning. I bought these hands from a place down past Hernando." It was Brannon's rehearsed explanation. He had forged papers to back up the story, and felt this would get them on their way. "Somebody had a slave run off around here?"

"Naw, don't reckon." The other spat tobacco juice. He was short, heavy, bearded, dressed in tattered clothes. His eyes had the greedy glint, Brannon thought, of a pig. The other two were also ragged, in slouch hats. *So they're not catchers? Just who...*

"An' we don't keer whar y'got these niggers, ner whar yer goin'. Fact is, we're needin' you t'hold still now, see whut y'got in yore pockets, feller. Man sez he kin buy slaves must have considerable money on him, don't you fellers reckon?" An evil grin showed broken teeth. "Jist you raise yer arms high, whilst we see whut yer carryin'. An' don'tcha even thaink 'bout grabbin' thet pistol, er I'll blow you t'bits."

My God, these are robbers! Just plain outlaws, out to accost whoever's on this road. He was reminded of the notorious Harp brothers and their ilk, who had terrorized the Natchez Trace a generation before, half a state east.

And he had only a few coins on him, so they'd be disappointed this time. *But wait: the slaves...*

"An' don't none a you others git enny notions t'git outta line, neither. We don't keer how big y'are," indicating towering Artie. "Move atall an' we'll blow a big hole in ya." The runaways stood, still frozen, their eyes wide in fear.

One of the other men searched Brannon, removing his pistol and taking the coins. He also took the ownership papers for the runaways. The man smelled of old sweat, tobacco and whiskey.

"Nothin' much here, Jake," he announced. "Reckon he done spent it all on these here niggers? Er mebbe on wimmen an' whiskey."

"Damn. Might of. But niggers is worth a bunch, we git 'em up t'th right buyers. Oh, y'd oughta check his boots, Caleb. Might have a wad hid in 'em."

"Got no money," Brannon insisted. "Like your man said, I spent it all on these hands. That's why we're walking: no money to ride the cars or hire a wagon."

"Naw, thet don't wash, neither. Y'got no light, sneakin' a buncha niggers north. Honest man'd have hisself a lantern. Reckon thet makes you one a them ab'litionists, 'bout th' lowest thaing a white man c'n be.

"But thet don't matter none, neither. Not our problem, feller. An' don't matter if y'got ennythaing in them boots er not: they's good boots, and reckon we'll take 'em."

They'll find the knife. And to take the slaves, they'll have to kill me. The realization struck him like a blow. He looked to big Artie, who'd moved a step between the third man who had his shotgun pointed, and Caleb, the one who'd searched him. A hard look passed between guide and runaway. It said they'd fight.

"You can't take my boots: it's ten miles to Memphis." *Need some kind of diversion here.*

"Reckon we kin. Daid man don't need no boots, ennyway." The shotgun came up, and the man cocked the hammer.

Tom Brannon was not a violent man. His involvement with the Cotton Route had been and still was one of principle, and a sense of the rightness of the cause. He was prepared—had to be— to defend himself and his charges, but the need had never arisen. Nevertheless, he'd practiced the quick draw of his pistol until it was automatic, and the swift reach into his boot for the knife.

Only now the pistol was gone, and the ugly grin on the face of the man behind the shotgun told him there was no respect for law or rights or anything else but greed there. He would die.

Suddenly the slave Artie whipped his arms out, grabbed both the other men by the backs of their necks and brought their heads together in a crashing, blood-spurting collision. The man Jake jerked his gun toward the huge Black.

In that instant, Brannon's hand went to the knife as it had a thousand times. He lunged for the man, point first, felt the resistance of cloth and flesh, surprised at his hand coming hard up against the other's chest. No rehearsal for that, or the sudden grunt, widening of the eyes, the realization by the man that he was dying. He stumbled, dropped the shotgun, clutched at the knife as Brannon jerked it out, stabbed him again.

And again. A fury took hold of the guide, the teacher, the compassionate, principled savior of freed Blacks, and he couldn't stop himself. Blood flew, and still he stabbed the writhing body.

The other two robbers were down, and Artie was kicking them in the head, a crunching, sickening sound as the others watched, open-mouthed. Then the two lay still.

"You all right, Mist' Tom?" Artie asked, viewing his blood-spattered arm and the chest of the fallen robber. Then for the guide, reality began to set in, with the actuality of the blood, the sticky, angry red.

"Yes, I'm... yes, I guess so. I..." Suddenly the world reeled before Brannon, and only Artie's strong arm held him up. His knees were water, a swirling blackness enveloped him, and the scene of butchery faded.

They were somehow beyond the road now, in darkness, and someone was giving him water, supporting his head. It was Naomi, one of the slave women, who spoke to him in soothing tones more than words. He could barely make out her features, and saw just the outline of the others, with Artie sitting leaned against a tree, head down.

Gradually the encounter, the violence, the blood awareness returned, and Brannon's mind swam back toward functioning. He raised up, feeling the blood leave his head too soon, but steadying. Thanking the woman, turning toward the massive figure slumped near.

"Artie, you all right?" The huge head raised.

"Most, I reckon. Never killed nobody b'fore. Sho' no white folks: jist allus tole 'em 'yassir', 'nossir'. Hadda take whutever meanness they put on us. Don't reckon you never, neither."

"No, but we had no choice. Those men were robbers, killers. They'd have taken you all, and to do that they'd have killed me. We have to put this behind us, move on out in time to get to town before daylight." Things were coming more into focus for him. "How long was I out?"

"No more'n five minnits," Naomi assured him. "We blowed out th' lanterns, drug them men off in th' woods back other side th' road. Got they guns. Oughta give us time t'git gone, 'fore ennybody come after us."

"All right, then." He searched landmarks for the familiar path, found it a few feet away. "Let's get moving." He reached, helped Artie to his feet.

But the ambush, the violence wouldn't leave his mind as they hurried on north. And a dawning horror at his own animal-like rage, his mad, killing instinct taking over his reason, his humanity, bore him down.

Where did that come from? How could I have done that? And Artie, a gentle, kind man. He crushed those heads like melons. But thank God he did, or we'd both be dead, for certain.

No, we did what we had to. And even though aiding runaways is against the law, that had nothing to do with any of this. Just robbers, preying on innocent people, for whatever they could get off them. Probably would have killed me just for my boots, if I'd been alone.

So Tom Brannon reasoned on the long way to Memphis and relative safety. And he hoped big Artie was able also to reconcile his necessary actions to his sense of humanity. But he was not to forget or rationalize, expunge this savagery from his being.

Not ever.

~ * ~

At the safe house, Tom turned the runaways over to the elderly couple who had the hidden basement, where they'd await the next guide on their way north. He took time to assure Artie again that they'd done the only thing they could have, and thanked him one more time.

There was food, but the big Black man hardly tasted it, so bewildered was he still at having killed the robbers. He went about in a sort of daze, despite the group's benefactors' assuring him that all was well, and that they'd all be on their way the next day.

Nothing in his past had prepared Artie for the sudden burst of anger, hatred, that had driven him to this violence. He'd always been a quiet man, peaceful in manner, the opposite of the image his size suggested. Where had the rage come from? When had he stepped over that invisible line into deadly action? Even his former owner, a planter east of Vicksburg, had never seen him express more than mild irritation at some inconvenience. But of course he'd burned inside with the desire for freedom, like all of them.

He eventually began to suspect that the bottled-up resentment at being treated like an animal, though controlled, had just erupted at the robbers' callous assuming that they could simply wreck the dedicated work the guides were doing. Yes, risking their own lives to get him and the others to freedom, to come up against greed, depravity from men with no respect for anyone, not even themselves.

And this episode frightened him: when might this happen again? He'd been told the runaways would be treated fairly up in the free states, but what if that weren't true? Could he submit to further degradation at the hands of domineering whites as a free man? He'd known their eventual goal wouldn't be any Promised

Land, but what if it were *all* a lie? A white man's fantasy tale told to enslave them further?

Artie prayed to his God for his soul, prayed for forgiveness for killing the two men, but his heart told him he'd done the right thing. And gradually he calmed the inner battle that raged, became again as close to the gentle ex-slave, the man he'd always been. At least to others.

They were kept for two days in the safe house, rested, fed well, clothed, then put in chains as a ruse and slipped away at darkest night to the Memphis docks. Their 'owner' was one Elbert Barksdale, a prominent merchant with secret abolitionist ties, who boarded a steamboat with them to travel the river north. He had forged ownership papers on each Black, and would deliver them to a factory owner in Illinois, across from St. Louis.

The plan was to dock at the last port before that free state, disembark as slaves bound for a supposed plantation owned by Barksdale, then slip across the state line to freedom. This procedure was only one of the ways the Route people delivered their charges, changing them often to avoid detection.

Artie talked quietly with Naomi, the former cook who'd come off the same plantation as he. She, along with the others, was frightened at all the secrecy, the fear that they'd be discovered at any moment, sent back, or worse. He assured her, calmed her nerves, seeming like the rock the group could hold onto to get them through this. He had no idea what lay ahead, but trusted in God and urged all of them to do likewise. Hadn't He taken care of them so far? Of course He had, and would continue to do so.

Besides, they were completely in the hands of these benefactors, so what other choice did they have? None, so they should stop worrying, be thankful, keep their hopes high.

Artie noted the steamboat's progress against the steady current of the river, the side-wheel paddles driving them northward in that constant, straining battle with the brown water pushing against them. He supposed the work the Route people were doing was like this boat, driven as the steam-forced pistons, the walking beams that drove the dripping wheels, against the unrelenting system of slavery. Just why only those who helped the runaways were so willing to risk it all, and no others, he couldn't fathom.

Weren't they all God's children? His mother had taught him they were, and that He loved all His creatures. Why couldn't the whites see that? Artie had lived long enough to know that most folks, from the most exalted to the meanest, just needed somebody to put down, to make them feel superior. And of course it was easiest to see Blacks as those necessary victims.

The boat docked after several days at a small landing on the eastern shore of the river. Barksdale herded the group, still chained, onto a wagon, which he drove himself, out away from the river. Onlookers appraised the 'slaves', noting Artie's size with what had to be envy. *Man's got hisself some good help, wherever he's bound.* Which one had to assume was a big plantation, perhaps being cleared of dense forest, perhaps already established, but expanding, to need the new help. Must be far on east, though, since nobody knew Barksdale here.

Eighteen

The reverend Harlan B. Sewell had arrived in Memphis in the late summer of 1860 with only a few dollars to his name. He'd answered the call to the tiny South Memphis A.M.E. church after its founder, Reverend Ezra Timmons, had died. He'd needed to leave the scene and memories of his misfortunes, as well as his need for employment. And had, even in this troubled pre-war time, decided on the southern church, certain the need here would be greatest.

And even armed with his impeccable Harvard credentials, he was wary, with the talk of impending secession and even war. And wondered how he, a Yankee, would fare in this city.

His appearance before his congregation was not what they'd come to expect. There were no fire-eating sermons, no brimstone, no haranguing, just calm, reasoned, Scripture-based Christianity. The dwindling attendance burgeoned.

And Headmaster Archibald Bancroft of the Shelby Institute, having learned of the pastor's presence, persuaded him to teach classes in religion there. At first Sewell had demurred, pointing out that he had no training for such a responsibility; he was no teacher.

Undismayed, Bancroft had showed his new prospect some of the actual classroom teaching by such dedicated staff as Tom Brannon, who taught math.

"He had no teaching experience either, sir, but our students are now ahead of most whites at their ages."

The reverend was still in doubt, although he'd found he could not subsist on the pittance the church could pay. He'd already been searching the area in vain for additional employment, anything, including common labor. *I'm not above any drudgery, since I believe it's God's will that He's led me here.*

But then, with a barely-concealed smile of triumph, the headmaster had ushered his hesitant charge into Anna Blake's English classroom. Her students were not only showing a clear grasp of the King's language, they seemed to have lost their farm and plantation patois. She had them speaking so well, if one closed his eyes, he couldn't have guessed they were Black.

And Miss Blake herself: Harlan Sewell actually gaped, and presented to this striking lady the appearance of one not quite in possession of all his faculties. She immediately pegged him as a fiery exhorter, and was dismayed that Bancroft had actually hired him to teach there.

Upon questioning her employer as to this apparition of damnation's qualifications, he replied simply:

"Harvard."

It was her turn to be speechless.

She'd nearly had to force herself to attend church that Sunday, to hear for herself what this anomaly had to impart. And was shocked at the best sermon she'd ever heard.

~ * ~

Jenny Blaine, despite her sobering, reality-based assessment of her beau Jethro Bennet, still viewed him as the only male likely to come within her sphere of existence. She dropped hints that she would welcome a more serious courtship. Jethro seemed oblivious to them, indeed as he appeared to be of much that occurred around him. Unless it pertained to the hammering of iron, any subject elicited a baffled expression on his long face.

Susan and the sisters had wrangled an extended trade through neighbor Ingrum for the essentials of a worn, patched blacksmith's forge for themselves, and had installed the firepot in a brick base. They had contrived a bellows of cured cowhide and barnboards, and through Jethro, had found a chipped-edge anvil. Now the youngest sister spent some time at the man's shop, often accompanied by the hopeful Jenny, learning more of the basics she'd acquired from Will McRaven and his mother.

And no scrap piece of iron fallen from a passing wagon went unclaimed by the sisters. No lost horseshoe or castoff wagon tire, perhaps worn completely through, escaped their claim. Susan began to master simple projects like wagon braces, single-tree hooks, a stove poker. The demanding forge welding was still beyond her, and the mysteries of hardening and tempering steel would perhaps become understandable, but not yet. Miss 'Quilla had a better knowledge of steel than either Jethro or Will, and Susan vowed to mine that lady's store of information as soon as she could.

In those days steel was rare, most smiths case-hardening iron with heating and the slow absorption of carbon from pulverized charcoal, bone or old, crumbly leather. It was a smoky, smelly, time-consuming process. Occasionally a worn file or broken scythe blade or castoff piece of railroad steel would come into a smith's possession, and he could experiment with it to produce knives, chisels, or forge-weld it onto softer iron tools such as axes for their cutting edges.

But gradually Susan, using the charcoal they made by immersing live hardwood coals in water, became familiar with the rudiments of the craft. She often pointed out that if a piece wasn't right, she could always heat it again and start over.

Jenny, even with these visits to Jethro's smithy, had made little progress in nudging him toward the altar. *Just too much like that Darrell, God rest him.* Why couldn't the man just respond? She knew she was no prize, now in her late thirties, but surely Jethro realized he'd never win a beauty queen.

What she would never know was that this man, although a Nashville native, strongly disapproved of slavery, and had come to the deep South only because that's where the need was for smiths. Resulting from his stern, originally Northern parents' prejudice, he had come to associate all in this region with the slave-owning planters. It was a misconception he was just not sharp enough to identify.

He knew nothing of course, of the Blaine sisters' activities with the Cotton Route, or his attitude would certainly have changed. But try as he'd have liked to, he just couldn't stammer out the questions to learn what Jenny thought of the odious institution.

And so their non-relationship weathered along unchanging, while she grew more frustrated and he viewed the coming storm clouds of secession and possible conflict, with dread. It just wouldn't do, he reasoned, for him to ally himself with a Rebel if it came to that. What would his parents, still living, think? He could never go home, that was for sure. And even if Miss Jenny turned out to be amenable to his secret abolitionist views, he knew his father, at least, would never accept her into the family.

Best wait then, as he'd done these years. He liked her, liked being with her, even if they couldn't seem to have conversations. And yes, he had other, less chaste fantasies, in which Jenny Blaine, unclothed, played the principal role. That he wanted her, wanted her slender body, both excited and confused him. He alternately viewed her as a desirable woman, and as some offering from the Evil Tempter himself, to lead him astray. Didn't the Bible say women were the downfall of all men?

But surely if he courted her properly, then they were married, then it'd be all right. Wouldn't it? He'd never received any coaching from his stern father on the subject of sex, nor spent much time among the other boys of his youth; they delighting in teasing him and taunting him for his clumsiness and his stuttering.

It was embarrassing, being with her. And excruciatingly lonely, being without her. Then this war talk... *yes, best wait this out*. But he was approaching forty years old: how much time did a man have for such as this? So confusing, all of it...

Jenny had almost taken matters into her own hands, alone with him, out away from others. But she'd stopped herself each time. It wouldn't do to try to seduce this bashful man. What if she failed? The shame of it would about kill her. After all, she wasn't one of those women men panted after, like dogs in heat. No, even if he never told, which she was sure he wouldn't, she just couldn't take *that* chance.

~ * ~

As for the Blaine sisters' close ally Anna Blake, she in time was able to see beyond Harlan Sewell's initial dumfounded reaction to her, to the sincere clergyman underneath. She was, that first time she heard him preach, pleasantly surprised that he was not a rabid exhorter, but a reasonable, thinking man, with thought-provoking points to make. Gradually her original assessment of him changed, although she still resisted any more contact with him than necessary.

As time passed, Sewell's reputation spread, and not only among the Black churches. Soon, even white ministers in Memphis were asking him to come help with revivals, special services, notably Reverend John Kellog, and some even down in nearby Mississippi. Despite his color, his manner and the touted (by others) Harvard education ingratiated him to these congregations. Even if grudgingly.

Anna wasn't sure just why she was still put off by him. Was it his obvious education, when she had no formal training herself? *Harvard.* The college that was held up as the pinnacle of learning in the entire country, among the finest in the world. That he had managed such an education in an irregular manner did not disturb her: one of her race took any and all opportunities to learn. *As should one of any race, indeed.*

No, perhaps it was she who had come to a place among the whites of the region that almost let her believe she was one of them... *Now that's nonsense of the worst kind. I'm constantly reminded of my color, every time I venture away from this secure sphere.*

When he asked permission to call on her, she initially refused, claiming an overload of work. That was mostly true, even with the scaled-down demands of the Route, but it wasn't the real reason. And analyzing her feelings, she finally concluded that she had been alone for so long, despite the impossible adoration of Tom Brannon, that she just wasn't ready to accept the first eligible male who presented himself.

So we'll be cautious here; if anything's to come of this... situation, it need not be hurried. Despite the rather obvious attempts at matchmaking for him the ladies of the church are devising, I doubt the reverend will leap into anything soon.

Or if he does, that settles that. I have lived alone as an adult for fourteen years, and literally owe no man. I can live my life as I have, giving my love and life only to these children.

Yes, I can.

But I must admit to being somewhat flattered that this educated specimen is so obviously taken with me. So different from Tom, with his idealistic, transparent near-worship, that can have no resolution. Tom must find himself a suitable wife, and get on with his life. Or is he too, wedded to our cause (both of them)? Perhaps. Dear Tom, you are a rock, as our Mr. Hyde has described you. But I doubt that marriage to a rock would ever be comfortable for any woman. She smiled at that picture.

But perhaps God had a hand in bringing this Mr. Sewell here, she reasoned: *I believe he thinks so. Could be, I suppose. I'll have to think about that one. I've plenty time to think, after all.*

If only thoughts of the man didn't fill so much of my time.

~ * ~

For his part, the minister had determined upon his first sight of this woman, to spend his life with her. With no disrespect to his late wife, he felt he'd been led here not only to fulfill his calling, but that God had surely planned this.

Accordingly, he'd resolved to take whatever time necessary to ingratiate himself with Anna and eventually to win her. So far that tack had met with resistance, and he wasn't sure just what he was doing wrong. Was she so dedicated to her work that there was just no time for a man? Did he somehow repulse her? Was he possibly even being overly polite? He couldn't know, but trusted that same God to work this out. *May it be Your will.*

Harlan Sewell devoted many extra hours to his church, calling on its members, participating in every community service imaginable, urging his congregation to higher levels of involvement in God's work. And he immersed himself in his teaching, spending time with each student, being available to confer with everyone regarding his/her faith journey.

And he was sincere. A few times he did catch himself wondering if this evident devotion would impress the desirable Anna Blake, but instantly chastised himself. *This is God's work, all of it. I'm not here to entrap this woman with my show of compassion... or am I?*

The weeks, months passed. She continued to attend the little church, now packed every Sunday and Wednesday night. She was unfailingly polite, never rebuffing his attentions, but never welcoming them, either. Anna made Harlan feel like an importuning teenage boy, never sure what impression he was making on the object of his desire. *But this is ridiculous: I'm middle-age, supposedly sure of myself, able to handle any situation. Except this one.*

Meanwhile of course, the looming spectre of war was on the horizon. Fire-eaters in several southern states had actually seceded from the Union, a move they were convinced was entirely legal, since these states had come into it voluntarily. Just how these moves would affect the residents was yet to be seen.

And when the Confederate States of America was formed in February, those in Mississippi hoped the rights of the citizens there would be restored, after a steady clamping down by the Federal government in Washington. The last real champion of the South, the late Andrew Jackson, now had no successor there to stand up for the region.

And the new president, Abraham Lincoln, seemed set on the Republican plan to make the central government even more powerful. And of course the abolitionists in the North demanded that the evil slave owners be punished for their sins, preferably by Federal power.

But these momentous events took place as if distant from the dedicated teacher and the hopeful minister, who both trusted they'd be left alone to do their vital work. Educating Black children was, they both believed, a thing that simply *had* to be done, if there were to be any future for them.

Anna eventually took her concerns about Harlan to her friends the Blaine sisters on a visit to their farm. She'd ridden the train with Rosanah's widowed husband Malcolm Johnson and his two children, whom she often minded. They'd go on to the

McRaven plantation by hired buggy, after another visit with yet another of Tranquilla's daughters and her husband, Doctor Marion Rossell, there in Hernando.

Jenny couldn't understand why the girl didn't just grab the minister and be done with it. Susan's advice was a little deeper.

"Girl, you gotta make up yer own mind on somethin' big as this. If th' man's th' right one, it'll work itself out, 'thout a doubt. But don't you go talkin' yerself into nothin' here, er y'll regret it long's you live. Yer sayin' y'got plenty time t'decide, an' you do: so take ever' minnit of it, t'be sure." She hugged her friend.

Kate was concerned with the situation, and had the perspective of more years to bring to it. She knew Anna's biological clock was ticking; she was mid-thirty already. And whether or not the couple would have children, she knew that adapting to each other would be harder than if they were young. From the way the girl talked of this Sewell, she found herself wanting to meet him herself. Not that she had to approve, but well, she had sort of assumed her usual mother role, almost as if Anna were family.

That winter, with neighbor Ingrum feeding their stock, the sisters declared themselves a holiday and took the cars to Memphis. They joked about passing judgment on the reverend as if their opinions would really matter.

"May be a hell raiser in th' pulpit," Susan conjectured, "but Anna says not."

"Well, if th' girl's got her head in th' clouds over him, he could prob'ly preach devil worship an' she'd like it," Kate offered.

"Now, you two're talkin' like th' man's some sorta freak outta a circus," Jenny defended. "She wouldn't be 'tracted to him 'less he was a gentleman. Never seen a Black gentleman, but there's gotta be some. An' *Harvard:* ain't no preacher in Miss'ssippi been t'Harvard, I'd wager."

So the three rural ladies disembarked and made their way to Anna's house, to crowd in for the weekend, which turned into a movable hen party. The Black girl was now their favorite human being in the world, and the four were more like sisters than any group ever had been, with the possible exception, Anna noted, of her years with the McRavens' Sarah and the late Rosanah, growing up.

Of course the Blaines spent their hard-earned crop money, and that from the sale of calves, and that from butter and egg sales as well. And did not regret a penny of it. They also sat among the congregation at Harlan's church that Sunday, and beheld the man of God for the first time. Jenny promptly fell in love again. Kate was cautiously impressed. Susan didn't say a word to Anna, but hugged her hard after the service.

As far as the sisters were concerned, God was at it again, with these two. And if not His hand in it, how in the world else would a Black Bostonian *ever* find his way here, to meet a freed Mississippi farm girl, and one every bit as sharp as he was.

"If she don't marry that'n," Jenny declared on their way home, "I'll black m'face an' go after him myself."

"Her decision," Kate stated.

"Shore, but y'saw th' way he was with her," Susan pointed out. "Take a mighty d'termined woman t'stand agin' th' kinda courtin' Harlan's doin'."

"He wa'nt that obvious," Jenny protested.

"Oh, he was," Kate disagreed, "it's jist th' way educated folks go at things, I reckon. He ain't 'bout t'let our girl git away, an' whether she knows it er not, she ain't 'bout to let him, neither."

And all three sisters were glad.

~ * ~

The supposed planter Barksdale turned his charges over to a contact just south of the Illinois line, a clerky sort who'd add fictitious, scattered former residences to the names of the former slaves. He asked them what last names he should record for them in the nearest county courthouses, and they came up with either their former owners' names, or ones they'd chosen. Artie decided he'd become Abner Boone, after stories he'd heard about the frontiersman.

The group was housed temporarily with a farmer who put them into a barn until they could be moved further north. Their destination would be with a factory owner named Blankenship, who would provide employment, housing, and who also operated a company store. There, they would be paid in scrip, redeemable at the store, much as sharecroppers were.

When they finally arrived in East St. Louis at the company housing, Artie and three others were crowded into flimsy board structures, each with two beds, a cast-iron heating stove to double as a cookstove, a privy, a tiny yard and a cistern. They were told to report at six the following morning for work, which would continue until six at night. Minimal blankets and additional clothing could be bought at the store, against future wages.

Since none of the former slaves could read, their last guide stayed with them for two days, explaining the system to them, getting them settled. Then this man, minister of a small church, departed, leaving them to the new system.

That first morning in the factory, Artie was assigned cleanup chores, wheeling a big cart from belt-driven metalworking machine to machine, gathering up borings, cuttings, scrap. This he dumped into a giant hopper, where it was conveyed to a melting crucible, to be prepared for re-use.

The lighting was almost nonexistent in the big building, with the few windows spaced far apart. A few gaslights illuminated some of the machines, but the overall gloom of the place made for a scene filled with accidents.

To later generations, such working conditions seemed primitive, dangerous, which indeed they were, but such was the norm in mid-century America, as industrialists built factories, rushed products to completion to meet the needs of the expanding nation. Workers, both white and Black at the bottom of the social strata were treated as necessary but expendable cogs in the massive wheel, too similar to slaves.

But I'm free, Artie kept assuring himself as the days, weeks, months passed in almost numbing sameness. *I can walk away from this anytime I choose, nobody come after me, go anywhere.*

If I could just pay what I owe at the store.

~ * ~

The Reverend Kellog, impressed by the boy Abel's intelligence, approved of his entering the Institute. Very quickly both Tom Brannon and Anna Blake, having also recognized the young man's potential, had assigned him extra work, so he could move ahead faster. Both teachers were to see their protege excel, and they'd laid the plans for him to go north for further education.

That would be quite difficult, but Tom knew he could smuggle the lad to Chicago with him as his body servant. There he knew of a college he was sure he could get Abel into.

"He'd have to work his way, of course… money's always the obstacle, Anna. But I've relatives who can help locate him a position. It'll take time, but I believe he can become just about anything he sets his eyes on, once there."

"I hope you're right, but I've been getting reports that the life most places up north our people find isn't what we'd hoped. At least not in the factories; Let's pray your connections work out."

But war was still years away when Abel finished his studies at the Shelby Institute, with the uncertainty of his future. Tom Brannon was as good as his word, traveling with him to his home in Chicago, where with the help of extended family, and in the increased job market, both work and college were managed. Both Institute teachers felt they'd done their best in this case, and it was a good feeling. Their only regret was that they couldn't do as much for the many, many others they'd helped to freedom.

~ * ~

Perhaps the reverend Harlan Sewell's most notable contribution to race relations occurred a half year after his arrival in Memphis. The aging minister at the Red Banks Presbyterian Church, Knox Thomas, had heard of this gifted preacher, had traveled to meet him. Eventually, he convinced Sewell to come help with a planned revival. That such events were mostly at more evangelical churches did not daunt the elderly Scotsman. *When in Rome...*

The tall Black man's appearance behind the pulpit had been a surprise to the congregation and the visiting attendees. All were shocked, some indignant, some at first angry at this presumptuous trickery, as they termed it. But their pastor began defusing the resistance by introducing his guest as a Harvard graduate, which took his listeners aback.

Then Harlan Sewell assured them he was not an 'uppity nigger' out to prove anything, but a sincere child of God, just as he was certain every one of them was. And his sermon was moving, even spellbinding. His manner of dropping his voice at critical junctures had them straining to hear every syllable, and his perfect use of the language widened their eyes. *Maybe this is indeed some of God's doing.*

Harlan himself was nervous, but nobody could have told it. And at the end of the service, both ministers welcomed the faithful in an altar call, prayed with them, and many responded. Definitely a departure from the usual Presbyterian worship service as they'd known it.

Outside, members of the McRaven family, as well as others of the sympathetic community and Reverend Thomas, engaged all of the potential troublemakers before they could talk themselves into indignation.

"Can you believe it, Fletcher, that man's prob'ly better educated than th' biggest preacher in th' biggest church in th' state."

"But Will, he's *Black!*"

"And I saw you hanging on every word he preached. You know a man of God when you see him, Fletcher, and I know you agree that his being here has God's hand in it." Tranquilla's eighteen-year-old son slapped his friend on the back, moved to another gesticulating neighbor.

John McRaven, the eldest son, was a respected physician, and he too, helped quell any animosity he saw brewing. So did Joseph Brunson, from Kentucky, whose elder daughter Will was then courting. These and others redirected the several dissidents, and generally turned the situation around to positive.

Tranquilla had watched Anna Blake after the service, and saw immediately the relationship with the Black minister.

"You'll come stay with us, of course, both of you," she put an arm each about Anna and Harlan. "And you, sir, are most welcome. Reverend Thomas had said he had a surprise for us tonight, and I'm delighted."

"Thank you, Mrs. McRaven. Anna has told me much about you, and I've looked forward to meeting you." He bowed over her hand.

"And we've another surprise for you," Anna fairly beamed.

"I know what that is already, dear girl," her friend replied.

~ * ~

The wedding was early in that year of 1861, at the McRaven plantation, among high-running talk of more secession, even of war. But that thundercloud of disaster was in the future, they hoped, and nothing marred the joy of this occasion. Tranquilla only regretted deeply that her husband could not be present to see their protégé married to this wonderful man.

The Blaine sisters were of course in attendance, and Susan managed to dance every available male's feet sore, including her favorite Harvey. Jenny was in a state of euphoria, a bit giddy at the festivities, the like of which she'd only imagined. Kate smiled, talked, beamed, even danced a little. This gathering was unlike any she'd heard of, with Blacks so welcome, so much a part of it. She and Hetty Barnes got to know each other well, those several days the wedding lasted.

Finally, in the company of Malcolm Johnson and his two young children, the newlyweds left in his carriage for home, the little cottage near the Institute. The Blaines and their plantation chatelaine waved them off in the lingering warmth of the occasion.

Nineteen

War had come. The long-talked-of secession of Southern states was a fact, and the Union's response to the shelling of Fort Sumter had been all-out war against them. And with a stubborn hope, the Confederate leaders had refrained from ordering the invasion of the North after the first Southern victories, to end it, sure the Union would give up and let the new country go in peace, its Constitutional right.

That was not to be. Lincoln was determined to hold the Union together, and the government in Washington refused to recognize the Confederacy's legitimacy. This despite one Supreme Court justice confiding to the president that the new country was entirely legal. Lincoln ignored him, even deporting one dissenting congressman and jailing another.

The first battles seemed to demonstrate that the South was highly superior to the Union in warfare: better generals, more committed troops. But Lincoln persevered, ordering ships built to enforce the coastal blockades, eventually to strangle the Confederacy. He tried, then discarded general after general, and not till near the end of the conflict did he discover the dogged Ulysses Grant, who with superior firepower and men, began to win decisively.

The war was full of commanders' blunders, wasted manpower, shortages, a repeat of practically every conflict human beings had ever waged against each other, and seemingly never learned from. Brutal, senseless, full of propaganda and calculated manipulation of the citizens on both sides, the blunt forces engaged, circled, advanced, fell back, orchestrated by politicians and manufacturers out to profit.

Newspapers on both sides printed outrageous accounts, quite often highly inaccurate, of their respective victories, of the rightness of their causes, of anything that would sell their advertised products, inflame their readers. Objective reporting gave way to impassioned rhetoric, inciting fights, riots and instability everywhere.

On the farms of the South, the shortages were acute almost from the very beginning. Soon the Confederate money was worthless, and the ancient practice of trading became the norm. With so many of its young men gone, the region's infrastructure began to disintegrate, and this got worse each month, week, even each day.

But the will of these people held on, far past any reason, simply because they could not envision defeat, could not prepare themselves mentally for life so different from anything they'd ever known or imagined possible. The holy Cause, the imagined invincibility of their armies, their government, embodying their way of life, just had to succeed.

Didn't it?

The Blaine sisters at first continued their lives in the sameness of routine, plowing, planting, weeding, harvesting, with the battles distant and seeming unreal. The dark earth must be turned, the seeds planted, the cloth woven or traded for, the roof mended, despite blood flowing on some faraway battleground, to them about as close as the moon.

But then there was Shiloh, and the returning few they actually knew, minus arms, legs, crippled caricatures of themselves, only part young men. And there was the capture of Memphis itself, and the clamping control of the big river, and the war came very close.

Now the dreaded foraging began, now the necessity of hiding food and livestock even from their own troops, became a reality. Now the war was at their doorstep. And the months groaned past, as the tightening jaws of this crushing, unnatural force engulfed them.

And so the years passed, with the toiling Blacks on the plantations, on the farms, hopeful of freedom, fed lies of prosperity to come, believing their liberators, their protectors were coming, were near. Older and more experienced counselors among them warned that much of this would be hollow, disappointing, only a different but equally hopeless existence. They shook their graying heads, wary of this white man's cataclysm.

~ * ~

Some months after the Union occupation of Memphis, Harlan Sewell and Tom Brannon drove a shaky cart pulled by one ancient mule, several miles out of Memphis to a white friend's farm to cut offered firewood. They were welcomed, helped, fed, and were returning with their hard-won load, when they passed, or tried to pass, a Union encampment.

"Woah, thar," an officious corporal challenged. "What y'got thar, you an' yer nigger? Looks like farwood t'me, and we're needin' farwood." He winked at his two companions, who stood grinning.

"Sorry, this wood's for our church and school," Tom replied, eying the road ahead. "It's not for sale, sir."

"Well, looks t'me like you could always get yer slave thar, t'cut you some more, and we ain't talking *buying* wood, no. More like you *donatin'* that cookwood to th' Union Army, ain't we, boys?"

"I am no man's slave, sir. I am a minister of the Gospel, serving God."

"Well, ain't you th' fancy talkin' one, now. Don't make no difference what you call yerself: one Black face might's well be another, right, boys?"

Tom requested that they see the commanding officer of this unit, but the ruffian told them they'd deal with him only, and that it was already decided.

"Now just you drive that ole cart through that gate yonder," he gestured, "an' we'll just fergit all this here... misunderstandin'. Yeah, like it never happened, which it didn't, did it?"

Just then there was a thundering fusillade from Confederate cavalry charging into the camp, leaping over hedges, shotguns and rifles aimed. Colonel Winfield Darby, attached to Bedford Forrest's command, called for instant surrender, claiming superior forces just behind his.

The surprised commander of the unit, staring into the muzzles of those shotguns, immediately ordered surrender.

"Wise decision, Major. No need for useless bloodshed. But I fear you'll not like our prison accommodations, since your armies have robbed us blind of our livestock and crops. Leave your weapons and horses, and form up, please." He actually bowed to the disheveled major, who'd emerged from his tent half-dressed.

Tom and Harlan felt like cheering. *Odd,* Tom thought, *Here a Black and a Yankee are rescued by the enemy. Or I guess they're really not the enemy, just here and now.*

But Darby rode closer, asking if these two were attached to this Union unit. When Tom answered in the negative, explaining their situation and the proposed hijacking of their firewood, the colonel seemed displeased.

"Sir, you speak with a Yankee accent, and here you are with a Union encampment. I sincerely hope you are not a spy, because we deal summarily with enemy spies." His hand was on his holstered pistol.

"Sir, I think perhaps I can better explain our situation," Harlan offered, in his rich baritone. "I am pastor of..."

"By the Almighty, I've heard that voice! Have you ever been near Byhalia, sir?"

"I have. My wife is from near there. And I..."

"That's it! You're the preacher from Harvard, that revival. I was actually one who came forward, Reverend. My sincere apologies, sir. And my compliments to Miss Anna. I'd heard of your marriage." He bowed low. "An honor, sir, and my apologies also to your friend." He turned and waving his hat, galloped after the shuffling Union troops, being herded by his men.

The two woodcutters excitedly discussed this rescue, for it was just that, by a surprising ally, and shared their amazement at the tangled situation and its outcome.

~ * ~

By 1863 there was no hope of peace for the ravaged north Mississippi region, no hope of a swift end to hostilities. The remembered boasts of a month-long campaign of Yankee-chasing echoed hollow and foolish as the South's young men died, and could not be replaced. And now, after the definite turned tide of Vicksburg and Gettysburg just a day apart that summer, it seemed only a matter of time till Dixie would be strangled, defeated, crushed under the superior hordes from the North.

And Will McRaven the poet, engaged to Cammie Brunson, after surviving most of the major battles in the East: Second

Manassas, Sharpsburg, Fredericksburg, Chancellorsville, had fallen the second day at Gettysburg. Fallen at the edge of a peach orchard, the branches of which had been stripped of green fruit by hailstorms of rifle fire. The plantation family was devastated, and it was all Tranquilla could do to keep the enraged thirteen-year-old Harvey at home.

At the outbreak of hostilities, Jenny Blaine's beau Jethro, from minimally-divided Tennessee, loaded up the essentials of his blacksmith shop and disappeared. In the direction of Nashville again and his pro-Union family.

"Never knew he leaned much, one way or t'other," Kate observed.

"Wal, if he had, he'd of fall'n over, he was that tall an' gawky," Susan dismissed the departed non-suitor. And surprisingly to these two sisters, Jenny didn't seem to grieve for him.

"Just wasn't 'nuff of a man, I guess," was all she'd say of him.

So the even tenor of their lives had returned for a time. A short time.

But as the conflict had heated up, Hiram Hyde, director of the Cotton Route, deemed it expedient to return to New England, effectively shutting down the operation until the war's outcome could be known.

"We are not abandoning our sacred cause," he intoned, "but with the prospect of a God-guided victory for the Union, surely the obscene practice of slavery will be declared illegal. These Southern tyrants will receive their comeuppance, and our work will be vindicated at last."

"What if the South wins?" he was asked.

"God forbid. But in that instance, we shall renew our efforts, and continue in goodwill and with that same merciful God's blessings." And Memphis saw the last of the austere Hiram Hyde, ahead of the storm, as it were.

The Blaine sisters watched all these events lurch forward, from the euphoric patriotic zeal of the neighbors to the stark reality of those same neighbors' husbands and sons killed or maimed, to the shortages, the doomed Confederate money, the unexpected Union victories. And if times had been hard for their marginal livelihoods before, now grinding poverty faced them.

Both Union and Confederate foragers raided, confiscating mules, corn, provisions of all kinds. And when daring Southern cavalry raids cut Union supply lines, those armies took more from the suffering farmers: retaliation or simple shortages—the end result was the same. It became routine to hide the one remaining cow in a tangle of brush-grown woods, the crated chickens, the little remaining preserved food. Even the resourceful sisters had not far to go to present to the foragers the appearance of absolute destitution, with nothing to give.

For them and others in the region, the ultimate end became a looming, inescapable reality, if not yet realized: the South would lose, was losing. And of course hardest hit were those in the direct path of the war. The Hernando/Holly Springs area was to change occupying hands thirty-two times before the war ended.

~ * ~

After a skirmish right on the edge of the Blaine farm, the sisters ventured out of the root cellar where they'd taken refuge. The acrid smell of gunpowder hung in the air, and the eerie quiet belied the still-lingering smoke of the fight. The women took stock of the torn ground, the bullet-ridden barn and house, and shook their heads.

They'd been raided by Union troops, foraged by Confederate troops, everything visible taken. The worthless paper receipts they'd received in return were duly stashed away, but none of them believed in the promised restitution. It was hard treatment for a family enduring a hard life they'd become accustomed to.

"Guess you c'd say we're lucky," the practical Kate observed. "Still alive." She viewed the dormant kitchen garden, fields awaiting plowing, planting the hoarded seeds. But their luck hadn't included being able to hide and keep their one remaining mule. The Union army needed it, they'd been told, despite the fact that these women plainly couldn't survive without that plowing.

"They jist don't keer," Susan had spat. "One thing t' take a few off a plantation, leave some. 'nuther t'leave us without a way even t'scratch th' ground. Makes me wanta go start m'own war."

It was in this angry, resentful, hopeless frame of mind that this tough farm woman had stumbled across a badly wounded Union solder, hidden in dense briars. Her first thought was to let him die, or even put him out of his misery with a shotgun blast.

She hadn't done that.

Any more than she'd have ignored the runaway slave girl Celie, those years ago. Despite her—their—hardscrabble lives, despite their having killed, the Blaine sisters were not cruel.

"But jist what in God's name we gonna do with him?" demanded Kate, hands on hips. Jenny was cleaning blood off the unconscious soldier, who appeared to be around 40 years of age. Susan had stitched the saber wound with the man's own housewife kit, after washing it out as best she could. The women had improvised a stretcher and carried him to their house, where Jenny applied whiskey to the place.

"Well, we ain't about to jist let him die, Katy. Reckon we c'n turn him over t'the Union doc at Hernando..."

"If there's Federals there. I'm thinkin', way they backed off here, our boys have got th' town, now. An' they'd send him off to a prison camp, where he'd die, sure."

"Kinda a good-lookin' feller," Jenny observed, "shame t'let him jist die off, when we'd oughta help him all we kin."

"Oh, there y'go, girl: so if he was ugly, y'd shoot him? Ain't no hope for you, Jenny." Susan rolled her eyes, as she'd so often done at this sister's romantic fantasies.

The resulting solution was to tend to the man themselves, having hidden his uniform, and when he roused, cautioned him to say nothing if visitors came, a giveaway with his Ohio accent. That way they hoped they could pretend he belonged to whatever army was actually in control, and was too weak to be moved. Beyond that, they hadn't come up with a plan. He thanked them feebly, eventually took some of Jenny's magic broth, began recovering slowly.

Which should have worked, in the confusion of wartime, survival, the general chaos there in the middle years of the conflict.

Except that three nights later, a pounding on their door awakened the sisters, prepared them for their agreed-upon story. Susan opened the door over the muzzle of her shotgun, and a lone Confederate soldier fell through it, leaving his blood on the floor.

~ * ~

The boy Seth had grown, there at the Illinois mill. He was now in early teenage, a strapping lad, long used to carrying the sacks of grain, meal and flour. Like his father, he was becoming adept at maintaining the mostly wooden machinery of the mill, and more often the aging miller left much of the operation to them.

His own sons had not chosen to follow their father's trade, and were farming with their young families close by. When the conflict erupted, this extended family drew closer, letting the rage, the violence, the people's war of hate and lies, circle them at a distance.

With the months, then years of fighting, Enoch saw some of his freed-slave counterparts enlisting in those Union armies that would accept them. He thanked God he was too old to fight, and that Seth was, he prayed, too young. His years with the Northerners had dulled his resentment of his former life station, though he would never forget the harsh treatment of the planter Calloway.

Enoch had never remarried. Memory of the bright, talkative Reenie, mother of his beloved son, remained vivid in his mind. He looked forward to the time this life would end, pleasant as it had become, and he could be with her again.

He'd talked about this hope with the miller, a man inclined to deep meditation.

"Allus heered God's people, us, 'd be together in Heaven, Mist' Adam. Whut you thaink 'bout that?"

"Well, our Bible does not specifically state that, Enoch, but given His mercy, and the promise of His holy Son, we who believe, and live that belief, will indeed see that paradise. It follows then, that we will be together, since Heaven is a place, or a state of being. So yes, I would say you can look forward to seeing your wife there."

The miller did not always agree with the tenets of his church, but did not express his concerns, believing completely that harmony was a precious goal, and to be preserved. Despite some things that troubled him, he had reached a place in his life where a good digestion, an adoring wife and a growing number of grandchildren, constituted the ideal. This side of that heaven, of course.

Seth's life was not that tranquil. Outside this community, Blacks, however free, were treated as beasts of burden, given the very meanest jobs, underpaid. Here he might joke, laugh, engage in adolescent fun with the white youths with a sense of equality. But venture just a few miles to a town outside this secure circle, which he did on occasion with the miller on necessary errands, and the hostility was like a dark cloud.

He'd been told this early on, and experience proved it. White folks just did not like being around Black ones, unless like here, their religion governed every activity, and except for a few sour old specimens and the odd rowdy child, life was good. *Just don't push it, boy, or y'll git y'self burnt.*

~ * ~

Nathan Bedford Forrest was worried. Two of his trusted young cavalrymen were overdue from a scouting mission west toward Hernando. Stuart Nicholson and Bobby Payne both knew that region well, having grown up just east, in Marshall County. The Hernando rail stop was vital to the Union supply lines, and the now-general wanted to hit it, wreck it, set the Union's Mississippi campaign back precious months.

He also wanted to raid north, up the big river as far as his hard-riding troops could push, cutting other rails, decimating outposts, harrying the ever-converging blue armies. Perhaps even drawing others of them west and away from the superior forces bent on crushing Robert E. Lee's forces in Virginia.

If he could hit Hernando with a trusted subordinate, that should feed rumors that he himself was there, while actually raiding far north, cutting telegraph lines, remaining a moving target no one could pinpoint.

Unfortunately, his right hand commandant, Winfield Darby, had been ambushed at Holly Springs while visiting—and yes, courting—one of the McRaven daughters, young Tranquilla. That left a big hole in the general's staff: Darby had been a VMI graduate, fierce, calculating, highly successful.

Forrest looked closely at his riders. There was one, a young Texan, a bit wild, who'd come with a herd of cattle across the Mississippi River and stayed to fight. Ambrose Larkin was a captain, but seldom bothered with insignia or took his rank seriously. If he could be disciplined, given a command, perhaps he could manage Hernando.

But first, the general had to know the situation. And his scouts were behind schedule. Stuart Nicholson was a favorite, and was the son of Mrs. McRaven's sister Candace. Forrest had traded horses with Robert before his death, and knew the family well.

Candace was also a widow, and Forrest had assured her he'd watch over Stuart closely.

"He'll be with my staff, ma'am," he'd assured her, knowing however this wouldn't mean safety, in this war. And unfortunately, the general's own brother had been killed in that rout of Union General Sooey Smith earlier that year.

He sent for Larkin, whom he remembered Darby had spoken highly of. And while he waited, he questioned another aide.

"What d'you know about Ambrose Larkin, Lieutenant?"

"Larkin? Oh, he's th' sharpshooter f'm Texas. Good man, but he doesn't follow protocol that much. Made captain, you may remember, just recently."

"Yes. You been in a scrap 'longside him?"

"Not directly, but from what I hear, he's cool under fire."

Just then the subject of their conversation knocked at the farmhouse door that was Forrest's headquarters just then, well east in Mississippi. The aide admitted a tall, somewhat slouched figure with wild yellow hair, chewing on a straw.

"Cap'n Larkin r'portin', Gin'ral," He gave a languid salute, attempted to straighten. He wore no captain's bars, and his uniform, like those of many of Forrest's command, was not recognizable as official Confederate issue. The commander smiled inwardly. *Damn West Pointers won't give me 'n army t'fight with, but it's men like this'll get th' job done.*

"What I've got in mind, Larkin, is a raid over on Hernando, cut th' rail line, retake th' town, put up a block t'the Unions that've got th' territory, 'long with findin' Stu Nicholson an' Bobby Payne, get 'em back here. Now, I got other plans, an' I need a man can take a small force fast 'cross th' state, hit th' place like a real army, set 'em back 'bout half a year.

"And, there's this Union general Harwell Thorsen in Byhalia givin' th' folks hell 'round there, needs t'be replaced. Garrison there, so I don't expect you t'take that out, no more men than I c'n cut loose for this." He looked keenly at the young man. *Couldn't be more'n maybe 25, an' that's a stretch. Might clean up better, but no real need.*

"Me. You're sayin' I'm th' man fer this?" The trooper was surprised.

"What I'm sayin'. I'd wanted Win Darby on it, an' I'm 'bout ready t'come down on Holly Springs, string up th' bastard shot him. But this operation's more important, sorta a diversion tactic, while I tend to a buncha stuff on up in Yankee territory. Think y'can handle it?"

"How many men c'n we spare?"

"That's th' hard part: only twenty. Y'gotta scrounge up yer own force, mostly. Got a good man outta Pontotoc, Gus Varner, gittin' over a bad arm, c'n help you: Lieutenant. Maybe a few you can find along th' way. Rest'll be up to you. I'd say y'need about forty, an' y'll need t'find your own mounts, 'sides you an' that twenty."

He didn't show it, but Larkin was elated at this prospect. He'd joined the cavalry to fight Yankees, not pose in a uniform, and here was the chance to head up a lightning raid, Forrest-style, and maybe make a real difference in this grinding war.

"Oh, an' here's a list of folks y'can contact on th' way, hide you, feed you some, give you d'rections. Varner knows th' territory 'round him, but y'll need more'n that on west. Couple doctors, few others workin' with us too."

"One question, sir: how soon?"

"Yesterday." He stood, saluted, "Good luck, Cap'n" and offered his hand.

~ * ~

"I know this boy," Susan exclaimed, holding the lamp as Kate turned the limp body. "That's Miss Candy Nicholson's Stuart, was at Anna's weddin'. She's Miss 'Quilla's sister. He rides with Forrest, er he did; Looks most dead."

"No, he's breathin'. Shot through th' side, 'pears th' ball's still in him. Help me git him on back, put him in th'other bed, 'side th' Yank, I reckon." They got Stuart's shirt off, bound the wound, which was now only seeping blood. From his pale face, it was obvious he'd lost a lot.

"Girls, this's more'n we c'n handle," Susan stated the obvious. "But try t'keep th' hole in him clean: whiskey. Reckon I'll ride fer Doc Rossell, er he's gonna die."

"How'll we 'splain th' Union, there?" Jenny asked the equally obvious. The three looked at each other, at the comatose soldiers.

"Doc's Miss 'Quilla's son-in-law, married to her Mary Ann. Reckon he'll be all right with it: I know he's treated Unions b'fore, works with their doc in th' town," Susan decided. "B'sides, we ain't got enny choice." With that, she dressed, took her shotgun, mounted Stuart's horse, which was just a plow animal. *Long way down f'm th' blooded hosses them proud boys started out with. Er mebbe Stu was hopin' t'pass fer some farmer; prob'ly out scoutin'. Others must've not made it.*

The result of this dilemma was a successful operation by Dr. Marion Rossell, removing the bullet from Stuart's body, and his agreeing to help the Union man also, whose name was John Weller from Ohio. Weller also covered for the Rebel cavalryman, telling a Federal officer that the boy, who hadn't regained consciousness at the time, was a new recruit, on their side, name as yet unknown to him.

Later, it was agreed a necessity to hide Stuart in one of the few remaining crumbling sheds the sisters had used to hide runaways, until word could be sent east to Forrest, or whoever was in charge in the region. Rossel then told the resident Union doctor that the trooper had died, and that they'd buried him. The lie troubled him not at all.

Twenty

Ambrose Larkin and his small force, now self-named Larkin's Lancers, rode west on what mounts they could find, mostly plow horses. Twice they encountered small Union patrols, but each time their Indian scout Eli Dobbins had discovered them first. Using guerilla stealth tactics, the Confederates had raided them, taking their horses, leaving those men afoot to make their ways back to their lines as best they could. And so far they hadn't lost a man.

Larkin's second-in-command was Lieutenant Gus Varner from near Pontotoc. He'd mostly recovered from having his arm hit by shrapnel from Sooey Smith's artillery, and was now ready to resume the fight. He knew the roads well to beyond Byhalia where the hated General Harwell Thorsen was in command.

And earlier, Varner had heard dimly of those sisters, the Blaines out of Hernando, who were harboring Forrest's wounded scout. From what he'd learned, the other, Bobby Payne, had been killed. And he also knew a few available men they might recruit for the raid.

"Boys been a little young to sign up," he told Larkin. "An' now that they know this man's war ain't no picnic, they've held back. But there's a half dozen will welcome th' adventure, an' th' chance to serve under Forrest, even if t'ain't directly. Few gittin' over their hurts too, like me. I'd say we c'n expect as many as forty, with what we've got, time we git to Hernando." Larkin considered this.

Forty men, if we're lucky. Not enough to raid Byhalia atall, unless we c'n think of somethin' they won't expect. Well, go on first, hit the railroad at Hernando, find Stuart, then figger how t'take Thorsen down. Word we got through th' gin'ral's contact Doc Benson in Holly Springs, was that that'n was so hard, whoever th' Yanks replace him with's gotta be a sight better. Dunno 'bout that, but all right, if we can't git th' whole command, mebbe we c'n cut that snake's head right off.

Larkin had earned all his field promotions because of his daring, his uncanny sharpshooting, and the way his mind worked, coming up with novel and unexpected tactics his general had noted early on. He'd ridden with Colonel Winfield Darby until that officer had been ambushed, and had learned a lot of craft from the dashing legend.

East of Red Banks, the scout Eli reported an encampment of Union cavalry in deep forest. Just then, this region was highly contested and they had apparently chosen to hide rather than risk discovery and attack by the enemy out in the open.

"How many, reckon?" the young captain asked, planning.

"Mebbe fifty, looked like. Too many."

"Yeah, but sure would like t'git some more good hosses. Reckon we c'd spook 'em, chase 'em down there in th' woods, 'thout gittin' caught?"

The Indian's eyes glinted at this prospect: a stampede, leaving the Union men afoot, while Larkin's troops rode after the runaways, caught better mounts. Maybe some extras, for any other recruits they might gather on the way. And wouldn't have to risk losing a single man, done right.

"Couple of us git close, we c'd spook 'em all right, but they'll be guarded good. Looks like a job for you an' me, don't it?" Larkin never asked his men for duty he wouldn't go on himself. An expert rider, he was sure he could leap onto one of the fleeing horses bareback, and dodge enemy fire, there in the dark.

The sky was overcast, and this raid would be almost by feel, and there was the distinct danger that the galloping horses could slam a rider into a tree, maybe tear his leg off racing past it. Larkin told his other men to try to haze the horses toward a distant field, beyond reach of any retaliatory attack by the crippled Union cavalry.

He and Eli crept up to the corralled horses, timing their approach to the rounds of the three sentries guarding them. Eli slipped to his right, and Larkin to the left, each with a long, sharpened stick. They silently cut the rope corral in two places, leaving wide gaps, then slipped around, following the retreating sentries. Then, on a soft, owl-hoot signal, both jammed the nearest horses, which reared, snorted, and ran through the others.

The men retreated as the guards rushed to the corral, then raced around to the openings. Eli then leaped on a racing roan, grabbing its mane, swinging up. Larkin had spotted a bay stallion in the light from a nearby campfire, and searched the running mass for him. He dodged flying hooves to catch this horse, and just managed to hoist himself up on him, even shoving against another animal alongside for the final boost.

The stampede didn't slow, as shouts and even a few rifle shots in the air failed to stem it. The two Confederates crouched low, reaching the others of their troop, who joined in directing the runaways toward the distant field. Finally breaking free of the forest, they raced on, the wind cutting their faces, a wild glee filling them. The young Texan could hardly keep from whooping in joy.

Once on open ground, the horses were halted, saddles were changed, and Larkin's Lancers were considerably better mounted than before. They herded the rest of the animals on toward a plantation Varner knew, where they hoped to hide, rest, and present the owners with this extra horseflesh.

~ * ~

On the plantations and the farms across Mississippi, even the remote cabins, people were starving, having been raided for any and all their meager provisions. Grim hunters, the young and very old, brought the few rabbits and squirrels home, and the very rare deer, even groundhogs, raccoons and 'posums they found. Then of course the powder and shot ran out, and they had nothing but contrived bows and arrows. Some straggled into the nearest towns to beg for jobs, the lowest and meanest, just anything to buy scraps of food from merchants who were closing their doors, having nothing to sell or trade.

A descendant remembered his aunts describing that as the 'dying time', when hungry children were reduced to gnawing on boiled leather from old shoes, harness. Every nut-bearing tree was stripped, every berry bush, even edible and not so edible roots dug, devoured. Often a sort of bread was contrived from pounded stalks of whatever grass they could find, maybe combined with hoarded grains or moldy meal, crushed seeds, anything to fill their empty bellies.

Some older people recalled that the Indians had eaten insects, even worms, grubs, in lean times. And these were by far the leanest. And so rotting logs were eagerly overturned, as if the nonexistent bears had ravaged the forests, their crawling inhabitants gathered, devoured.

And of course the now-freed Blacks had it the worst—nobody wanted them, or could help them. All wasted away together, Black and poor white. It was a sort of brotherhood of the deprived, a sisterhood of the bereft.

Hard-pressed, both races took to robbery, little as that gained them. And the beginnings of feuds arose, the bitter enmities of the survivors that would last generations.

And the dreaded bushwhackers rode, robbed, loyal to neither side, raping the countryside, preying on any and all too weak to resist. Betrayals, hunger-driven unholy alliances were common. Even within families, one or more members often gave in to the need to survive by stealing from the others or by any other however degraded means.

The good times were gone, the thousand-candle balls in the big houses only faded memories, as former belles dug, hoed, planted precious seeds, hid chickens in the brush out of hearing, buried family silver, hoarded precious cloth. In this chaotic time, the faded gowns mocked them, were cut apart, re-sewn to cover their now lean bodies. Hands toughened, hardened, and their bitterness would last till they died.

And the aged? Well, they simply perished. Of starvation, broken hearts, wasting away dreaming of the old ways, which would never come again.

Ever.

~ * ~

Ambrose Larkin's little troop crossed below Byhalia, riding at night, finding dense cover in swamps, brush-grown low hills to hide in by day. Finally they reached the road north of Hernando, near the Blaine sisters' farm. The Texan and Eli left the others in deep forest where the hills began, and slipped along the darkened road, wary of Union patrols this close to the town they now held.

Dismounting, the two crept up to the dark farmhouse, the Indian leading the horses toward the barn. Larkin was able to get close enough to call out.

"Hello, th' house! We're friends, so don't shoot us. I'm Cap'n Larkin, with Forrest. We'll jist wait here till you c'n see we ain't th' Yankees, nor them bushwhackers."

A lamp was lighted inside, and Larkin started toward the house. Then he felt a hard pressure in his back, and a voice warned him.

"Jist you hold it right there, young feller, till we git a look at you," Susan Blaine's voice came. Larkin had jumped, but now grinned in appreciation of this woman's skill and daring.

"Miz Blaine, Gin'ral Forrest sent us t'find Stuart, an' t'do whatever we can t'slow th' Yankees down 'round here. An' you 'bout scairt th' life outta me, y'know?" He turned to her as she lowered the shotgun she carried.

"Well, you ain't no bluebelly, that's fer shore. C'm on in, son. Who you got with you?"

"Our scout, hidin' our hosses in yore barn, an' close to forty others. Oh, an' we're to try t'git rid of that devil Thorsen in Byhalia on th' way back, if we can." They went into the house, where the other sisters were up, lighting the cookstove fire. Larkin bowed to them, learned their names.

"Right pleased t'meet alla you. Gin'ral Forrest, he's known 'bout y'all since on back, says you'll do to tie to." *An' he knows more'n he's tellin' 'bout you too, but that's history, now.*

"Call yer man in, then, an' we'll have us a bite 'fore we go out t'where we've got Stuart hid," Susan instructed. "Time enough b'fore daylight fer that, an' we c'n figger how t'git him up an' gone with you." Kate opened the rear door and let Eli in. He nodded to the women.

They had a hurried breakfast of wild hog and cornpone, then set out with Susan toward the falling-in shed the women had hidden Stuart in. Only lately had they acceded to his wishes to be left alone, since he was armed: the women had insisted one of them stay with him while he recovered. They'd taken turns bringing food to him for the weeks he'd been mending.

"Dunno he's fit to ride yet," Susan worried. "I'd say find a wagon, put him in deep hay so th' stitches won't bust loose. Doc Rossell's some doubtful, but this's prob'ly th' only chance you got to move him, right?"

"Is. Hey, Stu, how y'doin'? See these good women'er takin' care of you. Here Bobby didn't make it?"

"He didn't, I'm afraid. Good to see you, Captain. Tell me how it's goin' with th' general's campaigns." The boy hid the revolver he'd trained on the approaching sounds back under his blankets.

"Got some big plans for goin' north soon. Part of our job is t'distract th' Unions while he rides up thataway. Oh, got some bad news, I'm 'fraid: Colonel Darby got hisself ambushed in Holly Springs, why I'm on this raid. Knew you two were close."

"Oh, that's bad; he was one of our best." Stuart was silent, remembering this mentor. "Yes, he was courting my cousin 'Quilla after his wife died. So sorry to hear that. Guess 'Quilla's ma will keep Angus, raise him like she's been doing."

"S'posed t' see them when we git t' Byhalia, figger how t'git rid of Thorsen. But first thing's t'put you in a wagon, move out 'fore th' Yanks find us. Got near forty men, wanta hit 'em here in Hernando hard's we can, then skedaddle east."

"Been thinkin' about that, Cap'n," Susan said. "Whyn't I drive th' wagon, be Stu's ma. You got 'nolder man along could be his pa? He c'd be our boy, got hisself shot out huntin'.'"

"Might work. We got Gus Varner f'm Pontotoc. But you wanta ride right up thar in th' open? Could git mean, th' Unions run onto us." He wasn't sure about this—woman in the thick of what could well be a shootout.

"I'd say, with Miss Susan along, it'd be the Yanks'll hafta watch out for their hides, Cap'n," Stuart informed him. "Wouldn't wanta be in her gunsights."

"Well, th' gin'ral, he thinks a lotta all you sisters. You know him b'fore th' war?"

"Not really, but we've kept track of him, from on back. That's a sharp feller; wisht Richmond would give him 'n army to work with. Man ain't ever lost a battle, way we hear it." Larkin affirmed that record, including some of the general's colorful episodes, while they were together.

But the young captain was concerned with the scout Eli's report that Hernando was heavily fortified, bristling with Union troops, cannon, and cavalry everywhere. A meaningful strike seemed impossible, a suicide mission by any logic. Wearing captured Union uniforms, a few of his men had also learned that bridges north and south of town were heavily guarded, eliminating the possibility of blowing them up.

"Guess we'll hafta pass on hittin' this buncha bluebellies, men. Ain't gonna git us all kilt for nothin'." He chafed at this reality, turning over in his mind any and all means of inflicting damage to the enemy. Maybe some opportunity would present itself.

The raiders contrived to steal a Union wagon that night, and liberate mules and harness to pull it. Again Eli Dobbins was able to slip into a barn between sentry rounds for the harness, while Larkin and another soldier timed their raid on the mule corral to lead two of them quietly away. They'd let a section of the pole corral down, then melted among the dozing animals, again while the guards were on the other side of the enclosure.

The sentry at the wagon yard didn't patrol, just stood there, watching, almost asleep from boredom. Eli moved quietly up behind him and knocked him out with a stout singletree, and five other troops wheeled the nearest wagon away. Later they smeared the U.S. Army sign over with mud, and were on their way.

The wagon meant they'd have to travel the roads, except where big fields could be used, avoiding suspected patrols. Scouts moved ahead to find ways through the woods and over ditches, lit by a half-moon.

Larkin sent half his men well north of the town, to try to find a deserted stretch of railroad track, to wreck, and if possible to raid a train, or at least burn it. No way had come to him to strike Hernando directly. The divided force was to meet well east of the town, travel together toward Byhalia full-strength.

Eli asked for permission to conduct a one-man raid of his own, though, back at the town.

"Galls me, Cap'n, havin' t'leave those Yanks fat 'n sassy thar. Like t'do a little damage to 'member us by."

"What you got in mind, Eli? Don't wanta lose you in some tomfoolery."

"Just a little fun, an' I'll be back in two hours, I guarantee it."

"You ain't, I'll come whup your ass 'fore they c'n hang you." The Indian grinned, raced away.

He'd seen the huge corral of cavalry horses very close to a tent city of Union soldiers, now asleep with minimal guards. Tying his horse, he slipped like a dark shadow among the animals, reasoning that the sentries would expect any enemy to come from outside. Quietly, he dismantled a section of the rail fence nearest the camp, having to lie prone twice to escape notice by a patrolling guard.

Then he pricked several horses with the point of his knife, causing them to squeal in pain and lunge toward the opening. He reinforced the beginnings of a stampede with blows to the rumps of more as he worked his way back through them to make his escape opposite.

More than a hundred spooked, wild Union horses thundered through the closely-pitched tents, ripping them apart, trampling sleeping troops, shaking the ground like an earthquake. Eli reached his own mount and sped away to rejoin the Lancers, well ahead of schedule.

"Didn't hardly miss me, didja, Cap'n?"

"You go somewhere? Orders was to stay tight here. Wasn't they?" Ambrose Larkin slapped his scout on the back.

Stuart Nicholson was cushioned on hay, after being carried from the fallen shed. Larkin was surprised that nobody had discovered him there, these many days, and asked Susan about that, since there were both whites and Blacks wandering the territory now, displaced from everywhere.

"Wal, this's not far f'm where there was a shootout some years back, buncha slave catchers killed. Folks've shied away from around here every since, 'fraid of ghosts an' all."

Well, I'm not gonna ask 'bout that, not a word. An' I knew you wimmen were hidin' that Yank soldier back at th' house. But Gin'ral Forrest would've beat my young butt hard if I'd come down on th' man, after hearin' how he spoke up for Stuart. Guess some Yankees'er better'n others, like some Confeds are.

Gus Varner rode with Susan on the wagon that night, with the story about taking their boy to Byhalia to Doc John McRaven, who they'd heard was the best with gunshot wounds. And they refined their details about how he'd gotten himself shot in the first place. Sure, climbed over a fence hunting, and pulled the rifle up after him and hammer snagged, gun went off. Happened to folks all the time.

Twice the cavalcade eluded patrols their scouts had seen, by detouring into woods far enough to remain hidden. Then, nearing Byhalia, one of them reported a large group, riding right toward them. There wasn't time to evade them, there being deep ditches on both sides of this hilly section of the road. Larkin determined to bluff his way, Bedford Forrest style.

"You two jist keep on, Gus, an' we'll all fade off either side, close enough, but outta sight. If it gits hot, we're in for a fight, no help fer it. Countin' on you both t'talk yer way th'u this'n, but they'll be all lit up with torches, an' we c'n pick 'em off if ain't too many of 'em.

"You all right with this?" Gus asked Susan. He was about to suggest she just get down and stay down, but she disabused him of that notion. Without a word, she produced her pistol from the shawl-covered waistband holster at her back, and hefted a breech-loading rifle the women had come by, from a later slave catcher who'd not been lucky.

"Reckon I c'n handle my part, Gus. That arm gonna slow you down?"

"Naw, been able to hit whut I aim at agin, last few weeks. But let's do ever'thing we can t'talk these Unions outta ennything rough." She agreed, watching the road ahead, which now included a torch-bearing lead rider.

"Halt, there!" a sergeant called, reining his horse a few feet ahead of them. "Where you people going, middle of the night like this?"

"Tryin' t'git our boy to th' doc, sir," Gus explained. "Got hisself shot climbin' a fence, an' we hope t'git t'Doc John 'fore he goes off."

"I see. Let me see that wound, boy." He rode close, reached, pulled the blanket off Stuart, saw the bandages, now tinged with red from the jolting of the wagon. "You say the hammer snagged?"

"Yessir, I stumbled some, an' it got me. Shoulda known better." It still hurt, so Stuart didn't have to pretend, with the pain.

"Yes, don't ever do that. Cousin of mine had the same thing happen." He peered closer. "But you're military age, and that could just as easily be a gunshot from a skirmish. Hope you folks aren't lying to me." He backed his horse, hand on his holstered pistol.

"Nossir," Susan spoke up. "We've stayed outta this here war. Never had no slaves, even helped a few escape. No, we ain't out t'do no harm t'th' Union, sir."

"Really? You helped runaways? I've heard there were folks like that, few and far between. Where'd you hide them?"

"Not in th' barn, nor th' sheds. Used th' swamp, on down f'm our place a couple times, pertended they was on loan, some of 'em. Didn't make us pop'lar with th' neighbors, none, I c'n tell you."

"I should say not." The sergeant debated this for a few moments, then decided, since a gut-shot Reb probably wouldn't survive, anyway. And if there were ever poor small-farm people, these were surely them. "Well, you folks go ahead. I've heard of that doctor, McRaven, I believe, working with our Union surgeon some. But get passes for your way back, and good luck with that gunshot: could've killed you."

Gus nodded, spoke to the mules, hoping this man wouldn't notice how well-fed they were, or the smeared over brands, wagon sides, which they'd splintered somewhat. His hand was inches from his revolver, and the rifles were out of sight. Susan's deep sunbonnet defied any identifying her as too young to have a grown son, although yes, there were teenage mothers all over.

Ambrose Larkin kept his rifle trained on the Union sergeant's heart, and his men also had chosen targets. Now they relaxed, hearing the sounds of receding hoofbeats on the dirt road. He rode back alongside the wagon.

"Looks like you two fooled 'em," he praised. "Been a right rough gunfight if y'hadn't of. You all right, Stu? Saw that feller pokin' at you."

"Little sore, but doing well's could be hoped for, Cap'n." He too, had clutched his pistol, there under the hay. Larkin nodded, rode on.

"Where'd you come up 'ith that 'bout helpin' slaves git away, Miss Susan? That's whut got us by." He was all admiration at this ploy.

"Jist thought it up. Figgered it'd set well with a Yankee. They think we're all big slaveholders, beatin' 'em regular, not feedin' 'em. Worth a try."

Behind them in the wagon, Stuart Nicholson suppressed a grin.

~ * ~

In Memphis, Harlan and Anna Sewell served alongside others from the little church and the Shelby Institute, ladling soup and giving bread to the throngs of homeless Blacks who'd wandered off the plantations. No one wanted these people, who had followed the Union armies as they swept through the region. Their dreams of being freed, taken in and fed by the conquerors and the apparently mythical Lincoln, with his hatful of gold coins for every field hand, had been only so much smoke, and now they were literally dying. Bone-thin, lifeless bodies were found daily in ditches out along all the roads south into Mississippi and farther into Tennessee.

It was heart-wrenching for both Sewells, but Anna felt it more deeply. Here was the cherished freedom, and it meant less than nothing. She reflected on all the years of danger, dedication, tireless work by the Route members. But so few had been helped, compared to these hordes. *We did all we could, but this is disaster, this grim reality, this waste of human lives.* Why couldn't the Union, now so near victory, somehow take care of those so many had cried out to free?

She remembered what Josh, the Taylors' slave who'd escaped through the Route years before, had said: *"Dat seem kinda two-*

faced". Indeed. And faced with these walking spectres, she would almost rather have seen them back on the plantations, at least fed and housed, clothed.

But no, this madness had to end. The good Christians in the North had to come to their senses soon, reach out to these stumbling, starving, rootless children of God they'd cried out to free. Had to, didn't they? Surely?

And in the meantime, she and Harlan, she and these few, must do what they could, with begged food, hoarded scraps of worn clothing, whatever shelter they could contrive. Give, when there was nothing to give. Feed, when there was no food; aid, when all aid was gone.

True, the stalwarts from the Route were doing all they could: John Kellog, the Baptist minister and his wife Miriam were there, feeding all they could at their church. Tom Brannon and his new wife came and served alongside the others at the institute, and wily Archibald Bancroft often produced food almost miraculously, from somewhere. Even Ike and Lola Evans, distant friends who'd provided firewood, journeyed into town as often as they could, bringing whatever they could grow or gather, to the Sewells' doorstep.

The surprisingly most adept at gathering food and clothing turned out to be Eli Dobbins, he of the nerves and debilitating timidity. Somehow he managed to elicit sympathy from the residents of the town, rarely coming away from an importuning, wheedling visit without at least a small parcel.

But daily, more dark shapes arose from slept-in doorways, under-bridge shelters, sheds, even woodpiles, to roam the streets begging, asking for work, lost, dazed.

At night their faces haunted Anna, and she was kept awake by the moans of the few they had been able to shelter in their tiny house. *When will it end? When can we breathe again? When will we have a semblance of sanity again?*

But there seemed to be no end. Many, many sickened and died, many more trudged up the dusty roads off the farms, out of the fields the blue soldiers had conquered. She saw the disdain, the pitiless treatment of her people at the hands of the soldiers, and lately, of the Northern opportunists flocking into the occupied town.

Yes, intent on riches, like black vultures in the sky, ready to pounce on any victim. They treated the Blacks worse than any Southerners she'd known had, in this chaos of their conquering. The disgust settled deep inside her.

Dear God, don't let all this make me cynical, hardened. Don't let it make me deranged. I need you, Father, to face these starving faces. Provide for us please, in our need. And somehow, she managed to stagger through another day, she and Harlan growing leaner, hungrier themselves, as they shared, did without, gave. And at night, seeking sleep, pressed tightly against this man of God, she drew strength from him and from her faith.

And there were the degrading insults to be faced, ignored if possible. The Union troops never failed to regard her as some white man's bed plaything, a description all attractive Black women had hurled at them.

"You come on with us, gal. We'll find you somethin' to eat, mebbe do a little work for pay, if you be nice t'us. Why, we like fancy gals, don't we, boys?" Guffaws, further insults. "Bet you got them bucks linin' up, dancin' 'round for a piece of you; why don't you get yourself some white, now we set you free? Be glad to oblige." Crude gestures, nastiness overflowing.

And Harlan, despite his proper English, his ministry, was universally looked upon as an ignorant, freed slave field hand, no matter how he put on this 'disguise', as they termed it.

"Don't you go puttin' on airs with me, you Black bastard! Ain't one of you worth th' powder an' shot to blow you all to hell. Git yer ass on back t'Africa, whar you b'long, an' quit dirtyin' this earth!"

Harlan bore this with all the dignity he could summon, turning away. *The other cheek, Lord: I'll turn it. I will. But You know I want desperately to rip this subhuman's throat out, consign him to the deserved hell the other filth he and his ilk have brought with them.* He'd shake his head to clear it, edging past or retreating, fearful of inciting more of a target for this kind of contempt.

~ * ~

The weary but successful Larkin's Lancers reached the McRaven plantation early, where the mistress somehow produced piles of biscuits, two hams hidden from foragers, fed them, directed them to a hidden swamp with an island in it, to hide. There they made plans to remove the hated general Harwood Thorsen. Young Harvey was able to give them specifics of the Union-held occupation of Byhalia.

Larkin hadn't been able to tackle the heavily-fortified Hernando garrison, but he and his troops had cut rail and telegraph lines, harried outposts, doing the work his general was famous for. And of course spreading the word that he was actually Forrest, who was feared, from Union general Sherman on down clear to the lower ranks. This Confederate raider was by then far north, a scourge of Union forts and their harsh occupying of towns.

Susan was also in on the attack that led to Larkin's shooting of Harwell Thorson in his headquarters office residence, who'd foolishly gone for his gun after being confronted by Larkin. His aides had rushed off to fight a decoy fire at a derelict cotton gin.

She and Gus had positioned their wagon in front of a store just as the fire broke out. In the chaos, they subdued a storekeeper, with help from two Confederate soldiers disguised as hangers-on, and filled their wagon during the confusion that followed.

This along with the confiscation of other Union stores, horses, mules, wagons, effected by others of the raiders. Altogether, the raid was a success, with no Confederate casualties. And the hated General Thorsen was replaced with a more reasonable colonel named Blair. Harvey lamented his not being able to join them.

That young man had also managed, over many weeks early in the year of 1863, to dig an escape tunnel from the plantation house, with the determined help of his two sisters 'Quilla and Ophelia. These ferried the loose dirt out and down beyond the house, scattering it, covering it with leaves and branches to disguise it.

The tunnel had allowed the escape the year before of Colonel Winfield Darby, who'd visited to see his young son Angus at their house. And not incidentally, to pay court to young 'Quilla McRaven.

Later on, a drunken band of undisciplined Union soldiers had raided the place, and the family itself fled through that tunnel to safety. And were barely able to put out the house fire the rowdy crew had set, with the help of Hetty and Sam Barnes. That reported outrage had been part of Forrest's determination to remove Thorsen.

And so a major blow had been struck by Ambrose and his men, concluding their cross-state raid, although by that stage in the conflict, it constituted only a postponing of the inevitable. And a later ruse by this ragged command had managed to retake beleaguered Holly Springs for a short period. Posing as Forrest himself with the aid of the townspeople, the rumor helped rout the occupying force, decimated by contingents being sent to repair the railroad both north and south. The Lancers had trapped a Union supply train in the town, stripping it of food, supplies, armaments. They'd held there until reinforcing blue forces retook the region, then melted off into the still largely-wooded region east.

Twenty-one

Horatio Barber, formerly known as the slave Abel, had found Chicago to be a rough, rowdy city, dirty, extremely cold, and generally unfriendly. He'd kept telling himself that any discomfort was worth it, just to be free. Free to walk the streets—well, some of the streets—and free to work and get paid. He soon learned that pay was less than his white counterparts received for the same work, but he was wise enough not to complain.

Although the only work he could find, despite the education he'd received, which had taken more years while employed as a laborer, was more labor. His hopes of studying law or medicine, or of becoming an actual college professor, just hadn't materialized. The supposed opportunities for Blacks in Chicago, he discovered, were largely myth.

But he saved every dollar he earned, except for contributing to the family he'd been able to stay with throughout college, food and lodging. Bare necessities only, toward a goal that had crystallized in his mind shortly after graduation. Not try another Northern city, for he'd heard they were all much alike: not ready for free Blacks.

No, he'd return to Memphis, to the southside neighborhood where his friends Tom and Anna, both now married, lived, those who'd taught him, encouraged him. And he'd teach at the Shelby Institute also, to help others like him reach their goals. Perhaps, in a few years, this intolerant nation would accept qualified people of his race. He could think of no better place to use his talents.

And this next chapter of Horatio's life seemed the best he could hope for, despite the war that was still raging, and the shortages, the reduced enrollment at the school, the doing without, which he'd become accustomed to in Chicago, but much worse. Horatio found himself toiling away beside Harlan Sewell at whatever degrading work they could find, for little pay.

He was constantly amazed at how well this man of God bore the insults, the condescension, the cursing, for no other reason than their race. Oh, Horatio'd grown up a slave, knew they were not considered even human, but not till Chicago, and now back in Memphis at the hands of the occupying Union soldiers, had it been so hard.

"We must bear it, Horatio, for our God will not allow us to suffer much longer. This war will end, and we can hope some semblance of civilization will return." The two men had returned to the Sewell cottage after a day of toil in a wagon yard.

"What if the South wins? Can it ever go back to the life we knew, suffocating as that was?"

"No, I fear our world has forever changed, and we must have faith that it will be for the better, no matter which side wins. Besides, I fear the inevitable conclusion, given the North's superior manpower, arms; a matter of time, surely."

"You fear the Union's winning? I should think the opposite." Horatio was shaking his head in dismay.

"Yes, despite the canker of slavery, which is also of course present to a lesser degree in the Union states, the planter culture here has been jewel-like. A Northern victory will result in a priority to destroy all aspects of that culture, the architecture, the art, music, literature. I'm afraid we will see hate-blinded, rampant, vengeful barbarism everywhere. There will be no distinction made between non-slaveholders, kind, generous souls, and the worst of the Simon LeGrees. The Northern soldiers, too often with the support of their commanders, already see the proud houses of the gentry as symbols of all they hate, and they're burning them wholesale.

"And the ruthless tactics of generals like Sheridan and Sherman, making war on the civilians, unheard of in history, will become the norm, with a South beaten to its knees, defenseless.

"I didn't know what to expect when I journeyed here from Boston, but I suspected a twisted picture of the region and its inhabitants from the propaganda of the press. What I found was actually a refreshing lifestyle, totally foreign to the driven, impersonal, industrial, often inhuman conditions of the Northern cities. Again, apart from slavery, I found this was where I was meant to be, and I fear it will become a wasteland."

Just then Anna Sewell called the two to supper, having returned from helping at a soup kitchen at the institute. Horatio was a frequent visitor to this couple, living at nearby Sayles boardinghouse. They washed up, then presented themselves for the meal, knowing it would be scant. To their surprise, there was ham, sweet potatoes, cornbread.

"Ike and Lola Evans, God bless them, came in from their farm and brought us food, just before I left to help at the school. I took some of it to donate, but we'll still eat well enough for a while."

"They're truly wonderful people," Harlan told Horatio. "Bringing food, supplying us and the Institute with firewood, always ready to help. I like to think of them as the real Southerners, not having much, but willing to give, to help."

"That's certainly not my impression of most of the planters," the young man demurred. "Oh, they were courteous to each other, but considered themselves above the rest of humanity, I'm afraid. And of course we slaves weren't even viewed as human at all."

"But there were and are exceptions, Horatio," the minister pointed out. "Our friends the McRavens freed their slaves many years ago, after educating them so they could compete out in the world. In fact, Anna was raised along with their daughters, as equal as any white children."

There was another reason Horatio had returned to Memphis from the barely-tolerant North. There was the girl he'd studied alongside at the Institute he'd become friends with, and he was quite curious about where her education had led her. Samantha Echols had been one of the outstanding students, and he remembered many of their discussions on everything from religion to commerce. After he'd left for Chicago, he'd written her several times, even suggesting she travel to that city when she was older, for its opportunities for those of their race.

Samantha had replied that she had no desire to move to that city, having heard that it was a cold, dirty center full of slaughterhouses and probably few who would welcome her. In that she had been completely correct, of course, and eventually their correspondence lagged, then stopped.

Now Horatio learned the young woman was indeed still here in Memphis, still single, and currently employed as tutor to a banker's children. And even with the war's devastation, that family had been able to keep her, seeing the excellent results of her teaching. *So I won't rest until I've at least tried to rekindle our friendship, whether successfully or not. She may have simply closed the door on what we shared, and is not interested in teaming up: two Blacks trying to break into the system.*

Not having experience with young women, he decided to confide in Anna, and ask her help. He had learned early on that this was a wise woman, and would surely steer him in the right direction through this uncharted territory of the heart.

And it turned out the Sewells had invited Samantha to their home often, and kept up with her in her new life. Horatio greeted this news with a feeling that perhaps this hoped-for relationship might indeed get off to a start: the stage seemed set.

"Simplest thing in the world to invite her to supper," Anna told him, "and we can make your being here a surprise. Of course it will be up to her whether she'll welcome rekindling the friendship, and you'll have to be prepared for her decision. She's quite the independent young lady now, knows her own mind."

"I expected nothing less, given her self-confidence as a child. I just hope I won't make too bad an impression, with my failed Chicago *Savoir*."

"Just don't give even a hint of superiority, which I know you won't. And try not to let your Northern experiences spill over. From what you've told us, that chapter of your life might best be put behind you; the two of you will be equal in every way, so be aware of that always." She gave him a friendly pat on the shoulder, sensing the nerves he was trying to control.

It was a Saturday, Samantha's half-day, and she arrived with a bouquet of flowers and even cupcakes, plainly but neatly dressed, very much the poised twenty-three-year-old woman of their diminished world. Anna met her at the cottage door, with a smile she couldn't quench.

"However did you manage cupcakes, dear girl? We haven't seen flour in months! Or shouldn't I ask, you devious thing? Come in now, and we have a surprise for you."

"Let me guess: you've discovered Jesus' miracle of the loaves and fishes for supper? Or your garden has somehow exploded into bounty while your backs were turned? I'm on pins and needles." She gave her mentor a hug.

And caught sight of Horatio, who'd risen, a tentative smile on his face. Not recognizing him, she was a bit taken aback, but recovered quickly. *About thirty, not bad looking, as if that should matter. Is our Anna playing matchmaker here? Surely not: she knows better, with me. But I confess to being intrigued.*

"Samantha, I'm quite sure you don't know who I am, and I admit I wouldn't have recognized you on any street. It's Horatio Barber." He took her hand, bowed in the old manner. She registered his deep voice, and for a moment thought it was Harlan who'd spoken. No, it was... it really *was* him, her old classmate. *Can it have been that long? And now here, in the middle of this nasty war? Surprise, indeed. And will he be all citified, surely with a family, here among the enemy-occupied lowly? Well, I'm glad to see him, anyway. Just hope he hasn't deserted his heritage, stained as it's been, for the other side.*

"Hello there, stranger. You're about the last person I expected to see here in our war-torn wasteland. Visiting? Or have you returned permanently to the scene of our youth?"

"Well, I enjoyed about all I could stand of Chicago; you were wise to decline to join me there. And I don't believe I made one friend there in over a dozen years, which may say more about my woefully lacking personality than about any prospects. I've known for some time that this is home, and always will be. And for you also, it appears."

"At least I haven't been seduced by visions of paradise up in the magic North... Oh, that didn't come out right: no innuendos." She realized how that must've sounded.

"None suspected. I'll admit to having tried to aim high, but I was slammed back down to earth soon enough. I fear our race may have another century or so to go for any kind of real equality. But tell me, if you will, how has your experience been here in Memphis?"

"No change from before, except our supposed status, with Lincoln's worthless declaration. And with this damnable war on, the white folks are suffering right along with us. I have a wonderful family to work for, the children are learning, they pay me, most of the time. That about sums it up." She shrugged.

Anna watched this tentative reunion closely, and couldn't guess how it would turn out. She took Samantha into the kitchen with her, leaving Horatio to Harlan and their endless talk of the war's progress. There, she enlightened the girl as to his singleness, and that he seemed genuinely to want to serve in the capacity of teacher at the Institute.

"Tom and I liked him as a student," she told her, "and yes, we still like him, although far be it from us to try to influence you, Miss Independence. Of course nobody is having much of a life just now around here, but surely this war will end soon. The reports we get spell the inevitable end for the Confederacy: The Union just has too much more of everything."

"Let's not talk about the war, dear Anna; I'm quite sure our counterparts are dissecting it thoroughly as we speak. Oh, my, turnips! And surely not ham? How in the world...?"

"Jenny and Susan Blaine actually walked all the way from DeSoto County with gifts for us, stayed over. They can't have much themselves, but they're so resourceful, I pity the Yankee forager who raids them. Kate stayed home to guard the place, but promised to visit us next time. They have this wily neighbor couple, the Ingrums, who also provide for them, have sort of taken them to raise, and he's always able to find provisions out of thin air. Not, I'm certain, always legally."

"I remember the sisters from before the war. Pioneer stock, if ever there was that. Apparently surviving, and true to form, sharing. God bless them."

"And Ike and Lola Evans have helped, too. It's folks like those who have made these years bearable, really. We see so many actually starving, dying by the roadsides, abandoned. It's enough to destroy a sane person's faith."

"Don't say that. The rest of us took to you and Harlan as our role models, our examples of the finest motives and actions. Tell me you'll never actually despair."

"I'll try; that's about all I can promise. We're just so glad your banker family has been able to keep you and at least feed you through all this. Are they doing well? Or as well as could be expected?"

"I suppose the latter. Mrs. Shelton gives what they can to the shelters, as you know, but they're making do like almost everyone. Now, shall we feed those hungry men?"

~ * ~

Horatio did indeed join the faculty of the Shelby Institute, although headmaster Bancroft warned him the pay would be little and sometimes not at all. He'd expected this, and continued to work with Harlan at whatever they could find. Which was usually chores no white man would do. The minister often reminded his friend that nobody had ever promised them this life would be easy.

Tom Brannon and his wife welcomed the young man, and it turned out that they had also been visited often by Samantha. Abigail Brannon saw the makings of a match between the two former students, and she and Anna conspired to help this along.

As the reverend would note years later, Horatio may have thought he was making the decisions, but with those two at work behind the scenes, that was a myth.

"One might even say the same for Samantha, though, my dear," Anna had informed him. "If ever there was a match to be made, theirs was it."

But it wasn't to be all smooth sailing. First of all, there was the young lady's independence—she wasn't going to tumble for the first eligible man who came along, she repeatedly told herself.

Then there was Hortatio's real concern that he wouldn't be able to support a wife the way a man should. Maybe after the war…

"I'm afraid there never will be a right time," Anna counseled him. "Doors aren't going to open magically for any of us when the shooting stops; it'll be much as it was before. Probably the best we can hope for is increased support for the Institute, and the little increased pay we can expect. So my advice to you is to launch your suit now, with the realization that you'll both have to endure a lot more making do, but with the hope that our situation will indeed get better."

"Well, I've given up on being treated like an educated person, but I hate that Samantha has to go through being insulted, treated like a non-human. I don't know how you two put up with it."

"What choice do we have? The occupying troops are much worse than the local whites, and now they're winning, so they'll grind us all down even more, Black and white alike. We're quite sure that they'll keep thousands of idle soldiers here for years on some pretense, and martial law will be no law, with no higher authority to answer to."

"I suspect you two married on the eve of this war, no doubt trusting in God to take care of you, whatever was to happen. And you're telling me to trust in Him the same way. Am I right?"

Anna looked at her husband for his reaction, albeit knowing what it would be. Harlan was a rock in his faith, in his life, and the two of them had weathered all the meanness, all the degrading treatment the war had thrown at them, and it had not shaken their love nor their faith.

"It's your choice," the reverend said, "but I'd say, if you don't at least try, despite all the thorns, you'll regret it for the rest of your life." And so Horatio had sent a note, asking to call on the lady. Which he feared she might refuse, and if she accepted, it'd be awkward in the white banker's parlor. Harlan and Anna didn't know the family, nor could guess what reception he might encounter there. *So it's into the lion's mouth, for better or worse. And if she won't consider me, that'll at least simplify things. But I won't give up easily. These friends can always invite her here again, and I'll make the most of whatever time I can seize then. And if the best we can have together is half what they have, that'll be paradise.*

And so it worked out that, after a nervous evening spent with Samantha at the Shelton house, with their children giggling at the earnest fellow come to call on their governess, other arrangements were made. Not that this family resented or condescended to Horatio, but both the hopefuls were quite on edge.

Abigail Brannon soon invited both of them to their house, they went, and were left completely alone, to talk about whatever came to mind. And a lot did.

And of course Anna and Harlan practically made it routine for the younger people to spend Sunday after church with them, to eat together, engage in lengthy discussions, and to get to know each other better. They watched the progress of the war closely, at once anticipating and fearing its end, and how that would affect their relationship.

First of all, we'll need a place to live, Horatio thought. Samantha could continue her work at the Sheltons, and he could teach as much as possible at the Institute, but he wasn't about to ensconce his new bride in Sayles' boarding house. And Memphis was jammed with aimless former slaves, adrift, hopeless in their new freedom. Living in root cellars, shacks, haylofts, alongside the roads leading to town.

At length, he resolved to wait until war's end, then he'd propose, now fairly certain she'd accept, and they'd tackle that concern together. As of course they would every hurdle that lay ahead.

Twenty-two

The war-between-the-states, the rebellion, the war of Union aggression, the un-Civil war, was over.

General Robert E. Lee had surrendered what was left of his army in April, 1865, after defenses around Richmond and Petersburg fell. In the ensuing week, he had tried to march his army south and west to join Joe Johnston, to continue the conflict from the cover of the mountains, but Grant's superior numbers dogged him, surrounded him, and finally at Appomatox, forced him to capitulate. A few days later, after Lincoln's assassination, Johnston surrendered to Sherman in North Carolina.

So began the long, tortuous labor of the Southerners' trying to rebuild their region, their lives. With martial law in every hamlet and town, with arrogant Union soldiers protecting Northern opportunists bent on ravaging the destitute region, Reconstruction, as it was derisively called, was worse in many ways for its victims than the war had been.

Planters lost their holdings for alleged or real unpaid taxes. Illegally elected officials, often illiterate ex-slaves with Northern carpetbaggers behind them, fleeced the starving population further. Little redress was possible for wrongs to the ex-Confederates, with the Union army ever ready to enforce the most outlandish claims by the Northern vultures. These opportunists came into the region with intent to plunder, and often with little but one bag, hence the name.

To the Blaine sisters, little was changed from wartime. They managed to pay their taxes barely, and lived as they had always lived, sparingly. The receipts issued by foraging Union troops during the war were largely ignored when they and others tried to claim replacements for their mules, wagon, other livestock, and the provisions continuously taken. Finally, they were given one mule, after repeated harangues by each sister in turn.

"Wore 'em down, I reckon," Kate declared. "Never git 'nother cent outta enny of 'em, but reckon we gotta do with what we got."

"Galls me fierce," Susan fumed. "Don't seem t'matter whether folks was slave-beatin' planters er dirt farmers like us; all treated like trash by th' Union, 'cause hell, they *won*."

"Heard Miss 'Quilla had papers claimin' more'n thirty thousand dollars damage, all tole," Jenny volunteered. "Fin'ly hadda settle fer six hunderd."

"S'prised she got that much."

"Well, that son-in-law of hers, th' lawyer, he kep' after 'em till they fin'ly coughed up that much. Won't enny of us git whut we lost."

There had been one pleasant result of the sisters' wartime experiences. John Weller of the Union army, late of their care, had written often, telling of his post-recovery assignment to St. Louis and a desk job, and his subsequent return to Ohio. The letters were to all three sisters, but his attention was clearly focused on Susan. That disappointed Jenny somewhat, but she was both curious and glad her sister seemed to be responding finally to the attentions of a man.

Susan had dismissed the first missives as just courtesy, but as they kept coming, she began to write in turn. Within a year of war's end, John Weller had asked if he might take the cars to Hernando for a visit.

"Well now," Kate marveled. "Reg'lar courtship happenin' here, girl. You serious 'bout Yankee John?"

"Truth be tole, I dunno," Susan answered. "Reckon I like th' feller well 'nuff, but don't know jist how t'might turn out. Have been thinkin' some 'bout a man an' little uns, 'fore I git too ole, but didn't see much chancet of it." She had maintained her friendship with the McRavens, and Harvey, now sixteen, was still her favorite friend. They had hunted together, worked together, become close.

"Wal, 'd hate t' see y'go off to Ohio, girl," Jenny lamented, "but I'd say, y'git a man'll take keer of you, y'better jump at it. Good un hard t' find, I kin shore tell you."

"Dunno 'bout that goin' off up North," Susan mused. "Cold there, folks talk funny. Ex-Confed, prob'ly be looked down on worse'n some th' snobby planters used to, hereabouts."

"Bible says 'Whither thou goest'", her sister reminded her.

"Yeah, but y'know, that c'd cut both ways. Reckon I'll jist hide an' watch, like always. John might mebbe git a look at all of us now, ragged, pore, wore out, an' say jist fergit it. Bound t'be gals in Ohio got a lot more t'offer than us ole maids."

Kate eyed her sister. Susan would be a prize for any man with common sense. Not much the girl couldn't do; now that her talents also included blacksmithing. Maybe still could have a couple young uns, unlike the two older of them. But going off up North, that'd be hard all right, after all the years they'd done for themselves, taken care of each other here. *Well, have t'see what happens, like she says...*

When the Ohioan arrived, it was in a new suit of clothes, and he was carrying packages for everyone. The women opened the gifts with unfeigned delight, discovering clothes, shoes, and hard-to-find items like scissors, kitchen ware, good soap.

"Well, John Weller, you've 'bout brought us Christmas," Susan declared. "Things must be prosperin' in Ohio."

"Doin' well enough, but well, it gets lonesome," he admitted. "You can't know how glad I am t'see all of you. Owe you m'life, and can't ever make up f'r that. Little enough I c'n bring a few things. Hope I got near th' right sizes."

"Oh, little cuttin' an' sewin'll set ever'thing t'rights," Kate assured him. "An' yer sure welcome. Been what, two years now?"

"Has. That desk thing in St. Louis about bored me t' death, but didn't last long. Now, I've heard from others b'sides you, how bad th' Union is treatin' you folks, an' it makes me ashamed. Lot worse on account of Lincoln bein' killed I know, an' that bunch in Washington runnin' wild. Wish there was more I could do, y'know?"

"Jist gotta let it wear out, I reckon", the practical Susan said. "Won't be fun, but we c'n handle it: always have." She left him an opening for whatever he had to say next.

John Weller was not exactly shy, but at forty-one, he had grown used to bachelorhood, and was not in a hurry to make his case. After moving into the tiny attic room, which would have been unheard of before the war, he threw himself into helping the women on the farm, planting, clearing, building fences. And after viewing their one worn plow and the middling mule, he walked to town one day and came back with a serviceable wagon and team, and a good turning plow.

"Now don't let me hear a worda protest," he warned. "I figure it's just fair, me havin' Union back pay, an' you folks not gettin' reparations for army foragin'. And like I said, there's no way I could repay you for puttin' me back t'gether that time."

The sisters were dumbfounded. They tried to cling to a pride that would refuse the gifts, but were unable to pull it off.

"Well John, fer a Yankee, you're a helluva man," Susan declared, and in front of her sisters, she hugged him, hard. His face reddened, and both sisters grinned.

The upshot of the visit, which included several outings: square dances, pie suppers, church socials, was that John Weller departed with a promise from Susan Blaine to be his wife, though at an indefinite date. The proposal had followed a hard day's work in the fields, when the two were seated on the farmhouse porch among the fireflies, long after the other sisters had gone to bed.

"But I got to tell you, John, I'll hafta study on that pullin' up stakes an' goin' off up to Ohio. Cain't ask you t'give up all you got there an' come here, but mebbe we'd both best think on it s'more 'fore we set it in stone." He'd agreed, reflecting that there were no stones in this part of Mississippi. And departed with a light heart and some heavy decisions to make.

~ * ~

True to his plan, Horatio Barber had asked Samantha to marry him, and she'd agreed. The news of war's end had everyone in a jubilant mood, even though the South had lost. There was hope, however vain, that with the Union restored, trade would resume, there would be prosperity, work for everyone, wages, rebuilding, a future.

They planned a wedding very soon, just as soon as they could find a place to live. Headmaster Archibald Bancroft solved that for them at least temporarily, by allowing them to set up their housekeeping in a small cottage he'd had built for home economics classes. The Institute was running at a greatly reduced capacity, and the focus had been reduced to more vital training in the trades, with homemaking phased out. The school had actually become little more than a major soup kitchen for the homeless Blacks thronging into the city. Anna and Harlan Sewell were still helping, with Horatio, Samantha, the Brannons and other concerned citizens in trying to clothe these refugees, feed them, find work for them.

In general, the occupying Union army still wanted no part of dealing with these tides of human deprivation. However, under hard pressure from abolitionists in the North and the pressing need, provisions did find their way to the destitute, through church groups and other institutions, with only occasional graft or interference. The obvious thinking was it was worth something to the army not to have to deal directly with this result of its conquest of the land.

"Teacher, huh? Come teach me, gal... I'm ready." From a dirty, disheveled tooth-gapped and drunken lout dressed in stained blue. The insults went on, the humiliation. But Anna endured it, tried not to let the degradation show. Samantha too, on the rarer occasions she was able to help, suffered also.

Even with their two men present, these were all stared at, muttered at, resented more by the Northerners than the natives of the city who'd grown used to them. It hadn't been easy before the war; it was worse now. What would life be like after this insane occupation was finally over?

Still, the reverend preached patience and humility from his pulpit, taught it to the students who, the war over, flocked into the school. *Nowhere are we promised this life will be easy. We must be truly thankful for the good we receive. God is just, in His own time. No, the liberators of our race are not pure or ideal, but God is just.*

Just.

The Sewells had had no children. They did not outwardly regret this, but of course knew their life would have been fuller with that blessing. But as with everything, the minister accepted what he saw as God's will, and Anna had no choice but to concur. They had practically adopted the couple Horatio/Samantha, of whom they were both intensely proud. And both could continue to pour their love and skills into teaching the children of others, and work toward that day somewhere in the future when at last their people would know true equality.

~ * ~

For the McRavens, the waning weeks of the war had held a crisis. Young Harvey and his best friend, Daniel McGraw, at fifteen, had both run off and eventually found their way to Forrest's cavalry in Alabama. They had successfully blown up a powder magazine in Byhalia, and escaped in the resulting melee with fine horses.

Two small kegs of gunpowder they'd stolen hadn't proven enough to blow a railroad culvert on the line running south to Holly Springs, but the caboose had disintegrated, and Union army payroll banknotes fluttered in the air. These, quickly gathered, had helped the Confederate scouts they'd met accept them into their ranks.

One set of family lore has it that the boys' parents sent word through their still-functioning clandestine connections and had them returned safely before they could officially enlist. Another, attested to by Harvey in his old age to a grandson, had them duly joining the Confederate forces and participating in Forrest's last battle at Selma, the only one he ever lost in the entire war. Then, given the surrender and the humiliating prospect of having to take the oath of loyalty to the Union, Forrest offered to expunge their names from the rolls.

They then slipped away, and along with an equally unrepentant Ambrose Larkin, who later married a local girl, returned to face their irate mothers. Family records are silent regarding their punishment.

But for this family, war and Reconstruction forever changed life. Gone were the high-fashion balls, the prideful cavaliers come on blooded mounts to court the many daughters, the old courtesy, the enduring legacies of the plantation era.

The death of her poet son Will had ravaged Tranquilla, who had endured, lost so much: two husbands, her closest daughter, both parents, and two sons as babies.

Young 'Quilla, torn by the loss of her nearest sibling, outwardly past her grieving for Winfield Darby, had later married Ed Richmond, a prewar suitor returned with a permanent limp. Her grandmother, having freed her slaves before the war at her husband's death, had also died a few months after the conflict. Sister Ophelia had tried—was still trying—to get into a medical school, and often assisted her brother John and brothers-in-law Marion and Lewis in their work. She became a widely-sought-after midwife in the region.

John, after the bloody nightmare of Shiloh in 1862—days following sleepless nights of hacking off mangled limbs, operating by feeble candlelight, trying to save dying boys—had taken to drink. He and the other doctors had formed a network of information—spying—that they then funneled to Confederate commanders, resulting in repeated but short-lived Southern victories. John had prided himself on holding his liquor better than his Union medical counterparts, with whom he often visited, while listening carefully to anything they might let slip about the plans of their superiors.

His wife Mary had died childless, pining for the old ways. Their ward Kate Walker, then grown, was urged, as was her husband by the dying wife, to marry and take care of each other. Shocked, at first they refused, but some time later this had occurred, and two sons were to be born to the couple. Neither of these married, and that branch of the family came to an end.

Eventually, the many other children and grandchildren of this family were to leave the land for the new mercantile and industrial roles of the surviving South, with one exception never to plow the soil again. That exception was Harvey, who married Sally Brunson, the younger sister of his late brother Will's fiancee, but eventually moved to the Arkansas River valley in that state.

Dan McGraw had also married a local girl, Catherine Babb, and they too, relocated to the mountains north of Ozark, Arkansas. The families were to keep in close touch over the ensuing years. In fact, Harvey's eldest son and Dan's eldest daughter were eventually to marry, to leave a wide range of descendants.

Tranquilla would keep in close touch with Anna and Harlan Sewell in Memphis, along with her extended family, many of whom had moved there. And of course would remain best friends with the Blaine sisters, while living on the remnants of her diminished plantation, until her death in 1879.

~ * ~

It was not long after John Weller's visit that he arrived again, unannounced this time, at the Blaines' farm. He was astride a handsome horse, and had but one small suitcase with him.

"Well ladies, I'm here," was all he said.

"Um, yes y'are," Susan replied, glad to see him, but mystified. "S'prised us." She didn't know what else to say. Neither did her sisters, who waited, bemused smiles on their faces. Only Kate was pretty sure what this meant.

"Now what I've got in mind, if it meets with all y'r approval that is, would be askin' if I c'd buy a piece of th' place for a house an' the start of a farm. I want to see if there's land joinin' this could be had first, an' that'd be even better. But I've sold m'place in Ohio, and have a few dollars for a start here. I'm hopin' some Federal money will help decide one of th' neighbors t'sell me a piece, add to this, maybe."

"Well then, John Weller," Susan had smiled, "welcome to Miss'ssippi." She gave him a huge hug.

In time a son was born to this couple, who indeed now occupied a new, painted house on the knoll from which Susan had first seen her future husband, wounded, in the briar patch below. This house was the combined effort of multiple friends and neighbors, notably Sedgewick Rossell, Doctor Marion's younger brother, returned from a steamboat job to reclaim their acres. John junior was to be the Wellers' only child, but would represent the North and South's coming together again. John would become known as a master carpenter and builder in the region.

Tranquilla McRaven's daughter 'Quilla and her husband Ed Richmond bought the Talbot place. They welcomed the help of Susan and John, along with the other sisters, in reclaiming it after Everett Talbot had let it run down in his declining years.

Everett had survived on through the war, his life constricting itself into ever-narrowing circles, until he'd lived mostly in one room and the kitchen. He had refused to leave the place, although there was no way he could maintain it. He did sell the Wellers that piece of land John wanted, enlarging the farm.

The Richmonds had years of neglect to undo, but eventually re-created a prosperous cotton farm of it. Everett had been tended in his last years by the ancient and widowed Blythe, who refused to leave her former master.

And Ophelia, the youngest McRaven daughter, denied entrance to medical school, had married Sedgewick Rossell, and became a noted midwife in spite of that rejection. He'd had a case of what was then termed 'war nerves', and had spent some years working on that steamboat out of Memphis before returning whole to the family's former plantation.

It had not been long before this brother had noticed the sister-in-law's then-grown sister, who was accompanying the doctor in his rounds. Sedgewick had then plowed renewed energy into rebuilding the old overseer's house, and mounting a suit for the girl. In this renovating of the place, John and Susan Weller aided mightily in turn.

The practice was for John to tackle the inside finish carpentry, then tend the baby while Susan helped split pickets for the fence, painted these and the house, helped clear and plow. Sometimes they'd leave the baby with either 'Quilla or Marion's wife Mary Ann, and all three would wage war on the overgrown land.

In time, the now-purposeful Sedgewick showed his postwar belle the house, complete with inside well pump and sink. *And* a doctor's buggy he'd acquired, rebuilt with the aid of Weller and blacksmiths Susan and Tranquilla. Ophelia was speechless.

Their engagement was announced at the wedding of her younger brother Harvey, at the bride Sally's father, Joseph Brunson's place. Their own wedding was a social event of the recovering Hernando region. Ophelia, in addition to her midwifery, healed many other sufferers in her own right.

Captain Ambrose Larkin, late officer of the Confederate army and his young wife, the daughter of another veteran in Tishomingo County, settled into a new log cabin there. He became a horse trader, his stock highly sought after in the region.

Others had not been so fortunate. Reverend John Kellog had received a large crate of foodstuffs from other churches in the region shortly after the war for distribution among the starving ex-slaves who thronged the city. The crate caught the attention of the military commandant of the local headquarters, zealous in his enforcement of martial law in that part of Memphis. The package was confiscated, under the ruse of suspected weapons intended for an imagined insurrection.

When the contents proved to be only food for the destitute Blacks, this officer allowed his well-fed men to seize it for themselves. John Kellog, rock-like in his faith and his devotion to justice, had surged into a towering rage at this atrocity, and denounced the Union command in his booming voice, face reddening, striding about, fists clenched.

And he had dropped dead of a heart attack before the leering, unrepentant soldiers.

After Union General Harwell Thorson's demise, Colonel Blair had taken command of the Byhalia post, and held it until well after war's end. He imposed strict discipline on the troops, and early on, made it clear he would tolerate no harassing of civilians or interference with his command. When drunken Union soldiers had burned a farmhouse, he had them shot. And when a Confederate spy had been captured, he had the man hanged. The message was clear: Blair was hard, but fair.

And after twelve long years, through some maneuvering by Southern members of Congress, the hated martial law was finally lifted in 1877. This involved a virtual sellout of the popular Democrat presidential candidate Samuel J. Tilden, who'd actually won the numerical vote. The contentious outcome ensured the disputed electoral votes would go to Rutherford B. Hayes, the Republican and 19th president.

But largely unmindful of the national events affecting and swirling around them, the average Mississippians faced each day as well as they could, whether as a matter of bare survival or gradual rebuilding. Some would eventually prosper, some would starve. Many would leave this war-torn land, as had Harvey and Daniel, for what was left of the American frontier.

Not the Blaine sisters. Until her death, Jenny Blaine continued to read every romantic novel she could get her hands on. She still dreamed of the cities of the North, of Europe, of travel and finery. And of some aging prince who might yet one day appear on a symbolic white horse.

Kate would smile at this, remembering all the events in the sisters' lives: the triumphs, the disappointments, the narrow escapes. And yes, the dreams. Everybody had dreams, whether talked out loud or not. She had certainly had her own, many of them, but no, she'd never let on, even to her sisters. No point in it, them being who they were, where they were.

But these nights, from her rocking chair on the porch, she'd often gaze upward at the canopy of bright stars, as mysterious as ever, as distant. *Mebbe th' stars themselves are actually God.*

They did seem to smile, and she was pretty sure God had smiled down on them.

Meet Charles McRaven

Charles McRaven is an historian, a former journalism professor, a restoration contractor, minister, stonemason, log cabin, blacksmith and timberframe craftsman. He lives with his wife Linda in the Shenandoah Valley of Virginia.

***Other Works from the Pen of
Charles McRaven***

A Piece of Ground - Revolutionary War veteran searches for peace, a place to settle. Finds love with beautiful planter's daughter, slights farm girl. Is hunted by sophisticated criminals who think he has their gold. Must use his sharpshooting skill too often to survive. Loses fiance to oily preacher, then other girl. Maybe.

Troublesome Creek - Sequel to *A Piece of Ground*, with hero following the girl he'd slighted to wilds of Kentucky Territory. Encounters mastermind of robbery ring he'd all but eliminated previously. Wins girl, leads pioneer settlement against outlaws, is badly wounded, saved by wife and friend. Hard justice, with collateral damage, but the settlers find justice.

A Place of Stone - Aging craftsman takes the road not taken to escape ratrace, fights. Drops out to mountain wilderness, finds peace, even faith. But there are complications, duties, and his desertion has its thorns. He almost dies in freak accident, is faced with impossible choice, one he cannot dodge.

Sagebrush Treasure - Haunted Civil War veteran is hunted by scheming range boss, finds refuge with orphaned sisters on their ranch. He teaches them gun skills, which they will have to use. He falls for the beautiful one, wins her, loses her. He and the hardened older sister hunt treasure, fight off marauders, hold the place together, aided by woman saloonkeeper, formerly the villain's ally.

Pricking of My Thumbs - Sassy girl carpenter competes in a man's world, but stumbles onto drug ring, is hunted, along with unlikely lover. The chase involves several states, betrayals, surprises, blood, finally ending with seeming security. But it all comes apart in violence, revenge. Can she win, with these odds?

Border Crossing - <u>Prequel</u> to *Pricking Of My Thumbs*, Wesley follows 'call' to Mexican border and gets involved in rescuing a drug/human trafficking kingpin's enslaved girl 'assistant.' Bullets fly.

Tranquilla - Civil War era trilogy about a woman 150 years ahead of her time, pioneer, emancipator, sharpshooter, horse racer, loses two husbands, bears eleven children, survives war and then Reconstruction.

Mountain Storm - Past middle-age first-time minister, Carrollton Lewis, takes a remote mountain church where he discovers deadly undercurrents far above his pay grade.

Hunted Man - Colin Barnes is a down-on-his-luck builder and things couldn't get any worse. But they're about to.

Montana Gold - Harlan Kemp vows independence, a Montana present-day mountain man, but greedy gold-seekers threaten, and a courageous, overlooked cowgirl teams with him against them.

Dear reader,

I hope you've enjoyed reading this story of life in the
changing South.

Your opinion is valuable to other
readers like you,
who may be looking for books like mine.

Please consider taking a few minutes to post a review,
however brief,
on the site where you purchased this book
or on the Wings ePress web page.

You may also want to visit my author page
at the Wings' website where you can find the other books
I've written.

Thank you!

Charles McRaven

Visit Our Website

*For The Full Inventory
Of Quality Books:*

Wings ePress, Inc

*Quality trade paperbacks and downloads
in multiple formats,
in genres ranging from light romantic comedy to general
fiction and horror.
Wings has something for every reader's taste.
Visit the website, then bookmark it.*
We add new titles each month!

*Wings ePress, Inc.
3000 N. Rock Road
Newton, KS 67114*